THEY TELL ME YOU ARE WICKED

For Marsha—

Thanks for supporting a
colleague and starving artist.

Alex Ay

THEY TELL ME YOU ARE WICKED

DUNCAN COCHRANE – BOOK 1

DAVID HAGERTY

www.EvolvedPub.com
Evolved Publishing LLC
Cartersville, Georgia

For my wife, Diane, without whom....

CHAPTER 1

They tell me you are wicked and I believe them, for I have
seen your painted women under the gas lamps luring the
farm boys.
> ~ Carl Sandburg (1878 – 1967). Chicago Poems. 1916

***

A CAR. THE BOY JUST WANTED A CAR.

For their sixteenth birthday, most guys on the North Shore copped
their own ride. They'd snag their driver's permit then drive to New Trier
High the next day in a restored Mustang, or a cherry Camero, or a convertible MGB, and slow roll through the parking lot. Tradition required
it along the lakefront of Chicago, except in families either too tight or too
punitive.

Which label applied to his dad? He had plenty of money and no reason
to Bogart it. Still, for his sweet sixteen the boy got an Apple II, to "help
him with his homework," his mom had said, as if that glowing box could
make him care about school.

All of which explained why he hung back in the night shadows,
smoking a joint. The suburban street waited lifeless, all the house lights
snuffed, but the Oldsmobile Cutlass glowed under the street lamp like a
lightening bug: high-gloss yellow paint on the doors and roof, hubcaps
to match, black air vents on the hood, a spoiler on the tail. Buffed out to
mint condition, it would stand up on the cover of *Car and Driver*.

He took a final hit off the roach, looked both ways, and crossed.
After a dozen silent steps on pavement still damp from a misting rain,

1

he test-tugged the driver's door, and it opened on squeaky hinges. The bench seat offered hard vinyl, slick and cold. The steering wheel was bound in leather, but it had turned viscous as oil.

"Can I?" he said to himself.

The owner must have been asleep and probably wouldn't even notice its absence. Borrowing wasn't stealing, especially if he refilled the gas tank. It would be no more than a test drive.

Behind, an El train screeched by, but once it passed everything was chill. He lowered the window to take in the vibe; the air smelled of tar and pine, and the street lamps buzzed.

The ignition popped with a flat-head screwdriver, and behind it he found the two wires—black and red—as his friend had said. On first touch the engine woke with a grunt. He eased the ball-head shifter to neutral and rolled silently back into the street, just like with the family's station wagon when he snuck out at night. He switched into drive, and a window lit up across the street. No sense waiting for a hand to part the curtains. Time to motor.

He tapped on the accelerator and six dials stood up on the dash. The engine rumbled loud in his ears, so he kept the tachometer under 2K and waited for the end of the block to pull the plunger on the headlamps.

At the intersection with Emerson he idled, feeling the pants of the motor, the shudder in the flanks. Sheridan Road had fewer traffic lights, but Green Bay offered a straight shot, primo to test the 350 Rocket engine.

He tunneled under the railroad that pointed downtown and turned right. Lights flashed yellow as far as he could see, shining off the wet pavement. On the right, the berm of the train tracks formed a barrier like the grandstands at a speedway, while to his left lay the pit row of gas, food, and tire shops, their neon signs the only evidence of habitation.

He punched play on the 8-track, and the Bee Gees sang "Night Fever" in a flaming falsetto. Eject. He coiled to throw the tape out the window but instead pocketed it as a memento. Nobody would miss *Saturday Night Fever*. On the radio dial he found *the Loop* and the vibrato of Eddie Van Halen's guitar.

I live my life like there's no tomorrow,

And all I've got, I had to steal.

He amped up the volume and stomped on the gas. The car leapt, and the tachometer climbed to 4K then slapped down as the engine shifted into second, third, fourth. Its noise blew away even the music while the windshield pinched the world into a rectangle of onrushing lights. Soon his hands numbed from the vibrations of the steering wheel.

He leaned back into the hard vinyl and squinted at the wind raking his face. The pot was taking hold, dragging the corners of his mouth into a perma-grin, filling his head with helium light. He passed the music studio where he took guitar lessons, the chrome of Stratocasters glinting in the window; the A&P where his mom shopped, its parking lot big and vacant; the stony Presbyterian church where his family dragged him weekly. He imagined wheeling the Cutlass past them, people turning at the hum of the engine and staring at the gleaming paint, waiting to see who stepped out, then nodding at him—no longer the boy in his parent's back seat.

At every manhole the car bottomed out, dropping his stomach with it, and on every crack in the pavement it bucked him off the bench seat. It handled nothing like the pathetic AMC Pacer from driver's ed. or his family's wood wagon, which creaked and swayed like hammocks. This ride held taut as a guitar string.

He didn't even see the pothole, only felt the car dip and lurch toward the curb, as for a second the Olds drove him. Then the tires grabbed and straightened. These gopher holes hid everywhere on the city streets, but he'd never hit one in a ride this tight.

It was no sweat until his left leg started to shake, at first just a tremor timed with the vibrations of the engine. Then it found its own rhythm, bouncing as though he was playing a bass drum. He tried to restrain it but couldn't. Luckily, the other foot controlled the gas.

When he looked up again, a garbage truck was crawling round the corner ahead, but with three lanes open he didn't need to slow. He ticked left a couple degrees, except the Cutlass didn't want to reset, fixing itself on a line to the curb and a huge elm, the trunk thicker than a phone pole. He stomped the brakes and tugged the wheel right with both hands, but the car fought back, fishtailing and mashing him into the door. As it spun, his head rebounded off something both firm and spongy.

Then everything blurred.

A jolt ended the slide. Lights trailed around him. He groped for something solid but found only the smooth and slick. All over his body felt bruised, and he heard himself panting as if recovering from a run powered by bone and muscle, rather than by gas and steel. He couldn't tune into his other senses. Finally, he grasped something cold and metallic, then held on until the dizziness faded.

He revived on the passenger side of the bench seat. The Cutlass lay in the oncoming lane, facing the wrong way. In the headlights, black skid marks stretched beyond his sight, and the scent of scorched rubber mixed with that of his sweat.

He slid back to the driver's side and checked all his mirrors. In the wing, he saw the curb that had saved him from wiping out into the tree. Other than the tire tracks, he couldn't see any damage. Still his stomach burned orange and acid.

Behind him, the garbage truck waited too, its brake lights glowing red. The cab revealed only darkness, but he sensed somebody watching.

The Olds idled low and ready, so he eased on the gas, but the tires turned only once and locked. What was the hang up? He tried again, with more gas this time, but the car lurched and fell. On his third attempt the wheels only ground, metal on metal.

Another look at the side mirror told him the truck still waited. The garbage man would see if he stepped out. At least inside the cockpit he hid from sight.

If his dad found out, he'd freak. The old man acted as though everything was irreplaceable. Once, when the boy accidently knocked over a lamp taking batting practice, his father grounded him for two months. After a wreck like this, he'd probably be banned from driving, and definitely wouldn't get a car of his own—ever. He'd be walking to school until graduation.

He stared at the little reflection of the garbage truck in the mirror. "Go on," he told it.

Maybe the driver wanted some sign he'd given up.

He threw the shifter into park and waited for the truck to move on, but it just sat there, its exhaust drifting in the window, a sweet scent that made him nauseous and dizzy again.

The dashboard clock ticked fifty times at least during the standoff. Then the truck driver's door opened, and a round man stepped onto the ladder, hanging there as though he couldn't decide what to do.

"Hey!"

His deep voice echoed off the street, threatening to wake up everybody within a mile. He sounded mad, as though he knew what had happened, but that was impossible. Nobody had seen the boy swipe the Olds.

"Hey!" the guy repeated even louder.

He descended a rung and waited as if expecting someone to step out and meet him.

The lights! They threw a pair of cones on the asphalt. The boy reached for the plunger to drain them, but his wrist cramped with a spark of pain from finger to shoulder. Since his hand wouldn't obey, the boy punched the toggle with a knuckle, killing all illumination inside and out. Once his eyes adjusted, he checked the side mirror again.

The man hung half out of his cab. "Hey, flyboy, you okay?"

Now his voice sounded friendly. Maybe he'd push-start the car, help get it over the curb's hump and pointed back to the duplex. Because right then, all the boy wanted was a do-over.

"Hey, if you're hurt, don't move."

The boy flexed his fingers, but they wouldn't stretch more than an inch, and his forearm ached, every movement winding the muscles tighter around a spindle. What if he couldn't drive? In the wood wagon he needed only one hand to steer, but the Cutlass had proven to be way too potent for that.

A glance back showed the garbage guy had descended to the lowest rung. How far back? Like the fine print said, the mirror distorted the distance, especially in the dark. By looking over his shoulder, the boy saw the driver waiting at least twenty-five paces away.

"Think fast," he said to himself. "Don't count on help from this gawker."

A siren crept through the open window, and the boy's mind went tense as his hand. Was it the paramedics or the police? Would one come without the other? The cops would definitely ask for his license and registration—check who owned the Cutlass.

In the slow crescendo, he locked eyes on the trash man, who walked toward the Olds, his head cocked to one side. No sense waiting on him or the fuzz. Hesitation meant fessing up, humiliation with his friends, and who knew what hell from his dad.

He clawed the door handle but couldn't close his grip, the cord in his forearm so taut it kept no slack for movement. Instead, he worked the lock with his right hand, then shouldered the door open, lost his balance, fell to one knee, and instinctively reached out the bad arm. The pain paralyzed him in that stance, like a runner on the blocks waiting for the gun. Behind, he heard the sani-man striding toward him heavy and slow.

"Don't move," he said.

Up close, the garbage guy looked old and rotund, way stronger than him, but slower, too. The boy forced himself to his feet, and the ground shifted. He stumbled and nearly fell again, but pausing gave him back his legs.

"I'm cool," he said.

Running seemed impossible, so he race-walked off cradling the lame limb.

"Hold on," the dumpster driver said.

At a half jog, the boy passed the windows to a flower shop with a neon yellow rose, and a record store with a spinning disc. He couldn't hear any steps or breathing behind but didn't want to look back in case he lost his balance again. Up ahead, the sidewalk ended at an intersection, the crosswalk glowing like a ladder under the street lamp. Even stoned and scared he knew enough to get off the main drag. To his right lay the darkness of suburban homes, their black lawns and big backyards an escape, so he veered onto the side street. It held a dozen places to hide—high bushes, shadowy corners, tall gates—but all still too close. And what if someone heard?

He scanned the street for a gas station with its lights dimmed or a restaurant with a side entrance, but he saw only more homes. All the businesses hid behind him with the Cutlass, the trash trailer, and the siren.

Which had stopped now, he noticed. Quiet had returned, as though the sani-man and the alarm, all those officious gnats, had given up. Still, he couldn't stop. Luck had landed him there, and he couldn't count on it to save him.

If he could just get out from under this. If no one found out, not his dad or his friends....

"Please God," he said. "Let me walk, and I'll get you back."

He didn't mean to wreck the car; it was just a joyride. The irony of that term ricocheted through his thoughts, his arm throbbing, head spinning, heart banging. How much could it cost to fix? Didn't matter. He'd save his allowance for months, if he had to, and drop the money (anonymously) through the owner's mail slot.

He could make this right, as if it had never happened.

CHAPTER 2

THE DEATH OF RICHARD J. DALEY on December 20, 1976 left a political vacuum in Chicago, the suction of which reached far beyond the city limits. For 21 years, as mayor and chairman of the Cook County democrats, Daley commanded Illinois' liberal voters. In the city, no one bought a business license without his say-so. Statewide, he made out the party's ticket then got out the voters to support it. Rumor even held that he'd swung the 1960 election to J.F.K.

After the mayor's passing, many Windy City politicians plotted to replace him, but no less likely candidate emerged than Duncan Cochrane, a self-made magnate of salted pork who owned the city's largest supplier of hot dogs, brats, and sausages. Unlike the majority of local pols, who had been schooled and disciplined by The Machine, Cochrane brought no political experience, but he imagined himself overstepping the party to become the state's next governor.

Only his first steps faltered. With six weeks left to the election, he trailed by ten points. Ten. This was why no big name politicians had run for governor, and why newspaper columnists had labeled Duncan the token offering. With his massive war chest, most pundits considered Big Bill Stratton to be unbeatable. So far he was proving them right.

That was why at the fundraiser to save his campaign, Duncan circulated like Tarzan swinging vine to vine, his hands always seeking a new hold, never releasing one before taking up another, shaking with so many people he couldn't track whom he was gripping. Voices converged and peppered him.

"How're you going to beat Big Bill?" they said.

"Same way I won the primary: enterprise," Duncan said.

"But what's your pitch?"

"This state needs a leader who knows how to use all the parts of the pig."

"How do we know you'll remember us?"

"Running a state's no different than a company: it's all about relationships."

"Will you be a friend to business?"

"I will."

"Will you forget your friends?"

"I won't."

"Can we count on your vote?"

"You can."

"We're counting on you to win."

"I know."

All the while, the meat and wine from the banquet soured on Duncan's palate. Something was missing. The Drake Hotel's ballroom sat properly attired: the tables laid with white linen and cream china; the podium chiffoned in red, white, and blue bunting. The guests lined up for seconds on prime rib and drained every bottle of red Bordeaux. Waiters all in white trundled by a sheet cake with "Cochrane in '78" written in icing over the eagle and crest of the state flag. An octet played swing music even though the floor offered no space to cut a rug.

However, in back sat three empty tables, and even with the lights lowered, Duncan couldn't overlook them. When his face ached from smiling and his hand throbbed from shaking, he worked his way to the rear and stepped behind a gold brocade curtain hiding a hallway.

He finger-combed his auburn-tinted hair, but its sprayed stiffness reminded him: hands off. Instead, he tweaked the buttons on his tuxedo coat and adjusted his silver cufflinks. He'd paid $2,000 for custom formal wear, and already he'd sweated through the shirt and scuffed the wing tips. He felt like a little boy dressed up for church.

"Dad."

Duncan turned to see his teenaged son, Aden, slouched in the stairway to a side door. His hair stood up in a military flat top for prep school, bringing out his blue eyes. Already he'd removed his blazer and hiked up the cuffs of his slacks.

"What're you doing here?" Duncan said.

"Same as you. Vegging out."

"I'm practicing."

Duncan extracted his speech from a coat pocket, squinted, reached for his reading glasses, then stopped himself. His consultants had used a large-print typewriter so he wouldn't look myopic in public.

The boy pulled loose his bow tie and undid the top button of his shirt.

"Don't relax yet," Duncan said. "We've got an hour to go."

"Not me. I need a chill pill."

The boy slumped in his chair and slipped off his black wing tips.

"Aden, I need you to play along for a while longer."

"That's why I'm here, to play along?"

"That's not what I meant."

"So why am I here?"

Duncan didn't want to say that he didn't trust his son at home alone, even at age sixteen. Instead he said, "To whom much is given, of him shall much be required." Before he could indulge a fatherly impulse to lecture about public service and privilege, a hand drew back the curtain.

His wife, Josie, surveyed them, hands on hips. "Why are you two hiding?"

"We're chilling," Aden said.

"I'm preparing," Duncan said.

She stepped between them like a school principal breaking up a fight, her grey jacket and pantsuit as blockish as any man's, her blush, lip stick and rouge muted.

"People need to see you," she said

"In a minute," Duncan said.

"Screw up your courage."

Enclosed by the airless curtain, Duncan smelled his own sweat overwhelm the soaps and deodorants.

"How many people do you think we got?" Duncan said to her.

"Five hundred?" Josie said.

"The room only holds three."

Josie turned to Aden, surveyed his dishevelment, and said, "Get dressed," then lifted him by the elbow and attacked his tie until he recoiled.

"I just wish I knew how we're doing," Duncan said.

"You want me to ask Lindsay?" Aden said.

Duncan peeked around the curtain to the entry, where his adult daughter used her blue eyes and orthodontist's smile to coax people into larger donations. Compared to the other guests, she dressed like a hippie in a sleeveless dress that fell like a slip and blond hair so straight it looked ironed.

"I'll do it," Duncan said. While Josie redressed their son, he stepped back into the open room.

His campaign manager, Kai Sato, quickly spotted him and closed in. He wore the uniform of tuxedo and cummerbund, although his collar and cuffs spread too wide for Duncan's taste. As a drama buff, Kai's wardrobe tended to the theatrical.

"Nervous?" Kai said.

"No," Duncan said, too quick and automatic to be convincing.

"Then don't look it."

"How'd we do?"

Kai turned to the crowd. His broad nose and olive skin appeared German, but his straight black hair lay restrained in a Samurai's ponytail.

"I'd say we got about two hundred."

"Thousand?"

"People. It's too soon to count the money."

Two hundred people at $500 a plate grossed them $100,000, a solid amount but not nearly enough. Subtract the hotel rental, the dinner, the French Cab, which tallied at least $20,000. It never seemed important when they were planning this shindig. Now, only big donations would get them to their goal of $250,000.

"I thought this was the best way to fundraise," Duncan said.

"It's copacetic. We'll shake down everyone on their way out."

Kai's word choice grated—these were friends and associates, after all—but his flippancy helped Duncan to ID the flaw in the room: it had a Presbyterian restraint, everyone chatting quietly, the scrape of knives audible above conversation. Even the lighting simmered. What was lacking? Enthusiasm.

"Is anyone here from Marshall Field's?" Duncan said.

"Don't know," Kai said.

Meaning no.

"What about the party?" Duncan said.

"Focus on who's here."

"Don't tell me The Machine is still bitter about us beating their man in the primary."

"I'll put together a confab, see what's shaking."

Duncan looked away. Sometimes Kai sounded like a teenager — all lingo and no content. He'd survived only twenty-eight years, almost the same as Duncan's eldest. His daughters called Kai a mod, while his son dubbed Kai a "closet disco queen." Still, the strategist had won three local campaigns. The problem wasn't Kai.

Even now Duncan caught himself frowning against the advice of his consultants who'd warned him never to look unhappy in public.

He scanned the room for joyous faces until an unexpected one stopped him. At the entry, next to his daughter, stood a thick man in a long, black leather coat. If he were a cow he would have been well marbled.

"Hang on, there's someone I need to talk to," he said.

He crossed the room with back pats and arm squeezes, weaving through the guests like Walter Payton evading tacklers, until he stood by the door.

"...with the American Brotherhood of Laborers," the big man said to Lindsay.

"Hello, Joe." Duncan offered his hand only to find it compressed in a grip that paralyzed his strength.

Years before, this bull of a man had lost most of the fingers on his right hand to a grinder; now he compensated by overpowering people with the good one. For such a big guy, Joe Sturmer's face looked small and delicate, with a child's soft nose, a receding chin, and pale blue eyes; but his grip displayed no such weakness. Union guys didn't soften their words, and the meat cutters spoke brutally after breaking bones all day.

It took all Duncan's concentration to maintain his candidate's smile.

"I hear the governor's started calling you *the butcher*," Sturmer said.

"Typical insult from a farm boy," Duncan said. "I take it as a compliment."

"Good, cause you know Chicago's a working man's town. We got to roll up our sleeves and plunge our hands into the fleshy parts." He turned to Lindsay, who stared up at them like a little girl overhearing her parents argue, stunned to silence but logging every word. "You probably don't know about this cause your dad's the boss now, but we used to cut up carcasses together back when he was a college kid."

"Proud to be hog butchers to the world," Duncan said.

"You got it."

The union man finally released Duncan's hand after winning his submission.

"You get some prime rib?" Duncan asked them both.

"Don't worry, I'm not staying," Sturmer said. "Nobody sent me an invitation, which is too bad. I hear you need more money. I might be able to help you out with that."

"You know I appreciate your support," Duncan said.

"Then how come you don't return my calls? Your secretary hears my voice more than my wife. Seems like you're ducking us."

Instinctively, Duncan straightened, giving him half a foot over Sturmer. "Not at all. With the campaign, I haven't been at my office much lately. But I want to hear what you have to say, you and... your people."

"I hear you, but the membership isn't so patient. You gotta understand, our votes aren't given, they're earned. People like us can't afford fancy fundraisers. We're workers, but together we pack a lot of strength."

An innuendo of snobbery, like his opponent and media critics. Why say it now, here? Every candidate needed fundraisers, and Duncan had to invite people with money. Yet another reason to get out of meat packing.

"You don't need to donate any more to get my attention," Duncan said. "I'll call you tomorrow morning, myself."

Sturmer stepped back but kept his gaze fixed on Duncan. "I can't wait to hear what you've got to say." He turned to Lindsay and offered her a delicate handshake. "Good to meet you." He then turned back to Duncan. "Talk to you soon."

He stalked through the hotel's lobby, leaving behind a medicinal odor of cheap cologne.

"He works with you?" Lindsay said.

Duncan shook his head and turned from his daughter, searching for the words to explain.

Before he could answer, Kai stepped in. "It's time," he said.

The lights dimmed, and Duncan ascended the podium to the ping of silver against glass. The lectern reminded him of a trial where he had to deliver his own defense. He'd need all his eloquence to save himself. He reached into his pocket for his reading glasses, then stopped himself and grabbed the speech, taking time to smooth the pages and regain his composure.

"Friends," he said. He looked over the audience to where his wife stood in back, arms crossed.

She nodded once to push him forward.

* * *

They drove home along Lake Shore Drive, the windshield wipers of the Cadillac Fleetwood Brougham beating away the mist off the lake. To their right, the infinite darkness of Lake Michigan merged with the night sky. To their left, the high rises of the Gold Coast shimmered like fireflies — habitats for the wealthy and powerful, the people who should have attended the banquet.

During the ride, Duncan and Josie rehashed the evening, noting who'd come, skipping who hadn't. They also plotted the next week — a charity auction she would emcee, a press conference he'd planned on curbing inflation — but only to confirm their dates and times.

Throughout, Lindsay and Aden sat silent in the back seat.

Halfway home, Duncan's adult daughter finally spoke. "Daddy, who was that man from the union?"

"Nobody important."

"Didn't he want to donate?"

"Maybe."

She leaned forward, put her hands over the front seat, and whispered in his ear. "That's good, isn't it?"

"Not with all the conditions."

"Like?"

Duncan reached for the radio and tuned it to WFMT, Chicago's classical station. "He thinks by giving me money now he can squeeze me later."

"So? It's not a loan. You don't have to pay it back."

A jaunty piano concerto distracted Duncan until he switched off the sound. "He's not someone I want to owe."

"But, Daddy, it's a fundraiser."

"He's not someone I want to owe."

"Duncan," Josie said. "How do you expect to raise money if you snub your biggest supporters?"

"I didn't snub him," he said, but in a subdued voice. "It's bad enough we have to beg our friends for donations, let alone getting in hock to my employees. I'd sooner spend my own money. And look where it's gotten us: five million to be ten points behind."

She laid a hand on his arm. "You remember the time I met Daley?"

He shook his head.

"With the League of Women Voters?" she said. "I went to the mayor's office to solicit his support for the E.R.A.

"I expected this powerful, charismatic figure, the one I'd read about for years in the *Tribune*. Instead, I saw a shlumpy little Mick from the neighborhoods. At first I couldn't believe it. How did this round, ugly man get to be mayor?"

She paused. "You remember what he told me? 'How many?' he said. "But I didn't get it. 'Votes,' he said, and stared at me over his broad desk. 'How many can you get me?' At first I got confused. I assumed he was mixing up the E.R.A. with suffrage."

She chuckled. "Then he explained. 'Miss,' he said, 'how do you think I got this office?' For once, I didn't know what to say. 'Votes,' he said. 'From people like you. You want my vote, I expect yours back. So how many?'

She shook her head. "I left convinced that no outsider could penetrate Chicago's political machine, but that was naive. He wasn't saying no, he was saying yes... but—"

"What's that have to do with the union?" Duncan said.

"All you're hearing is the but, not the yes."

Duncan fixated on the rumble of the highway slabs while trying to recover himself.

"Why not just ask?" Aden said.

Duncan checked the rearview, but his son was looking out the side window, so quiet he could have died. "Ask what?"

"For money."

"People don't spontaneously give me money."

"Do too. Dudes send you bread all the time. I saw the checks stacked on your desk."

"Small donations," Duncan said. "Not enough to keep the campaign going."

"What if you asked for more? I bet if you sent envelopes to everybody you know, you'd be raking it in. Like in church, you pass the plate and people throw in some moolah."

"It's not that easy."

"Seems like it to me."

Josie reached across the front seat to touch his arm again. "You have to have faith."

"In?"

"Us. Your friends. Your staff. We're going to win."

For six months Duncan had tried to escape the smell of salt pork on his clothes and the clang of heavy machinery in his ears, yet seeing that union thug standing in the doorway reminded him of all the degradations of his business. How could he resume his previous title if he lost? Returning to his company would be like begging an old girlfriend to take him back. People would hide their pity, but already he sensed it.

Still, Josie was right: self-doubt never got the job done. Twenty-five years in business should have taught him that, but business followed clear rules: you made a good product and sold it to willing consumers. How did you market the product when the product was you?

Politics operated differently. It canvassed Irish bars on the South Side, committee meetings in City Hall, lunches at Manny's Deli. The city limits held fifty wards, all with an alderman expecting some favor or tribute.

The whole state of politicos expected something. Too late he realized this, too late to save his campaign, and too late to save face.

They passed the dark expanse of Lincoln Park, dotted with street lamps, and the signs to Wrigley Field. Aside from the other cars, the city sat immobilized as in a photograph, the lights on but inanimate. Duncan concentrated on the white dashes directing him forward, until the freeway ended and he picked up Sheridan Road through the North Shore suburbs. The farther they drove, the bigger the houses became and the more deserted the streets.

At a stoplight, Duncan looked into the rearview mirror to meet Lindsay's blue eyes. "How much longer are we going to have you kicking around the house?"

"Till you win."

"Then what?"

She cocked her head and thought. "I'll move to Springfield with you, live in the governor's mansion."

"You think the state's going to support a freeloading daughter?"

"Of course! You'll be the boss."

"And we'll be on the public till. Voters shouldn't have to pay for your European tour."

"Springfield's not Europe, Daddy."

They passed the Northwestern campus with its brick buildings covered in vines—the Ivy of the Midwest—where Duncan had first learned about salesmanship.

"What if we gave you a job?" Duncan said. "Head of sanitation."

"You should hire her as your fundraiser," Josie said. "She brought in more money than any of your staff."

"I'd rather plan your parties," Lindsay said.

"Fine. What'll we do when we win?"

"Rent out the Pump Room, with free food for everyone."

"You'll need to raise more money first."

Even focused on the road, Duncan could feel Josie's stare, the one that said he'd become intolerably sullen.

"I'll drive," Aden said.

"I don't think I'll get a personal chauffeur," Duncan said.

"How'll you get to work?"

"Walk. The limo would be as long as the two blocks from the mansion to the Capitol."

"That's why we'll dump the limo."

Duncan slowed just before his house and parked halfway up the semi-circular drive. When he stepped out into the cool mist, the road shone an ebony gold under the street lamps. Even his home glowed, the white of the Tudor gables reflecting the porch light.

"What would you recommend?" Duncan said.

"Something cool, like a Camero," Aden said.

"I'd be impeached in the first month."

"There you go," Josie said. "Now you're thinking like a winner."

CHAPTER 3

DUNCAN AWOKE TO A SCREAM. Its punch hit quickly and retracted—or had it come in a dream? Outside, darkness persisted, though moonlight seeped through the drapes. From the hallway, a band of light glowed under the bedroom door. Then something whimpered just past it. It sounded foreign, the pitch high and tight. The children hadn't called in the night for years.

"What's going on?" Josie said, groping for the lamp on their nightstand.

The digital clock read 2:34.

After his eyes adjusted, Duncan rolled, stood, and ran across the room, his pajamas flapping against his legs, the night air chilling him through the thin fabric. In the hall he found his eldest daughter, Glynis, crouched, knees to chest.

He squatted and palmed her back. "What's wrong?"

She replied with a gasp between sobs. In her room, the covers drooped off the bed, and a pillow lay on the carpet. Otherwise nothing looked disturbed. Next in line stood Lindsay's door.

He pushed it open and flipped on the overhead.

A pillow was covering her face, and her hands curled on her chest defensively. She never slept that way, instead curling into a ball on her side, a holdover from childhood when she sucked her thumb obsessively. The blanket hung off her, revealing her nightgown, which twisted around her thighs.

Even after Duncan removed the pillow, his daughter didn't move, her eyes half closed, mouth open. Her forehead felt cool, and on her throat he saw a red depression. He touched the spot lightly, but she didn't flinch.

"Lindsay?"

No reply. He pulled her to his chest and rubbed her back, but she didn't return the hug, her body still and limp. Up close she felt thin, her ribs a washboard under his palms, and she smelled like peaches—from some cream or soap probably. No way to tell if that was unusual. These days he rarely held her for long since adult children reacted like cats, skittish of affection.

He embraced her for some time—five seconds or a minute, he couldn't say—before her chest expanded. It happened slowly and only once. Had he imagined it? He held his breath until it came again, a swell that proved she could still breathe.

"What's going on?"

He turned to find Josie standing in the doorway.

"Get Bill," he said.

His wife's footsteps thumped along the carpeted hall and cascaded down the steps; then the front door slammed against a wall. Soon a cold breeze filtered up the stairs.

While waiting, Duncan tallied Lindsay's every breath, which came irregularly. He tried to count the seconds between but couldn't get a steady rhythm. How much longer could it take? Bill Connolly—their neighbor and the kids' pediatrician—lived barely a hundred yards away. If Josie ran, she'd be there in seconds. Then what? She'd bang on the door, maybe twice, wait as he dressed—but weren't doctors trained to respond quickly? They should have come already. Instead he heard only the mantle clock ticking downstairs. He would have gone himself, except only his warmth and comfort were keeping Lindsay alive.

Then a new body touched his, Glynis wrapping around them from behind.

"Where are they?" he said.

"Gone," she said.

"Go get them."

But Glynis remained.

Anger swelled inside Duncan, which he tried to repress but couldn't. Didn't she sense the urgency? As he searched for words to animate her, footsteps sounded below, two sets, which climbed the stairs, turned the corner at the head of the railing, then thumped through the door.

Bill arrived grey hair askew, pillow creases still on his face. He wore a burgundy robe and carried a leather satchel. When he and Josie sat, the weight of four people compressed the bed so that it groaned beneath them.

"Let me see her," Bill said.

The doctor gently separated them and laid Lindsay on the pillow, but Duncan retained one of her hands so she could still feel him.

"Her throat," Duncan said, pointing.

The doctor ignored him and checked for a pulse on her other wrist, then put his ear to her chest. After listening at least ten seconds, he pushed aside the sheets that covered Lindsay's legs. They shone pale and opaque, the blue veins visible beneath her skin. She'd always been fair, but looked almost bloodless now. The doctor began squeezing her muscles from the feet up, compressing both her calves, then her thighs, using two hands, then pausing at her waist.

"You may want to wait outside," he said.

He looked at all three family members, who neither moved nor replied, then stared at Duncan.

"I need to undress her, and what I find could be disturbing."

Duncan wanted to hold tight to Lindsey's hand, her warmth the only sign that she yet lived, but he forced himself to his feet. He pulled Glynis off the bed, but she hung limply in his grasp. As he pushed her to the door, Duncan looked back to see his wife still seated.

"Josie," he said.

"One of us should stay."

After steadying Glynis in the doorway, Duncan crossed the room and lifted his wife by the elbows. Still, she pulled toward her youngest girl.

"Come on, you heard what Bill said. There's nothing we can do," Duncan said.

"How do you know?"

"Bill will call us."

With an arm around her waist, he led Josie to the hall, where he grasped Glynis with the other hand. Together they walked downstairs and stopped in the front hall.

Josie stood in her nightgown, arms crossed, and looked at everything but her husband. "We should call the police," she said.

She looked about her as though searching for a phone, then walked toward the kitchen, where one hung beside the refrigerator.

In a moment, he heard the dial spin three times. Meanwhile, he looked to Glynis, whose Cubs nightshirt came only to her mid thighs. "Let's get some clothes," he said.

With a palm on her back, Duncan steered his daughter up the stairwell and past Lindsay's door. Instinct compelled him to look inside, yet only a minute ago the doctor had shooed him away. He resisted the urge and pushed Glynis into her room, then went to the master suite. From the closet he grabbed the first clothes he saw: grey slacks and a white shirt. Even with them he shivered, so he added a cashmere sweater.

In his wife's closet, dresses, pants, blouses, and suits hung limp. She'd want something warm and comfortable, so he grabbed a yellow, terry cloth robe.

Back in the hall, he paused outside Lindsay's room and pressed an ear to it but couldn't hear anything. He imagined the doctor listening to his daughter's chest with a stethoscope, her recoiling at the cold metal. As quietly as he could, Duncan turned the doorknob and peered inside. Bill hunched over Lindsay's neck, slicing it apart like meat.

Still, she didn't move.

Unconsciously, Duncan gasped.

When Bill looked up, anger creased his forehead. "Duncan, please."

Duncan closed the door, then forgot why he'd come upstairs.

A door opened down the hall and Aden emerged, squinting out of one eye, his flannel pajamas twisted around his legs. "What's happening?" he said.

A moment later, Glynis opened her door as well and stood stiff and silent next to her father in a Brown University sweatshirt and jeans.

"Come downstairs," Duncan said.

"Why?" Aden said.

"Just follow me."

In the foyer he found Josie pacing along the cold tile floor and helped her into the gown, then steered the children away from the stairs.

"We should pick up," Josie said.

So the two women walked through the downstairs, turning on lights, putting away books and mail, leaving Duncan with his son by the front door.

"What's happening?" Aden repeated.

Duncan stood silent, searching for words to explain, until a siren pulsed high and low in the distance, like the intake and exhalation of Lindsay's breath. Once he opened the heavy front door, the volume grew until a police car pulled into the driveway with an ambulance just behind.

They switched off their sirens, yet their lights strobed the surrounding homes in red and blue, probably waking half the neighbors. An officer stepped out first, a man no older than his daughters, with a blond buzz cut and a slender build, followed by two paramedics who reminded him of the TV show *Emergency*. The thinner one wore his hair shaggy over his collar; the second sported a crew cut and a linebacker build. He carried a satchel the size of a tool chest.

"Upstairs," Duncan said, then "third door" and watched them disappear around the landing.

At his elbow, the officer asked, "Who else is in the house, sir?"

"My wife and daughter. Josie, Glynis!" His shouts came out louder than he intended and echoed through the hallway.

A moment later, the women emerged from the kitchen. They moved to the living room where the family sat on a pair of floral couches, women on one, men on the other, with the young cop between them.

"Tell me what happened," the officer said.

How to begin? Duncan awoke to a scream and found his daughter asphyxiating, possibly.... Bill said what he found could be "disturbing." Did he mean she'd been...? None of it made any sense. In confusion, he turned to Glynis.

Despite the sweatshirt, she hugged herself against the cold. She glanced at her father, then at the officer, and said, "I heard something bang against the wall."

"What did it sound like?"

"Heavy."

"Like a piece of furniture? A person?"

"A person. Maybe."

"How long ago?"

"I don't know. Ten minutes?"

The clock on the mantle read 5:20.

As the officer guided Glynis through a recitation of the morning, Duncan wondered why she hadn't woken anyone. She'd been living at home since the campaign began, but before that had been on her own for several years. Had she grown so accustomed to taking care of herself that she didn't even think to get help?

"In what state was the victim?" the officer said.

Glynis put a hand to her throat. In the lamplight, and without any makeup, she looked pallid and frail. "I heard something... Lindsay moaning or crying."

"Lindsay is —"

"Our daughter," Duncan said. "Our other daughter. She's upstairs, in the bedroom...."

He couldn't bring himself to call her the victim. Since the paramedics arrived, he hadn't heard anything, which had to be a good sign. He imagined Lindsay sitting up in bed, sipping a glass of water while the stocky medic checked her blood pressure and Bill applied a warm cloth to her forehead. Surely she had revived by now. Except she bore that incision now in her throat, which would need patching.

"What'd you do next, miss?" the officer said.

"Went into Lindsay's bedroom, and I saw them. She lay still and... he just stood over her."

"Who?"

"I don't know. He had a flashlight in my face. I looked at Lindsay. She wasn't moving. I couldn't... the light was too bright. I didn't know, so I... I...." She shook her head and mouthed words to herself silently.

In the pause, Duncan looked to his son, who leaned forward, palms pressed between his thighs, listening intently. Duncan squeezed the boy's knee, but he flinched at the touch.

"And what did he do?" the officer said.

"Ran."

"Which way?"

She threw one hand toward the back of the house.

Someone had broken in, and Glynis hadn't mentioned it until just now? Duncan stood to look in the kitchen.

"Sir, please stay here."

"I want to check the back door."

"An officer will take care of it." He turned to the radio on his shoulder and said, "Dispatch, this is unit two. I'm on a 242 in the forty-one hundred block of Sheridan Road. Have other officers respond Code 3 and search for an unidentified male, description following."

"Won't that take too long?" Duncan said.

The clock said that five minutes had passed.

The officer ignored his question and turned back to Glynis. "What did he look like, miss?"

"The light was too bright."

"You didn't see him, sir?"

Duncan recalled walking down the hall, flipping on the light in Lindsay's room, finding her on the bed. He hadn't seen or heard anyone besides Glynis.

"No," he said.

The officer turned to Aden, who leaned forward, hands on thighs, as if ready to spring.

"You, son?" he said.

"I was crashed out," the boy said.

Overhead, a door opened, then footsteps descended the stairs. Everyone fell silent and still until Bill entered the living room. The doctor looked first at the officer, then at the two women, and finally at Duncan. On the collar of his robe lay a thick droplet of blood.

"I'm sorry," he said.

CHAPTER 4

FOR THE NEXT SEVERAL HOURS, police swirled around the Cochranes like debris in an eddy, each new arrival circling from Lindsay's bedroom, to the back door, to the front entry. On occasion, one would glance toward the family — still seated in the living room — nod knowingly, then look away. When the police chief showed up shortly after daybreak, he reassured Duncan that he needed all of them to search for his daughter's killer.

Chief Dunleavy had a ring of white hair, a full beard, and half glasses, which he peered over as he spoke. Dressed in cords and a thick wool sweater, he looked more fit for a university lecture hall.

"Sorry to take you through this again," he said.

"What more can we tell you?" Josie said.

For the first time that morning, her tone and face showed her exasperation.

"I've got to understand the sequence of events," the chief said.

He turned first to Glynis, who over the hours of questioning had compressed ever more tightly until she sat knees to chin. Duncan knew she felt intimidated, but an unconscious conviction stirred in him that if he listened closely he could deduce who did this and why.

"You saw a man in Lindsay's room?" the chief said.

"Yes."

"Describe him."

"I couldn't see. He shined a light at me."

"How big was he?"

"Your size, I guess."

The chief stood probably five-nine and weighed no more than 150 pounds, no match for someone Duncan's size if it had come to a fight.

"Did he say anything?" the chief said.

Glynis opened her mouth but hesitated.

"This is too much," Josie said.

When Glynis' lower lip began to quiver, her mother took her hand and squeezed it until it turned red.

"What use is interrogating us?" she said.

"Anything you recall will help," said the chief.

"He just shined his light at me," Glynis said.

"And what did he do?"

Glynis sat silent, forcing Duncan to intervene.

"By the time I got there, the man had run off."

The chief turned to Josie, who sat with her arms folded staring into a corner.

"You didn't see him, ma'am?"

"I already told you, no. How is this helping?" she said.

He ignored her question and turned to Duncan.

"How much time passed?"

Duncan listened to the tick of the mantel clock and began to count, testing his estimate.

"Twenty seconds, thirty? I was asleep."

When Glynis first screamed, he'd been slow to rise, waiting for Josie to react, fumbling out of bed.

"If I'd gotten there ten seconds sooner...."

"He ran down the stairs?"

"I think so."

"You heard him?"

"No."

"How about any slamming doors or breaking glass?"

Duncan stood and walked to the mantle, ran his fingers over the round head of the clock, felt its smooth wood, listened to its incessant ticking.

"I don't think—"

"He was totally stealth," Aden said.

The boy stood from the couch, his head darting between the adults.

"I didn't even hear him, and he strutted right past my door," he said.

Josie grabbed his hand and tried to pull him to sit next to her, but instead he faced his father and spoke only to him.

"He probably freaked out and booked. No way you could have caught up to him, Dad."

"Sit down," Josie said and yanked him down next to her. Despite his resistance, she kept both hands clamped down on his as though she could contain him in them.

The chief turned to the first officer to interrogate them, who sat next to him taking notes. They spoke inaudibly and then turned back to Duncan.

"Could one of you come with me?" the chief said.

Duncan looked to Josie, who was pulling Aden's hand to get him to sit, and motioned her to stay with him. Before they spoke again, the chief led him to the upstairs hallway.

"I need you to tell me if anything's missing or out of place."

They began in the master bedroom, although Duncan knew no one had entered it. To get there, the killer would have run right past him. Still, he surveyed the king-sized bed, the covers thrown toward the center, the walnut vanity where Josie's jewelry box lay closed, the nightstands covered in books (his with two volumes from Kai: *Rhetoric* and *How to Win Friends and Influence People*, hers with *Augustus* and *The Prince*). It looked exactly as he'd left it hours before.

Next came Glynis' room, which looked the same as when she'd left home for college, the wallpaper and bedspread still a pale blue check, her bookcase filled with trophies for gymnastics and tennis. On the wall hung her favorite photos: of Billie Jean King shaking hands with Bobby Riggs after the Battle of the Sexes, and Olga Korbut on the balance beam. Glynis could have judged better whether anything was different, but Duncan didn't want her subjected to any more questioning now.

Back in the hallway, Lindsay's door remained closed. The chief paused outside it. "I'm sorry, but we need your eyes on everything."

Duncan nodded and steeled himself. When the door swung back, beddings covered Lindsay from top to toe, her body an outline under a quilt in the family tartan. An officer stood by her bedside in a military at ease, feet apart, hands clasped behind his back.

"Tell me anything that's odd, even if it's just askew," the chief said.

They circled the bed. On the bookshelf sat a photo of Lindsay in a white dress with a high-necked collar from a high school production of *A Doll's House*. She'd acted all through college and might have continued in community theater if she hadn't been so consumed by his campaign. On her dresser lay a silver brush and mirror that she inherited from her grandmother. The teeth had trapped some of her blond hair, and Duncan reached for it.

"Don't," the chief said.

Duncan froze with his hand inches from the brush.

"I'm sorry. You can't touch anything."

Duncan nodded and stared at its silver gleam. Try as he might, he couldn't recall if he'd seen it out before that night.

Even with his back turned to her body, he could feel a warmth creep over him, seeping through his clothes and skin to lodge in his spine. Her smell, too, enveloped the room, that peach tang he'd noticed before. He paused to soak in this last, lingering essence of her.

"You need a break?" the chief said.

Duncan shook his head and moved to her closet. Clothing overflowed from the hamper and onto the floor, including the evergreen dress she'd worn the night before at the fundraiser. The curtain rod sagged under the weight of jeans and shirts, the shelves above with sweaters arranged by color, including an Irish cable knit he gave her for her last birthday.

"Anything?" the chief said.

Duncan turned to say no when he noticed the picture above her bed, a framed print of Degas' ballerinas. It was her favorite, though she'd never been an athlete or dancer, lacking the grace of her sister. Instead she'd studied art history and planned to work in a gallery after college. If only he hadn't called her home, hadn't involved her in the campaign. He slumped to her bed and ran his hand over the blanket, felt her form beneath its rough wool. As he reached to pull it back for one last look, the chief pulled his hand away.

"Let's move on," he said.

Aden's room came next, but it looked so disheveled that nothing stood out. Posters covered every inch of the walls and ceiling—most of bands staring balefully back at the viewer—but some featured pinups, Farrah Fawcett in her red swimsuit, and other women wearing even less. On the floor, records overwhelmed the carpet. Clothing, like lava, spilled from the closet, overflowed the dresser drawers, seeped from under the bed. Ordinarily, Duncan ignored the mess, but seeing it with the chief felt embarrassing.

"It looks... typical," Duncan said.

Downstairs, they walked through the dining room, where the table featured a linen runner and sterling candlesticks, then the den with its TV and stereo, his study, where Cochrane '78 posters and bumper stickers filled every flat surface, and finally the living room with its collection of frosted crystal by Lalique on the sideboard. Not one item missing, not one out of place. Last they entered the kitchen, where a half dozen officers stood, sat, and kneeled around the back door.

"We're assuming he broke in here," the chief said, pointing to a fracture in the glass just above the doorknob. Fingerprint powder hung in the air, glistening in the early morning light, but choking Duncan.

"One problem, chief," said a female technician squatting by the door. "All the fragments are outside."

The men stared at the tile floor, which shone clean and glassy.

"So he *left* this way," the chief said. "Any other signs of forced entry?"

The young cop pursed her lips and shook her head.

The chief turned and looked at Duncan over his half glasses.

"Are there any other doors?"

"Just the front."

Duncan turned toward the entryway, where an oak door stood thick as a drawbridge, then back again to the rear yard. Through the glass, parallel fences marked the property line all the way to Lake Michigan, which lay calm and grey, while above it a gauzy haze gave way to golden sunlight. Still, dampness pervaded the house, as though rain loomed and the moisture was building up inside.

"When'd you last use this entrance?" the chief said.

"A couple weeks? It's been too cold."

As he said it, a shiver passed through Duncan.

"You keep it locked?"

"Of course."

"And you checked it last night?"

"I... can't remember."

The chief nodded and pointed beyond the door.

"We also found footprints in the sand. Anyone else been in your backyard lately?"

In the dim light, Duncan saw only a jumble of swirls and depressions like mini dunes.

"Shouldn't have been."

"Bare feet," the chief added.

Duncan recalled seeing Lindsay the month before on a beach chair, a straw hat covering her face, a thin blanket over her pale legs. She aped the pinup girls from the '50s, more teasing than tempting. Could someone else have seen her too? He looked away to dispel the memory.

The chief crouched on his haunches, fingers to his lips, tapping them lightly like a professor considering a problem.

"It's someone who knew the layout of the house. Who should we be looking at?"

"I... have no idea."

"She have any boyfriends?"

Duncan shook his head, only to have the question regurgitate on him. Would she have told him if she did? He knew a little about Glynis and her dates, as much as he wanted, but Lindsay had always veiled her romantic life. Even in high school, she rarely mentioned boys, and then only on accident. Privately, he preferred it that way.

The police chief looked up at him, frowning.

"Let's ask her sister."

* * *

"Lindsay was never into guys like that," Glynis said.

"Like what?" the chief said.

She glanced from the policeman to her father and back. Still seated on the living room couch, she looked isolated now. Josie had taken Aden upstairs, which relieved a bit of the pressure. Her irritability just made Glynis more reticent.

"She didn't want to date anyone seriously."

"How about unseriously?"

Glynis did another double take then shook her head.

"She saw guys as... a distraction."

"She go out with other people?"

"A few old friends from high school," she said, "but no one who'd...."

Glynis licked her lips but did not continue, so the chief turned to Duncan.

"Does anyone else come here? Housekeepers, cooks?"

"We don't need those," Duncan said. "There's a gardener who comes twice a week, but he's never inside. I doubt he's even seen Lindsay."

He glanced out the front window, where dawn illuminated the yard, its magnolia cut back for the winter, the azaleas deadheaded, grass browning.

"Anyone else, friends or people from work?"

"A few from the campaign, my manager, Kai. No one who'd do this."

"Regardless," the chief said in a calm tone, "we'll need a list of anyone who's visited in the last couple months."

"Of course."

Duncan glanced to the mantle, where the clock read 7:20. Could only two hours have passed? The morning felt endless.

"Anyone else we should talk to? Anyone who might resent or dislike her?"

While Duncan thought, footsteps banged down the stairs and skidded through the hall until Aden slid around the corner in socks, a hand on the door frame to hold himself upright.

"I know who she was seeing," he said.

They all turned and waited as he scanned from face to face, drawing out the moment.

"Some guy named Tom," the boy said. "I heard them on the phone last night."

CHAPTER 5

AFTER TALKING TO THE CHIEF, Duncan retreated to his study. Despite a closed door, he heard police stomping throughout the house. Quietly, he sat at his wide oak desk and surveyed the room, its piles and posters a chaos of unfinished business. Despite so many choices, he couldn't think what to do. No office work prepared him for burying a child. After many minutes sitting inert, he grabbed a tablet and listed people to notify: the funeral home, the florist, his minister, his siblings, other relatives. First, he called Kai.

"I need the morning off," Duncan said.

"No can do," Kai said. "You've got a network show at nine, the Rotarians at ten, and a major party donor right after. No way we can reschedule all that."

"Then cancel them. Something's come up."

"What?"

Heavy footsteps rattled the ceiling—more intruders in Lindsay's bedroom.

"I... it's personal. Just... I need time to take care of some things."

Kai stayed silent for at least ten seconds before answering, "Ohhhh-kay." It was the closest he'd come to disapproval, even as they languished in the polls.

"What about the afternoon?" Kai said. "We've got a dozen more confabs."

"I'll let you know."

The next several calls went more smoothly. The funeral director guided Duncan through dozens of choices about the type and timing of the burial.

The florist worked even more efficiently, though she asked him to stop in later. Rev. MacLeod proved more difficult to navigate, being trained in condolence. "But how are you *feeling*?" he kept asking. "Spent," Duncan wanted to say, but didn't.

After several hours trapped in his office, Duncan felt confined and restless. Yet when he stepped outside, he found a young female technician at the kitchen table with Josie and Glynis, rolling their fingers on an inkpad. His daughter's face showed exhaustion and fear, yet his wife's remained pinched and impatient.

"What's going on?" he said.

"They want our prints," Josie said, "like we're the criminals."

Duncan sat heavily and let the tech lead him through this foreign ritual.

"We'll need a cast of your feet, too," she said.

He looked outside to the sand drifts and beyond, to where the lake and sky merged into a monochrome of grey. A gust of wind stirred a haze of sand and dead leaves.

"How much longer will all this take?" Josie said.

"You'll have to ask the chief, ma'am. Should I get him?"

"Don't bother."

Duncan turned to his family; he planned to suggest they step outside for a walk when a creak overhead distracted him. He followed the sound to the front hall where two men in loose jumpsuits lugged a black plastic bag down the stairs. It stretched long and slim, sagging in the middle like a suspension bridge, with the bearers acting as pillars. From their awkwardness, it could only be one thing.

"Where are you taking Lindsay?" Duncan said.

"The coroner will be wanting an autopsy," said one bearer.

"Don't we... can't we see her first?"

The men paused, looked to each other. Just as the first opened his mouth, the chief emerged from Lindsay's bedroom and trod down the stairs.

"It'll only take a day or two," he said. "When the coroner's done, we'll transfer her to the funeral home."

"We can't see her?" Duncan said.

"You wouldn't want to."

As he steered Duncan by the elbow toward the living room, the bearers left, slamming the door after them. Through the front window, Duncan watched them carry his daughter toward a white van, swinging the body bag like it held rice or grain.

"She's that bad?" he said.

"Wait till she's cleaned up."

Cleaned of what? Only hours ago, she'd looked fine except a few bruises.

"I need to go out," Duncan said.

* * *

First he drove to the flower shop where he ran into Barbara Lyman, an old family friend, who asked why he needed a dozen bundles of chrysanthemums. Staring at her cordial grin, Duncan faltered, then explained, "A family affair."

"Campaign secret?" she said, with a wink. "Don't worry, I won't spill."

Next he stopped at the dry cleaners to retrieve his black suit. The owner, Mrs. Hannity, saw him weekly since the campaign started.

"Nobody wears black these days," she said, "but it's such a classic look. You can bring it back in style once you're elected."

When he returned home, two television crews occupied the sidewalk. He drove between them and stopped at the top of his circular driveway. Both reporters rushed him, thrusting microphones and demanding details.

"Ask the police," Duncan said.

He pushed past them, but they pursued with a vigor he could only have fantasized about for his previous press conferences.

"How are you feeling?" asked a middle-aged man with sprayed down hair.

"As you'd expect," he said.

"Will you drop out of the race?" asked a bottle blond with eyelashes longer than God could make.

"I haven't decided."

He escaped into the house, slamming the door behind him. In the hall, two things stood out: a stark quiet, and the stench of bleach.

"Anyone here?"

"Upstairs," Josie said.

Duncan followed the smell to Lindsay's room where Josie sat on the bare mattress, running her hand over it. A small brown stain remained where her head had lain hours ago. Before he could walk to her, she wiped away a tear and turned to him, her face contorted by the strain of composure.

"What are you doing?" he said.

"The police took her bedding."

"It was... nothing we'd want to keep."

"It's all we have left of her."

"That's not true."

As he cast about the room for other mementos, he noted how composed it looked compared to his tour with the chief.

"Did you clean the house?"

"It was filthy. Those people turned over everything but the dirty laundry."

Duncan shook his head, then thought how ridiculous his own morning had been, both of them acting as though the day comprised a list of chores. He sat next to her and put a hand on her back, but she didn't react.

"No... " she said.

She stood and walked to the window, keeping her back to him, and pretended to study something outside. Like his, her Depression-era parents equated emotion with weakness.

"I need a break," he said.

"From what?"

"The campaign."

She continued to face the window, revealing nothing of her thoughts.

"So you're quitting?"

"Just taking a few days off. I... we need to get through all this."

"There's no time. You've only got six weeks left."

"I'll wrap things up quickly."

"Let me handle everything. You focus on the election."

"I can't. Not until this is settled."

She sighed and pushed away a piece of hair from her face.

"You don't need to quit. I can manage."

"But I can't."

***

Duncan finished the day in his office with a call to Kai.

"I don't know how to say this, but I'm going to need some more time off."

"I know. I heard. I'm... sorry."

"From who?"

"Reporters," Kai said. "They've been calling all day, so I've postponed everything and asked for privacy."

"It should only be a few days."

"Don't sweat it. The staff and I can maintain. How are you holding up?"

Before answering, Duncan listened to the wind whirling outside and watched the trees blow and rebound. His parents—good Scotch Presbyterian—always forbid crying in front of others. Even in these circumstances, the rules seemed to hold true.

"The best we can," he said.

"You want me to tell the media anything while you're off?"

Overhead, the vacuum whirred to life, blotting out the stillness.

"That I'm not quitting."

CHAPTER 6

TWO DAYS LATER, Duncan scanned the chief's office: the Formica desk, the faux wood paneling, the plastic-covered love seat, everything clean and new but cheap. Across the hall, a man slept on a concrete bunk with his back to the bars, close enough for his snoring to be audible, the smells of his vomit and alcohol mixing with disinfectant. Duncan would not have imagined the chief sharing space with the town drunk. Then again, he never expected to be part of such a scene.

"We've generated a lot of leads," the chief said.

He tapped a manilla folder an inch thick with papers, the only thing visible on his desktop other than a penholder and telephone.

"Somewhere in here's the man we want. It's just a matter of figuring out which one."

He walked around the desk to sit in a folding chair opposite Duncan. Even in the office he dressed like a college professor, all earthy corduroy and woolens.

"Anytime a case goes public it generates a lot of calls, and we have to follow up on all of them. It takes time, but we've got everyone working."

Even sitting tired Duncan, his weight too much to support, as though the force of gravity had multiplied over forty-eight hours. The wood sapped him, the seat hard and cold against his thighs, the back cutting into his spine.

"Who are you talking to?" he said.

"We're starting with her friends, from the list you gave us."

The names came from a closet in Duncan's memory, friends from the community theater and Lindsay's high school. Five years had passed since she'd attended New Trier. Who knew if she'd kept in touch with any of them? Plus, the school contained thousands of kids.

"Anyone in particular?" Duncan said.

"One. I want to ask you about him, but you have to keep it to yourself. We don't want any leaks. People in this community are very... sensitive."

Duncan exhaled the vomit and bleach, trying to think what to say. Instead, he nodded.

"Good. Your son said he overheard Lindsay phone a 'Tom.' Does the name Tom Dalrymple mean anything to you?"

Duncan recalled a boy from her senior year: tall, slim, with dark, curly hair.

"We met him once or twice."

"How?"

"They went to a formal."

"What do you remember about him?"

"A swimmer, I think. Polite. From a good family."

The chief flipped open the file and jotted notes.

"When'd you last see him?"

"You'd have to ask my wife or Glynis."

"So he hasn't been to the house recently?"

"Not that I know of, but I've been away a lot. Were they... seeing each other?"

"He said no, but my sense is he had an eye for her."

"A lot of people did," Duncan said.

Since her teens, grown men had ogled Lindsay, stopping on the street for a double take, glancing furtively at her if they stood with other women. Their impudence had always annoyed Duncan, who'd glare back, but she'd learned to ignore it.

"Duncan," the chief said, using his first name for the first time. "Statistically, seventy percent of homicide victims know their killers. With women, it's usually somebody they dated or married."

He tapped a pen against the sole of his shoe as though measuring time.

"I understand," Duncan said, "but she didn't like men like that."

"Like what?"

"Killers."

"What about someone from college?"

"Most of her friends are back in New York."

"She must have mentioned somebody."

In her four years at Vassar, Lindsay never introduced her parents to any boys. On the phone she'd talk about friends, but she dwelled on academics and politics. Her years there appeared to him like postcards of someone else's vacation, everything pretty and serene. Had Duncan been remiss in overlooking his daughter's friends?

The relentless tapping brought Duncan back. He scanned the office for photos of the chief's family but found none. The shelves contained only books while the walls held plaques from the Rotarians and Masons.

"Do you have children?" Duncan said.

"Two boys."

"How old?"

"Thirteen and seventeen. You're wondering why I don't have any photos?"

Duncan nodded, caught in his amateur sleuthing by a pro.

"I don't want them exposed to the people I see."

Duncan felt chastised for his curiosity, then recalled why he'd asked.

"Yours are younger than Lindsay," he said. "When they get to be adults... they have their own lives. Your seventeen-year-old's probably taught you that already."

The chief nodded and—for the first time—broke eye contact.

"They live with their mother," he said. "But I see what you mean."

Duncan leaned back in his chair and sighed, feeling that he'd proved his point but still lost the argument. He'd failed to protect his daughter, and in his own house. No amount of rationalizing would relieve that.

"You should talk to Lindsay's roommate, Sandy Pantalion."

Plump, unkempt, bashful Sandy. Although the girls couldn't have been more different, they'd lived together Lindsay's last two years of college.

"And Lindsay acted in some plays."

As Tzeitel in *Fiddler on the Roof* she'd dressed in a tattered shawl and headscarf to sing "Miracle of Miracles" with her groom, a slender Oriental boy. Had Duncan seen something between them? At the time he passed it off as acting.

"Her art history professors, too."

The chief scribbled, then waited with a neutral expression. He didn't give away much.

Duncan inspected the walls, where photos linked the chief with local celebrities: George Halas on the sidelines of a Bears game, Mayor Daley, state assembly members past and present, mostly republicans. Not that it mattered. Duncan had taken more grip and grins than he could recall, often with no idea who he was gripping or why.

"What about a stranger?" Duncan said.

The chief crossed his legs at the knee—a professor's affectation—and set down his pen.

"From the autopsy we know your daughter asphyxiated. Someone broke her larynx."

Against his will, Duncan pictured his daughter's neck swollen with bruises.

"How—?"

"The coroner couldn't say what hit her, but something with a lot of force. The only injury he'd seen like that came from auto accidents where somebody hit the steering wheel."

A gust of wind set tree branches scratching at the window. The night before, Duncan had lain awake listening to the world breathe. At his side, the rise and fall of Josie's chest trembled through the mattress; above, the heater rattled its metal lungs; outside, the wind passed in a whistling gasp. All the world struggled for breath as he lay counting his own, waiting for the effort to become too much.

"Whoever killed her was motivated," the chief said.

"You think he *wanted* to assault my daughter?"

"He walked straight to her room."

"But why?"

"The coroner saw no sign of sexual assault," the chief said, and tapped his foot again, this time more slowly. "But *something* was driving this guy."

"So you're sure it's not a stranger?"

"Pretty much. That should make the investigation much easier though. We'll focus on people she knew. That way, I expect we'll have things wrapped up quickly."

CHAPTER 7

DUNCAN TRIED TO MATCH PACE with the other pallbearers, yet even with six of them the coffin left him straining. He leaned to counterbalance the weight, but his palm slipped on the metal handle, frozen dry and slick by the fall chill. Then he straightened his back, but this put all the stress on his shoulder. The burial plot waited fifty paces away. Surely he could hold on that far for the last time he'd be this close to his daughter until they met in heaven.

To his left, Aden carried the other side with military precision. The boy wore a new black suit from Marshall Fields since in the two months he'd been away at school his chest had grown two inches. His face too looked more manly with a buzz cut than the long hair and thin mustache he'd worn when he'd lived at home. He should have been back in class already, but his long weekend had been extended for the funeral.

Ahead, Rev. MacLeod waited beside the grave. In place of his usual robes and collar, the pastor wore a charcoal grey suit and a fedora, which felt anachronistic, too informal for a funeral. Yet he'd been extremely generous throughout the week, handling most of the arrangements, stopping by twice to check on the family, even spending an hour counseling Glynis the day before.

"Grief is irrational," he'd told Duncan. "It comes upon us at unexpected moments and in inappropriate ways. Don't judge your feelings. Let God hear them all. He will respond."

Still, Duncan found his ministrations lacked something: a personal connection that only those who knew the crime intimately could provide.

Talking to the police chief satisfied him more, if only because it promised some resolution.

Around them everything looked dead: the grass brown and crisp, the trees denuded of leaves, the sky grey and cloudless. Even the wind lacked life, carrying no scent of flowers or sound of birds, only the smog and traffic of the city. Surrounded by a phalanx of graves, Duncan felt nearly dead as well.

Finally, they set down the coffin, yet when he straightened Duncan still felt he bore its weight, and dizziness overcame him. The world swirled until a hand gripped his arm: Aden, who steered him to the circle of mourners.

At the back of the crowd stood Chief Dunleavy in a black wool over-coat, an Irish tweed cap pulled low over his eyes. Watching him watch the mourners, Duncan wondered if his motive was protection or detection. He'd said the killer hid close to Lindsay. Could he be one of the guests?

Among them stood Chicago's Mayor, Michael Bilandic, his head lowered so that his silver hair shone even in the dull light. Surrounding him clustered a dozen aldermen and other city officials Duncan knew only from photos. Even U.S. Sen. Charles Percy showed. Why had they come, for some political advantage? Surely none resided with the dead. When he suspended the campaign, Duncan meant temporarily, but he'd come to like the isolation. He hadn't realized what a burden he'd been carrying until it lifted. That morning, the *Tribune* reported Big Bill Stratton had stood down as well. The governor hadn't said for how long, but it didn't matter. If neither of them said another word, would it change the result?

"Who may separate us from the love of Christ?" said Rev. MacLeod.

His voice resonated throughout the open space.

"Shall tribulation, or distress, or persecution, or famine, or nakedness, or peril, or sword?"

For many minutes the reverend quoted scripture dramatically, as though God Himself stood in attendance. Finally he set down his Bible and invited speakers to the podium, fashioned from a music stand tottering on three legs in the uneven grass.

First came Glynis, who minced on high heels, then leaned on the wobbly tripod for balance.

"You're supposed to resent your kid sister, especially when she's so pretty, but I loved Lindsay. I used to call her the Bionic Woman since she looked just like her, but she also wanted to be strong."

While she recalled Lindsay's beauty and drive, Duncan took in Glynis' own aura. Even made up she looked unkempt, her hair coming loose from its clips and the seam of her stockings crooked. Worse, her legs trembled, as though without the platform she might crumble. By the time she finished, Duncan exhaled with relief, except on her walk back to the crowd her heel caught in the dirt, and she had to grab Josie's arm for support.

Meanwhile, Aden took her place at the podium and stared at the audience until everyone went silent. For the first time he looked unsure, stuffing his hands in his pants pockets and hunching his shoulders as though he expected a bad reception.

"She was my sister too," he said.

He shrugged, looked down at the empty music stand, then back at the audience.

"I'm not going to say how cool she was, cause she could be a real square. Sometimes she'd play the fuzz with me, like if I tried to sneak out late or stall on my homework, but it was cool. I knew she was just doing it to keep me in line."

Aden looked uncomfortable, as though his new suit bound too tight. Probably it arose from all the attention—he disliked being watched by adults—but in his darting looks and stammering delivery Duncan sensed something deeper, a shame that he hadn't done more to protect his sister. After going on about her overprotectiveness, he nodded to himself, compressed his mouth into a tight frown, and looked to the crowd.

"So I guess now I'll have to look after myself," he said and walked back to his place with his hands still pocketed, shoulders hunched.

Josie followed him and—after composing her notes and herself—offered the first faint smile of the day.

"At age eight, I told my father I wanted to be president. He laughed and patted my head and explained that girls didn't have jobs, they had families. Truth is, most working-class girls felt lucky to have homes. We nearly lost ours to The Great Depression. World War II saved us when our farm became a Victory Garden, and my mother suddenly became employable. She saw Norman Rockwell's picture of Rosie the Riveter on the cover of the *Saturday Evening Post* and later read Mrs. Roosevelt's column encouraging women to take jobs, so she became a secretary at the Fleischmann Company in Peekskill.

"After that, I practiced my reading with the first lady's columns about war and trips abroad. She taught me to dream of better than typing or sewing.

"That lasted until May 14, 1945, when Mrs. Eleanor wrote about the E.R.A.: "I doubt very much whether it ever will be." The byline read Hyde Park, just up the river from our farm. I had just turned eleven, but I've remembered the words ever since. They crushed my hopes in a single sentence."

She turned to face her children, who stood stiff and immobile, as though accused by the tale. Compared to them, Josie looked poised and proud. Even in her black dress and heels she stood straight and defiant, as though she were giving a birthday remembrance or a wedding toast.

"I vowed that my girls would never feel those limits. That's why we sent Lindsay to Vassar and why I encouraged her dreams of becoming curator at the Art Institute. When she said that she planned to buy all the Georgia O'Keeffe's and Camille Claudels, I told her she should open her own museum."

Finally she lifted her veil to stare at the mourners, her skin pale and taut with effort.

"We can't let her death paralyze us," she said. "My daughter's gone, but she hasn't left us."

When his turn came, Duncan walked slowly to the podium, then paused to view the cemetery, which stretched away as far as he could see, a minefield of headstones. At the gates, news vans idled, coughing out exhaust, but they lurked too far away to intrude.

"My daughter was...."

He looked down at the page in his hands, but it offered nothing. The day before he'd locked himself in his office for hours and tried to write a speech, then just some notes, and finally to find even one appropriate quote from the Bible, but the words eluded him.

" ...bionic. She took the poor parts that we gave her and improved on them, built herself into... a remarkable girl. She could have been doing anything now: acting, curating, studying. Instead she came home to be with her family in a time of need, sacrificing...."

Sacrificing: not the word he intended, but it had escaped already, hanging in the air like the smell of chrysanthemums from her funeral bouquets, so he continued.

" ...sacrificing herself for us."

He scanned the mourners, but few would return his look. Most studied the ground, crying silently or nodding to themselves. Except one. In back, a young man peaked several inches above the others, his wet eyes raised to the heavens. Even from far away he looked handsome with dark, curly hair and a sharp, Germanic nose and chin. Sensing Duncan's stare, he smiled weakly and looked down. Then recognition came. Though he'd filled out, Tom's face hadn't changed since he'd picked up Lindsay for the dance years before. Duncan returned the half smile but resolved to talk to him after the service.

Suddenly he noticed the silence and saw everyone watching him. "As a little girl, Lindsay used to sit beside my desk while I was working. She'd keep quiet but would stare at me with such intensity I... couldn't concentrate."

A breeze ruffled Duncan's blank notes, and he slapped them flat before continuing. "Now I feel like she's still watching me, waiting for me to explain all this...." He gestured to the crowd, the cemetery, the bare trees, then waited for inspiration, but his thoughts remained clouded and vague.

Finally, Rev. MacLeod guided Duncan from the podium until Aden took over and escorted him back to his place, keeping a firm grip on his father's arm.

"Please, if you would, join me now in the Lord's Prayer," Rev. MacLeod said.

The familiar words helped Duncan again find his voice:
"Our Father, who art in heaven,
Hallowed be thy name.
Thy kingdom come,
Thy will be done,
On earth as it is in heaven."

* * *

An hour later, the mourners gathered at the Cochrane home, sipping single malt scotch and ale, eating Cornish pasties and cucumber sandwiches catered by McDowells. While Duncan accepted condolences at the front door, Josie mingled in the living room. Glynis and Aden had both disappeared, probably upstairs to their rooms. Hospitality demanded too much of them now. Thankfully, the mayor and other politicos had begged off the luncheon, so after everyone arrived Duncan felt free to see the guests he wanted to. He found Tom Dalrymple seated on the stairwell with a half dozen young women.

"I'm glad you all came," Duncan said.

They answered with nods or murmurs.

"You're Tom?"

"Yes, sir."

He stood for a handshake and loomed several inches taller than Duncan. His shoulders expanded to the limits of his black suit, although his hips and legs tapered in comparison. His body looked capable of the cruelty the police had described, but his expression remained kind.

"Can I speak to you in private?" Duncan said.

In his office, Duncan ushered Tom to the leather sofa and took a place opposite, crossing his legs to signal that he intended a casual conversation.

"It's been a while. What, four years?"

"I think so."

"What have you been doing with yourself?"

"College in Michigan."

"And what's next?"

"I start grad school this fall."

"In?"

"Mechanical engineering."

"Lots of jobs in that."

"Yes, sir."

Duncan studied his face a moment and saw how hard he was working to restrain his emotions.

"What about sports. You're a swimmer, right?"

"I'm done with that now."

"That's a shame. What happened?"

"I ran out of eligibility."

"Yes, of course."

Tom shrank in Duncan's presence, collapsing into the beaded red cushions as he sipped from his tumbler of scotch.

"I hear you and Lindsay were getting reacquainted."

The young man nodded and took a hit of Glenlivet, though his face betrayed no pleasure in the taste.

"Were you dating?"

"We were friends."

Tom emptied his drink and looked about for more, so Duncan took his glass, walked to the bar, and refilled it with Bicentenary Highland Park. Before he could speak again, Tom drained half of it.

"Look, Tom, you don't need to be so... demure about it. I know Lindsay had boyfriends. I'm just asking: were you two romantically involved?"

"Did she tell you that?"

"No, the police did. They think you might know something that'll help them."

"I've already told them everything."

"Actually, they said you were uncooperative."

"That's not true! I answered all their questions. Same as yours."

"Then why would they say that?"

The young man stood and walked to the window, jingling the ice before slamming the liquor.

"Because of my dad."

He turned to Duncan, his face in shadow with the window behind him.

"He told me not to get involved."

"Why?"

"He's afraid I'd end up... I don't know. It's not like I have anything to hide. Lindsay and I... hung out. Then the police came at me about how I called her the day before she... died. What did I say? When did I see her last? It felt like a movie."

Duncan studied the young man, whose frustration could not hide a shaky voice.

"You've never felt pressure like that before."

"What do you mean?"

"Math tests and swim meets aren't the real world."

"I'm not some sheltered college kid," he said. "I've done stuff."

He set the glass down heavily on the windowsill.

"But you've never lost someone close to you."

The boy shook his head and looked down. Duncan stood and refilled his own drink. When he turned back, Tom was handling something small but firm: an emerald band.

"She gave me this," Tom said.

"What is it?"

Tom rubbed it in his fingers, then pocketed it.

"A mood ring. It's supposed to read your emotions. The color reveals what you're feeling. It was just a joke. Lindsey didn't believe in it, but it definitely changes color."

"What does green mean?"

"Sadness."

Duncan returned to the sofa and waited for Tom to join him, but he stayed by the window.

"Why'd you call her?"

"When?"

"The night she died."

"Did she say that?"

"The police did."

The boy looked away for a good thirty seconds, but Duncan decided to wait him out.

"Just to talk."

"About?"

"We had planned to get something to eat, but she said you needed her... your campaign. So we talked about meeting up later."

"So you *were* dating?"

Tom's silence provided all the answer Duncan needed. Still, even as the young man stared into his empty palms, he seemed to await absolution.

"Do you feel responsible?" Duncan said.

"For what happened? No, why would I?"

"I do. It's a man's role to protect the women he loves."

"I don't see how —"

"I'm not saying you could have. I'm only saying... if you know *anything* that could help...."

The boy looked up and grabbed the tumbler again, rolling it between his palms so firmly Duncan feared it would crack the crystal.

"Sometimes," Tom said, "she acted... sad."

"How so?"

"She didn't like to talk about things. Like your campaign. If I asked, she'd say something vague about stuffing envelopes, and then change the subject."

"She felt sad about my campaign?"

"About the polls. She knew you were losing, and I think it bothered her. That other people didn't see you the way she did. So I assumed that was it."

"But now you don't?"

"I... don't know."

Duncan nodded and looked to his bookshelves, where photos showed Lindsay at every age from birth to death: in a crib, a play, a graduation. In the last of them, she gripped her mother and sister at an early fundraiser. They all wore straw hats with "Cochrane in '78" across the bands. He recalled his wife's speech at the funeral, of her ambition for her children, and her surety of their impending success. All the children on the North Shore lived with expectations of greatness weighing on them, including Tom.

"I appreciate your honesty," Duncan said.

He stood and walked to the door, turning the handle to crack the lock but using his weight to keep it closed. When he looked back, the sun shone off the lake sanctifying Tom in a halo of golden light.

"How long will you be in town?" Duncan said.

"All summer."

"So we can talk more later."

CHAPTER 8

THROUGH THE SHEERS on his living room windows, Duncan checked the front lawn and saw it lay empty — finally. For five days reporters occupied his yard, blocked the street, filmed the house, and made it impossible to leave. Many times the police had chased them away, but like flies they'd circle and return. The chief said he would have assigned a uniform to guard the house full time if he had the staff, but the investigation was consuming all his manpower. Instead, he offered regular patrols as the best substitute.

Perhaps the scavengers had finally sated themselves, though Duncan didn't trust that they'd finished picking at him. He walked to the kitchen and exited through the back door, where the new lock stuck and the new windowpane gleamed. A small brick patio gave way to sand and the lakefront, which looked grey in the overcast and merged with an equally monochrome sky. Wind whipped the waves into small whitecaps and sent the water slapping up the beach, almost like on the ocean. It smelled all wrong, though, more rotting fish than salt spray.

Fences led almost to the water's edge, forcing Duncan to use the thick, damp sand to cross his neighbors' back yards. The beach compressed under his tread, but his prints quickly filled with water and dissolved. He studied the sand drifts for footprints or debris but found only the peaks left by the wind. Five days before, the killer had followed this same path. Had he too used the tide to disguise his steps? In either direction he would have passed several other lots before reaching a cross street. Surely someone had seen him.

At the first turnabout Duncan paused and looked east toward Sheridan Road, where cars passed as usual. Most likely no one remained to see him, but he kept to the waterfront, bypassing a sign that warned "private beach." Homeowners allowed each other free passage. Convention dictated that they not ogle or speak to one other, yet as he passed the Brennermans, Duncan exchanged nods with the elderly husband, who in defiance of the weather wore shorts and docksiders. Whether due to discretion or embarrassment, none of the neighbors had called or visited the Cochranes for a week. Two days before, a basket of fruit appeared on their doorstep with a card that read only, "Thinking of you."

After two blocks, the beach ended at a cliff and a grass skirt surrounding two apartment towers. Duncan crossed the lawn, then Sheridan Road, and entered Plaza del Lago, a strip mall clothed in Spanish dress with creamy plaster, red tile roofs, and a bell tower. Across the parking lot waited a pharmacy that carried all the local newspapers.

Inside the store, a clerk glanced up at the bell's jangle, then just as quickly looked to the glass case below her as though contemplating a purchase. She had to be a teenager, pale and ponytailed, a stranger to him, yet a blush rose on her cheeks. Since the news broke, Duncan had grown used to that reaction. People on the street would see him and look away in shame, as though they bore some of the guilt. He passed it off as awkwardness, that they couldn't find the words. What could one say? "Sorry" didn't fit, yet no other word came closer.

Duncan skirted the front counter and headed to the magazine rack to check the headlines. The *Tribune* read: "Woman Slain at Loop L; Ford says Warren Conclusion Right; Blast Rips U.S. Oil Facility." The *Sun-Times* ran similar leads but nothing about him, Lindsay's death, or the governor's race. A weekly Kenilworth rag featured pictures of his house and the demure headline "Woman Slain Along Sheridan Road," but the first few graphs offered nothing new. Like their pestilent employees, the papers had finally moved on.

Duncan wanted to spare the young clerk from seeing him again but felt awkward about leaving without buying anything. Behind him, the shelves held all the usual remedies for headaches, constipation, sleeplessness. He reached for some aspirin, then noticed a vending machine by the door. Cigarettes cost only fifty cents a pack and could be purchased anonymously. Duncan hadn't smoked since his twenties when Josie harangued him to quit by refusing to kiss him if he smelled of tobacco. Still he could imagine their release, a mellow head rush that dulled the nerves. In his pocket he found two quarters.

The machine's handle felt stiff and sticky, so much that Duncan feared the contraption had eaten his money. Then a pack fell to the tray. He scooped it up and left without looking back.

Outside, cars congested the parking lot, so he walked to a small grass patch across the street. Under the canopy of an elm tree, he fumbled with the cellophane wrapper, tapped a cigarette free, and pushed it between his lips, then realized he had no matches.

He hated the thought of returning to the pharmacy but couldn't bear to toss the pack. Already his hands trembled and his throat bound in anticipation. At home waited plenty of matches but also his family.

Then he saw a woman nearing on the sidewalk, young and slender, with straight blond hair, tight jeans and a fringed leather jacket. More importantly, she held her fingers away from her body then raised them to her lips. When she'd moved to within a few feet, Duncan stepped from under the tree, startling her. She paused and studied him.

"Light?" he said.

For a moment he feared she recognized him, but no, she was just cautious. To show his harmlessness he extended his own cigarette. Reassured, she dug a lighter out of her purse and flared it for him.

"Cheers," he said.

As soon as she passed, he ducked under the tree cover again. His first puff tasted dreadful, like sucking on dry dirt, and he coughed up most of the smoke, but after the second came the rush. His head felt light, his tension dispersing with each drag. After finishing the first Joe, he lit another with the butt and sucked it down to the filter, then pocketed the pack and turned toward home.

This time he used the sidewalks along Sheridan Road, confident that no one would stop him. And they didn't.

On his front doorstep sat a cellophaned basket with cheese and fruit, which he carried inside and set on a table next to a half dozen other gifts.

In him, relief mixed with disappointment. The guard dog he'd expected now slept, uninterested.

"Anybody here?" he called.

His voice echoed off the tile floors but with no reply. He climbed the stairs and turned toward his bedroom, then tasted the cigarette's staleness. Since his own bath connected to the master suite, he used the girls' at the other end of the hall. In the vanity he found some minty mouthwash, but other cosmetics stopped him. One shelf held Lindsay's toothbrush, mascara, two shades of blue eye shadow, a smattering of barrettes and hair ties. Instinct said to dump the whole medicine cabinet before anyone else noticed, but he couldn't imagine throwing out anything of hers.

Back in the hall, he passed Aden's door. A day before, Duncan had dropped his son at the airport so he wouldn't miss any more school. Understandably, Aden had acted morose the last few days, staying in his room, listening to music, appearing only for dinner and then only as long as required. While waiting in the lounge for his flight, the boy had promised to focus on school and not Lindsay's death. If only Duncan could do the same.

At Glynis' door he stopped and listened but heard nothing. She behaved no better than her brother, skipping meals and sleeping late. The whole family dangled in limbo, uncertain how to move forward, unable to look back.

In their bedroom he found Josie splayed across the mattress, staring at the ceiling. Hearing him, she turned her head but stared without a word.

"They're gone," he said.

"Who?"

"The blood-sucking reporters. They've given up."

He sat beside her and laid a hand on her hip.

"What about you?" she said.

"What do you mean?"

"Have you given up?"

"On what? Lindsay?"

"The election. You've been mooning around for days like we could stop time."

"I hadn't even thought of it."

Outside, a breeze blew tree branches against the window so they scratched like a dog wanting in.

"If you wait any longer, it'll be too late."

Suddenly tired, he lay beside her and let his arm wrap around her waist.

"You don't think it would be undignified?"

"No, but quitting would."

He buried his face into her shoulder. In her hair he smelled citrus shampoo, then wondered if his own carried the stink of smoke.

"I don't have the...." he started, but the right word wouldn't come to him.

She pushed off his arm and rolled to face him.

"What good is mourning? It's your misery feeding on itself. Lindsay's death should fire you!"

"What if it's too late already? It's only been a week, but it feels like everyone has forgotten. What if we forgot, too?"

She palmed his chest, pushed him flat, and rolled on top to straddle him.

"Then you'll lose more than a daughter."

"You don't think... the union won't hold us to those promises. Not after what happened."

"They put no conditions on that bet. Their money's on you to win, not place."

"Have you heard from anyone?"

She shook her head and looked past him. "I never told you about this," she said, "but back when I was young, union guys kept me from getting... I don't know what."

She paused as though unsure whether to continue, then did. "I'd just turned fifteen, and on the radio I heard about these riots in Peekskill because Paul Robeson planned to sing there. A bunch of the locals fretted about an invasion of 'insurrectionary socialist Negroes,' and they caused so much trouble the concert got cancelled. The next day the *Evening Star* ran photos of men turning over cars and one of a teenager lying unconscious on top of a grave. It blew up into the biggest local scandal ever, so when the concert got rescheduled, I snuck out to hear it.

"The same rednecks tried to block the road until union volunteers formed a human wall around the grounds. They stood guard for two hours while we heard Pete Seeger sing 'This Land is Your Land.'

"Then we all boarded buses to escape the thugs, only they waited for us up the road. A couple blocked the way while the others loaded up like archers. My own neighbors threw stones that shattered every window. They sprayed us with glass until my face looked like I'd been attacked by razor blades.

"A bunch of police stood by and smiled. They had us trapped and helpless until the union guys reappeared with bats and tire irons."

She smiled wistfully until Duncan interrupted. "The meat cutters aren't that type of union."

"Not long ago, you were one of them."

"They're not our protectors."

"No, they're your workers."

He grasped her hands firmly and spoke. "This isn't upstate New York, and it's not the 1950s. We're not going to run into these guys at church or the local diner. The only place I see them is in contract negotiations, and they're not rough, they're hard. They wear rings thick as brass knuckles."

"But they're your biggest supporters."

"More like my loan sharks."

"You knew the terms when you took the money."

"We shouldn't have. I shouldn't have let you talk me into it."

"Who else would fund you?"

He placed his hands on her hips and adjusted himself beneath her. "What if we paid it back?"

"All of it?"

"Eventually."

"You really want to owe those people?"

"We do already."

She pushed his hands from her and stared down into his face. "You're already defeated," she said.

"I... can't see a way past this."

"I can. Get busy! When you're governor you can mourn. Right now you've got to act."

"All that's left are flowers. People drop them on our stoop and run as though a plague has struck our house. They look away from me on the street like I'm a leper."

"People run from grief. Show some passion and they'll respond."

He tried to look away from her stare, but she pressed down with all her weight upon his chest and gripped her legs tight about his waist.

"Damn it, Duncan, do it for your daughter!"

"How?"

"Be as vicious as her killer. Utter her name like a curse. Don't let people forget."

His chest ached from her weight, but he preferred pain to isolation. "You think that will be enough?"

"It has to be."

CHAPTER 9

A DAY LATER, Duncan stood inside the foyer of the Kenilworth Club with the police chief. When Dunleavy suggested meeting there, Duncan didn't understand why he'd choose a place walking distance from the police department, but now it made sense. The empty hall offered more privacy than any office or home. Even its stained glass windows hid the inside.

The chief left his overcoat buttoned, looking stiff and formal, interrogating Duncan with his eyes before he spoke

"Has anyone threatened you?" he began.

"What?" Duncan said.

"Your safety or your family's."

"Why would you think that?"

The chief stepped into the main hall — a typical Prairie style room with leaded glass windows, hardwood floors, and a low-slung roof of exposed beams. Something about the place felt familiar, as though it had hosted some civic event or fundraiser he'd attended.

"My detectives went over all the physical evidence and found... nothing. All the fingerprints we collected belonged to your family. The footprints on the sand were a men's nine, the most common size. And like you said, nothing was stolen."

Duncan craved a cigarette but didn't dare smoke inside the old wood building. "I don't understand. What are you implying?"

"This was no amateur burglar. He escaped without leaving any evidence, even though your elder daughter walked in on him. A typical thief would have panicked and made a racket trying to get out, but you slept steps away and heard nothing."

"So you think... what?"

"Organized crime has professional killers. That's why I asked about threats. Typically you'd get some warning."

"I... no, nothing like that. I doubt I've met an actual mobster. You mean like Al Capone? Why would they want to hurt Lindsay?"

"You are running for a major office."

The suggestion gripped Duncan like a hand around the throat, cutting off his speech and breath. "Who?" was all he could say.

"I'd hoped you'd know. So no one's contacted you?"

In his coat pocket, Duncan found a pack of cigarettes. He lit one, inhaled a lung-full, and waited for the smoke to lubricate the tension before answering. "No."

"I hate to ask this, but I have to. You know holding back will make it impossible for us to solve this case?"

"This isn't *The Godfather*."

"But it is politics."

"Not my kind."

Outside, a train chugged by, rattling the chandeliers, pulsating through the air, and overwhelming all other sounds. While he waited for its vibrations to pass, Duncan studied the roof's sag and the water stains on the rafters. The hardwoods too showed the damage from years of Boy Scouts and 4Hers. Decay could hide in any corner.

"Why are you asking me this now?"

"We can protect you, and your family."

"Too late."

"Not if we know what we're facing."

"You think you can stop an assassin?"

"If you tell us who to look for."

"I've told you everything. This isn't about the campaign. You're trying to blame us instead of... whoever. It's been a week, and all I've heard is speculation. Now you've got more conspiracy theories than the Warren Commission. Quit all the hypothesizing and find my daughter's killer."

The chief took it stoically, eyeing Duncan and waiting to respond. "We want this solved as much as you, but we're running out of leads."

He turned to one of the colorful windows and stared silent as Duncan looked in vain for an ashtray; the hall had been stripped, so he finished his cigarette and ground the butt to ashes under the sole of his loafer.

"I've resisted going public," the chief said, "but a reward might help."

"You want to buy information?"

"Some people need a reason to do the right thing."

Duncan walked to the bare stage and stared, then located his *déjà vu*: Lindsay's last night. The room looked just like the banquette hall, with a dozen sets of tables and chairs. That evening, he'd begged for donations while back home someone lay in wait for them.

"I need to talk to some people first," Duncan said.

"Your campaign staff?"

"No. Friends. I'll call them today and get back to you."

* * *

Winter had arrived overnight. Frost-edged windows, and wind-whipped trees. Outside the Kenilworth Club, Duncan raised the collar of his overcoat and covered his mouth with a scarf. What next? The Metra train tracks pointed downtown, so he hopped the first express. Inside, the cars were smooth, quiet, clean, and light. Riders usually respected the ethic of privacy. Still, to avoid notice, Duncan sat on the upper tier. For the next half hour he watched the skyscrapers of downtown grow from weeds on the horizon to tall timbers around him.

It all sounded farfetched: political payback, hired killers. This wasn't medieval Scotland, and he wasn't Macbeth. What would anyone gain by killing Lindsay? Only to drive him out of the race, and no one had suggested that (yet). To make sense of it, he needed advice from someone who knew both crime and politics.

After exiting the train, he craved a cigarette worse than ever. Not even ten, and it would be his third of the morning. This relapse was stretching into days. He huddled under an awning, moved aside his scarf, and enjoyed a long puff, but no more. After his first step across the street, a gust blew the butt to the gutter. In Chicago, the wind built momentum on the lake then funneled its strength down every east-west corridor like Walter Payton bursting through the line of scrimmage.

So it went for the next three blocks — calm, gust, calm, gust, calm — until Duncan turned west on Harrison, where the gale hurried him to the state's attorney's office. He passed through the lobby unnoticed, rode the elevator to the eighth floor, then walked head down through a corridor of cubicles toward an open door with the name plate Ron Turner. The office compacted a half dozen heavy, metal objects: battered filing cabinets, packed bookshelves, and a broad desk. Manila files overflowing with paper covered every flat surface. The piles stacked up neatly but without any obvious order.

Duncan's old friend stood facing the windows. His greying hair matched his pinstripe suit, but his body looked as lean and lithe as when he'd been nicknamed "Slim" and hardly filled out the grey pinstripes of his baseball uniform. They'd met as undergrads at Northwestern and had kept in casual contact since, political allies on parallel career tracks.

"Batter up," Duncan said.

Ron turned and stared.

"What are... did we...?"

"I need your help with something."

Duncan closed the door against the clatter and bells of office typewriters then replayed his conversation with the chief. Throughout, Ron sat silently, as though he were deposing a suspect, but when Duncan finished he leaned forward for his cross examination.

"Organized crime?" he said. The attorney's surprise registered in two rises and falls in pitch.

"According to the police," Duncan said.

"Hmm.

"What does 'hmm' mean?"

"Only that we haven't had a political assassination for — I don't know — forty years? You remember Mayor Cermak?"

"The mob killed him?"

"Officially, a crazed immigrant shot him, but some people blame Al Capone. There's never been any proof of that, though. Most likely he was aiming at F.D.R., who sat next in line."

"Anyone else?"

"Not unless you believe the J.F.K. conspiracy theories."

On the wall opposite hung a flag inscribed "Land of Lincoln" over an outline of the state. Another assassinated politician from Illinois, yet not even the most crazed historian implicated gangsters for that.

"So you don't believe politics... played a role here?"

"I'd say there's not enough evidence for an investigation. You want me to ask around?"

"Quietly. I don't want this on the news."

From his desk, Ron picked up a rainbow-colored slinky and began weighing it palm to palm. As a student, he'd often gripped a baseball even far away from the diamond, anything to keep his hands busy.

"I need to ask about something else," Duncan said. "Tomorrow, I'm announcing that I'm still in the race. You don't think...?"

How to phrase it? Even putting words to the thought felt dangerous.

Fortunately, Ron understood. "That it's a risk?"

Ron gathered the slinky, raised it over an open hand, and let it fall like cards. "Hard to say. If you're worried about publicity, though...."

"It's not that. If anything, the press might help. The chief proposed a reward, but that feels too much like a payoff."

"Or a provocation."

"We need to do something. The police are stymied, and the only power I have is notoriety."

"Still, be careful what you say in public."

"But you just said you didn't think this could be political."

"Probably not."

"Probably?"

"With so little to go on, what do you expect?"

Twenty years before, Ron excelled at plate patience. He'd foul off a dozen pitches to get one he could hit. Apparently, his instincts hadn't changed.

"Why do you want this so bad?" he said.

"What, Lindsay's killer? Why do you think?"

"No, to be governor. Back in school, you never cared about politics. When most guys were arguing about the draft and the spread of communism, all you cared about was making the college World Series."

"I want to bring some business savvy to government. I'm sick of all the inefficiency and—"

"I know your campaign slogans. I mean why *really*?"

Duncan looked out the window at the building blocks of the cityscape, its orderly grid disguising the anarchy within. "You wouldn't ask that if you worked in meat packing."

"It got you a house on the North Shore."

Ron picked up his slinky again, letting his thumb rattle against the coils until Duncan wanted to snatch it from him. Despite his office with a view, Ron lived modestly, with a two-bedroom on the South Side for a family of five. Duncan tried not to be showy with his wealth around his old friend, but Ron could recognize a tailored suit and handmade English Oxfords.

"I need something... more," Duncan said. "I can't spend the rest of my life as a bloody butcher."

"Is it worth risking your safety?"

"You think I am?"

Ron replaced the slinky on his desktop but kept one hand covering it. "No one's contacted you?" he said.

"Such as?"

"In this town, it could be anybody: aldermen, lawyers, unions."

"No, no one."

"Not even heavies from the party?"

"Why would they? I'm not part of the Machine."

"Fine, but pay attention to the people around you."

Twice in a day someone had all but accused Duncan of corruption, as though politics left an unbleachable stain. Then he thought of Lindsay's last night. "Wait. There's one guy. From The American Brotherhood of Laborers. He showed up at my last fundraiser."

"You talk to him?"

"Only for a minute, but he talked to Lindsay."

"What's his name?"

"Joe Sturmer."

"Dark, stocky guy with one good arm?"

"That's him."

The attorney moved to a filing cabinet and riffled two drawers before extracting a thick folder. He examined the contents for a silent minute but kept them to himself. Finally, he spoke: "What'd he say?"

"Nothing specific, just wanted my support on some labor issues, but he's left three messages in a week."

"You call him back?"

"Not yet."

"Don't. You don't want anything to do with him."

"You think he could have—"

"That's not what I'm saying. Just keep clear."

"Why do you have his file?"

Ron collated the pages and replaced them in the cabinet.

"Legally, I can't say, but you can guess."

Duncan picked up the slinky and stretched out the coils like a harmonica, unsure how it worked. "What should I do?" he said.

"Keep your circle small, nobody you don't know intimately. If you have to be in public, keep your personal life to yourself. Don't talk about the case, don't answer questions about your family. Be the most cloistered politician this side of the Pope."

When Duncan's fingers became entangled with the toy, he replaced it gently. "I'll keep things quiet, but I can't withdraw. Right now, it's all I have going for me."

"I understand," Ron said. "I've talked to a lot of victims and their families. They all think solving the case is going to bring them relief. That's... most of the time it doesn't. You're better off getting on with things. There's more relief in distraction than obsession."

Ron sat in the chair opposite him and leaned forward to close the gap between them. "I'll check with some friends, see if they believe the mob theory," he said. "Meantime, you stay on the opposite end of town."

CHAPTER 10

OUT THE WINDOWS on the 39th floor of the John Hancock Center, Duncan could see twenty miles in all directions. To the south lay the downtown high rises and the curve of the lakefront to the Indiana border. East, the lake stretched out like an endless blanket. West, the skyscrapers descended to a grid of low-rise blocks cut at diagonals by freeways. Below, traffic pulsed, a free flow through the city's veins and arteries toward vital organs and distant extremities. The life force of downtown Chicago continued, even if Duncan no longer flowed with it.

"What's happened since I stepped away?" he said.

"Nothing," Kai said. "Big Bill's kept his pledge not to campaign, and without any fresh blood the news parasites have lost their appetite for us."

Duncan turned from the view and looked over Kai's office furniture: plastic chairs curved like egg cups, a couch of molded foam shaped like an amoebic blob, hanging lamps in the form of bubbles. Even Kai's desk looked space-aged with chrome legs and a clear Plexiglas top. How could you get comfortable? Standing appealed more.

"That's good, I guess," Duncan said. "At least we're no farther back."

"Not at this point. The last *Tribune* poll put you ten points behind. Making that up in four weeks is... " he nodded to himself, "a push."

Outside, a seagull banked left and right on invisible wind currents, passing through the corridor of skyscrapers toward the lake. Its progress looked effortless, although the work lay not in the flying but in the direction, reacting to those invisible winds. Birds did it instinctively, but politicians rarely could.

"We've got our work cut out for us then," Duncan said.

Kai looked away. "I'm hip to what you're doing," he said. "No one likes to give up. Ordinarily, I'd suggest we play this out to the final curtain, but you've already been through enough. I've talked to the party leaders, and they're all down with your situation. No one's going to blame you for letting an understudy take over. In a couple years, if you decide to run again, you'll have center stage."

Like Duncan, Kai qualified as a newcomer to Illinois politics, a director of three civic contests who was running a statewide show for the first time. In pushing him to steer Duncan's campaign, party leaders called him a rising star. Now Duncan wondered. Could any outsider penetrate the network of Irishmen who'd ruled the city for decades?

"What about all the promises we made and the donations we took?"

"Don't feel like you're letting anybody down. Mitch Kupcinek has already volunteered to step in. All you have to do is say the word, and I've got press releases ready."

"Mitch Kupcinek is a city alderman," Duncan said.

From behind him, Kai said quietly, "Yeeeesss," dragging out the word to several syllables.

"Who we beat handily in the primary."

After another pause, Kai said, "Yeeeesss."

"Which means he can't win."

"No, he can't."

"Which means you don't believe I can either."

Duncan turned to see Kai staring at him with an expression of sorrow unlike any he'd seen before. For a theater buff, he didn't have much faith in the surprise ending.

"I think we've got to get real about this."

"Haven't people come back from big deficits?"

Kai picked up his phone and dialed four numbers — an in-house call — then said, "Join us."

A minute brought Parish Steves, the campaign's treasurer, tall, thin, and dark, with features that suggested pure African heritage. Though Duncan could appreciate his conservative style — blue suits, white shirts, red ties — Parish had always been stiff and formal around him.

"Let's figure out exactly how much work we have," Kai said. "The state has 5.7 million registered voters. Most likely half of them will come out in November. That means we have four weeks to turn how many, Parish?"

Without hesitation, the treasurer answered, "Two hundred eighty-five thousand."

Outside, clouds blew past on the invisible wind. When he stood still, Duncan felt the skyscraper swaying with the strongest gusts. How could you convince people to live in a building that wasn't firmly anchored? It took great salesmanship. Yet someone had it, because here stood he and thousands of others suspended four hundred feet above street level.

"What do you suggest?" Duncan said.

Kai's expression suggested a disappointed parent. "Breaking it down further, that translates to how many people per week, Parish?"

"Seventy-five thousand."

"Or how many per day?"

"Eleven thousand."

"Per hour?

"About four hundred fifty, assuming you never sleep."

"You suggesting we give up sleep?" Duncan said.

"You'll have to if we're going to raise enough money. How much do we have left, Parish?"

"Without looking at my figures I can't say precisely, but putting it in round numbers, you have about $23,412."

Probably due to the elevation, Duncan's mood had risen since he'd met with Ron. Out the window, he couldn't even see the street below, and whenever he looked down on the world he saw limitless potential. "What about all the money we raised at the Drake dinner?" Duncan said.

"It's already committed," Kai said. "Commercials are expensive, and we spent it all for a couple dozen spots on the networks."

"So if we have the air time already, why not use it?"

"Speaking to an empty theater isn't a performance."

"Won't the Cook County democrats throw us something?"

"Not likely. We're a one-man show now."

"If it's really a lost cause, I may as well finish it. I'd rather take the loss myself."

"You don't need to stay for curtain calls, though."

Sick of the theater metaphors, Duncan reached into his pocket, withdrew a cigarette, and lit it without asking Kai's permission. While he enjoyed its release he recalled the years before he knew the cost of ambition.

He'd met his wife during college. Although Josie attended Douglas in New Jersey, her roommate, Sissie, lived in Chicago and invited her there over summer break for a tour of blues bars, jazz clubs, and fattening foods. Instead of good times, Sissie got the flu, so Josie explored the city alone.

In 1954, everyone was talking about the Cubs' first black players, Ernie Banks and Gene Baker. On a hot day — the sixth straight over ninety degrees — when the wind was blowing out at Wrigley Field, Duncan scored tickets in the bleachers. He had just graduated Northwestern, having played his last collegiate game the year before, and despaired of ever having a team worth rooting for. He'd come to see the new double play combo, which announcers called "Bingo to Bango to Bilko." The beer lines took two innings, but the hot dog salesmen circulated in the stands. As he waited for an all beef frank to be passed down his row, Duncan spotted a woman sitting alone just ahead, shielding her eyes with a scorecard. In profile she reminded him of Eva Marie Saint, who'd seduced him in *On the Waterfront*. Josie had the same blend of schoolgirl innocence and womanly knowing, so Duncan signaled the vendor to send down a second dog, and he presented it to her with the formality of a butler.

"What's this?" she'd said.

"Chicago's finest."

The reference meant nothing to her, but she enjoyed the sausage. After he'd sat next to her, he talked about wholesaling them and his plan to open his own meat packing plant.

"All beef, kosher," he'd said.

"Will you serve it with all this?" she'd said, gesturing to the pile of tomatoes, onions, pickles, peppers, mustard, and relish that covered the dog.

"That's Chicago style," he said.

"No ketchup?"

He shook his head definitively.

Later, she told him why she'd listened. More than his looks or charm, she liked his seriousness, that he wore a cotton shirt with creased sleeves, and that his shoes shone from waxing. Compared to the frat boys at Rutgers, she said that he acted manly.

Somehow in that past six months—even before Lindsay's death—he'd lost that swagger.

As the smoke pooled around him, Duncan waved it away and turned back to his staff. "I need to finish this."

"We can't afford to keep everyone," Kai said.

"Then fire the consultants. I don't want ten people's advice. Yours is enough."

Kai waited an uncomfortable time before speaking. "Alright."

Again he phoned someone to join them. Before Duncan could finish his smoke, Margo bounced onto the couch. She looked like a farm girl with her red hair twisted into two pigtails and a plaid flannel shirt over jeans. Duncan could see why she ended up behind the camera. Despite graduating from Medill journalism with honors, she looked too country cousin for Chicago.

"During your break, Margo cancelled all of your appearances," Kai said. He turned to her. "How many can we reschedule?"

"Most. When do you have time, Mr. Cochrane?"

Duncan took a long drag and held in the smoke before answering. "I don't want to fade to black. I want people to hear me. I want Lindsay still in their thoughts."

Kai stared at a pencil he had balanced above his desktop, swaying it back and forth with a single finger as though to contemplate it from all angles. "You sure you're up to it?"

"Why do people keep asking me that?"

"Because it's legit. The last month of a campaign is the worst. Every day we'll travel. You'll be on camera most of the time. I can't guarantee no one will ask about... what happened. Reporters think like mosquitoes, always hovering and looking for an opening. If they find it, they'll suck you dry. You sure you're up to that?"

Duncan took a final drag off his cigarette and recalled his last talk with Josie. "Lindsay wouldn't forgive me for bowing out early."

"Then I'll schedule a press conference," Margo said. She smiled, bringing out the freckles in her cheeks. "It's too late for local TV, so let's do it tomorrow morning. You'll need to explain why you're returning, and you should expect some questions about...."

She looked to Parish and Kai for help.

"About Lindsay?" Duncan said.

"Yes."

With everyone else dodging the subject, Kai took over. "I could write something for you, but it'd be better if you came up with the lingo."

"There's not much to say. The police haven't arrested anyone, I don't have a clue who did it or why. The media have already reported all the details."

Omitting the police department's speculations about organized crime, of course, which he couldn't mention anyway.

"They still need a narrative," Kai said.

"They want bereavement," Duncan said, "so that's what I'll show them."

Kai stood and walked to a tablet of butcher paper hanging on an easel by the door. He tore off an old sheet containing illegible numbers scribbled at odd angles.

"Alright," he said, "just don't go too heavy on the sorrow. Remember, you still need to appear strong-willed. A little sadness is okay, but you're better off with anger or determination."

On the tablet, he wrote sadness, crossed it out, and next to it determination. "And there's no predicting how Big Bill is going to react. He may decide it's not worth the effort, but if you attack he'll respond."

"Let's stop calling him Big Bill," Duncan said.

"Just don't forget he earned that nickname."

Yet another phone call brought in Carl Verbover, the campaign's opposition researcher and expert on all things Republican. Limping over a cane, Carl brought an air of gravity.

"What's happening with the governor?" Kai said.

"Same as always: kissing babies and old ladies," Carl said. "Why, are we back in?"

Duncan had always liked the old man's spirit. After being cast aside by the Nixon White House during Watergate and blacklisted by his former friends in the GOP, Carl had switched loyalties. He'd worked his way up in the Democratic Party until he could pass for a lifetime member. Neither a divorce nor a near-fatal car wreck had deadened his enthusiasm, despite a permanent limp and disabling alimony.

"We're in," Duncan said.

Kai returned to his butcher paper and tapped his pen against it. "We'll need a new theme, something to explain why this campaign matters. Taxes and unemployment won't resonate."

"What about 'for justice'?" Duncan said.

Kai turned to his republic strategist and waited for an opinion.

"Novel platform for a democrat," Carl said. "It might play well with the farmers downstate, but I don't know how a liberal town like Chicago will respond."

"They're the ones with the most to fear," Duncan said.

Kai wrote the words "for justice" in bright red on the blotter, as though he couldn't evaluate a theme without blowing it up to poster size.

"It's got mojo," he said. "People always assume Big Bill—sorry—the governor is unassailable on crime. If we attack where he's strong, it might catch him unprepared."

When Bill Stratton ruled as state prosecutor, he'd made a name for himself targeting politicians in Chicago's Machine, inching his way toward Richard J. Daley but not close enough to strike before the mayor died. Even Otto Kerner, his predecessor in the governor's office, ended up in jail thanks to Big Bill. Everyone in the state's attorney's office knew it presaged a career in politics, but the public and the media bought it.

"The only people Bill Stratton ever caught were politicians," Duncan said. "The average person doesn't care if his alderman gets locked up. He wants to know he's safe in his house."

Duncan glanced around the room for objections but saw only nods of agreement.

CHAPTER 11

EVERY MORNING FOR A WEEK, Duncan awoke to see the VW Beetle parked in his driveway, its dayglo orange burning in the early sun. Lindsay's old car marked the bulls-eye of his bedroom window and the backdrop to his dining table. Besides being an eyesore, it blocked the way to the garage and forced the family to stack all three of their other cars in the front oval. Something had to be done. He found Josie in his office, sorting through stacks of mailers, posters, and stickers. Though already dressed in a pantsuit, her hair looked pressed down and flat, as though it needed washing but instead received spraying.

"What are you doing?" he said.

"Organizing."

"You don't need to do that."

"I want to help."

He watched her sorting things into stacks and recalled his first years in business when she temped as his (unpaid) secretary. "I've got a staff for that."

She kept working, ignoring his stare and focusing on the stacks of paper around her.

"Are you sure you want to keep doing this?" he said.

"I need to keep busy."

"Not like this," he said. "This campaign is...."

Before he could find words to explain himself, she interrupted. "I'd run myself if I could, but you know I can't."

"Just because you lost one election...."

She set down her papers to stare at him with rancor. "People won't vote a woman into office, not even for a petty position like ruler of Kenilworth. They're too sexist. You remember my opponent's slogan? 'The man for the job.' People got the message: don't let a girl govern you. He may as well have highlighted the word *man* in bright red."

"It was one race, one opponent, years ago."

"But I was better than him."

"You were a mother of three teenagers with no political experience. Your only job had been helping me at the plant."

"We made that business together."

"I know that, but other people don't. They didn't see how strong you are."

"They can't. I get the same chauvinist treatment when I talk to people about the E.R.A. Men don't want to hear from the League of Women Voters. They're too busy with their drinking clubs and golf games. As long as the old boy's network still holds sway, a woman will never get elected to a position with power."

He glanced at a flier, which included the seal of the Cook County democrats despite their early opposition to him.

"What about Jane Byrne? She could be the next mayor."

"Never happen. Some boy from Bridgeport will beat her."

"Aren't I just another boy?"

"You're the man who can push through the E.R.A. We just need three more states to ratify it, and you can get us Illinois. Remember how close we can last time?"

He nodded, knowing that argument would be futile.

"You can be our champion."

He turned to a mirror hidden behind the office door and pretended to check his hair. "We need to move the Bug," he said.

"The what?"

"Lindsay's old car."

"Where?"

"Not where, how. I mean sell it."

When he checked her reflection, he saw only the crown of her head as she bent over the desk again.

"No. I couldn't."

"It's in the way."

"Put it in the garage then."

Duncan looked to where their detached, two-car sat with one empty bay.

"Only till winter," he said. "Then we'll need the space."

"Wait and see."

He nodded and left her to her work.

Outside, the air hadn't begun to warm, and even the chrome door handle felt cold. When he fell into the driver's seat, the hinges squeaked, and the vinyl exhaled a groan. Not since their test-drive four years before had he been inside the Bug, an apt name given its size. It felt as cramped and uncomfortable as he remembered. He had to slouch to clear the low ceiling, and even with the seat scooted all the way back his knees hit the dash. The gearshift was too loose, the clutch too tight, and everything too small. But touching each part—the plastic grip of the steering wheel, the round knob of the shifter—felt like touching a part of her.

He'd offered to buy Lindsay almost any car she wanted—a Mustang, a Thunderbird, a Malibu—but she'd demanded a Bug.

"Remember the oil embargo?" she'd said. "We need to use less gas."

He'd argued every practical reason but didn't sway her.

"It's cute," she concluded.

By whose standards? Compared to his Cadillac, it looked like a toy. More impractically, she'd bought a convertible, even though Chicago offered only a few weeks between winter's snow and summer's humidity. Outside these transitions you either froze or sweltered. The soft top made it feel even lower and darker inside. To flip down the sun visor he had to duck. Under it he found a pin with a theta symbol in green.

How odd. She'd never liked the Greek system, and Vassar didn't tolerate sororities. He pocketed the button and looked into the back seat for other mementos. There he found a Cub's hat, probably dating from her high school years. The games always bored her, but she loved the manual scoreboard and the bleacher bums who enforced a shirtless dress code and a three-beer minimum.

What else could the car hold? He popped the boot only to find the engine, another proof of the Bug's ridiculous engineering. Up front, the "trunk" had little room, just enough for a lawn chair with sand in the joints and a white apron stained by grease and blueberry syrup.

Back in the cockpit, Duncan looked for other hiding spots. From the glove box he excavated a ticket stub to the Botanic Garden dated two weeks before and a pair of maps for the North Shore. Their folds cracked when he opened them, and the colors shone like new except for two circles in blue ballpoint. One covered Maple Avenue, a side street in Evanston a couple miles south, the other a spot on Green Bay Road, almost close enough to walk.

In the house, the curtains remained closed and the lights out. He walked invisible past the breakfast room where he'd seen Josie, and by Glynis' bedroom. If he drove fast, the trip would only take twenty minutes.

But when it fired up, the Bug roared louder than a prop plane. He shifted into reverse and immediately stalled, the manual transmission as foreign as an 18-wheeler's. It restarted even louder, and in the rearview he saw a cloud of blue smoke. A moment later he smelled the exhaust. No point stalling again. He mashed the gas and lurched down the drive, scraped the curb, braked with a squeal, and then peeled out. No one for a block could have missed his exit.

Driving the Bug felt like being inside a washing machine, with its round cockpit, screaming belts, and vibrations more violent than any spin cycle. Even with the top up, the wind's roar competed with an orchestra of rattles, the closest a man could come to the inside of a maraca. He vibrated and shook down Sheridan Road, uncomfortable even at 35 mph, cars whizzing past, potholes jerking the steering in every direction but straight. How could he have let Lindsay drive this toy so long?

Anxious to get off the major roads, Duncan turned onto Kenilworth Avenue, ignored the police department and the Kenilworth Club, and bumped over the berm of UP train tracks. After a left onto Green Bay Road, he paralleled the rails for a half mile, past dozens of mom and pop shops: a bicycle dealer and a hardware store, a flower stand with a neon yellow rose in the window, and a record store with a spinning disc. The circle on the map could have denoted several blocks, and large tree planters lined one side of the road, hiding the stores. Nothing caught him until the red awning of the Walker Brother's Pancake House, whose neon sign showed a cartoon chef flipping a dense flapjack in his skillet.

Duncan pulled into the parking lot and idled. Summers during college, Lindsay waited tables there, which would explain the apron but not why she'd gone back. She didn't need the job, with its hot, greasy kitchen and packed dining room, but said she wanted it for gas money.

"I could give you that," Duncan had said.

"But then you'd want to know where I went," she'd said.

At least a year had passed since her last shift. Duncan cut the engine and rolled down his window, letting in the baked apples of Walker's signature pancake—more like a pie than a breakfast—and the sizzling flesh of their sausages. He could go in, order breakfast, see if any of her old coworkers remained and recalled seeing her recently, but that would take time, and he didn't want Josie to know what he was up to. Plus, he had a press conference later that day.

The second circle waited half a mile away, so Duncan headed east on Lake Avenue toward the water. Along Sheridan Road he passed the pure white dome of the Baha'i Temple, its crenelated plaster shell as elaborate as a wedding cake. Sheridan followed the irregular curves of the lakefront, at points offering a clear view of the water, elsewhere tunneling through mansions backing up to it. Beyond the Evanston border lay Northwestern University, his alma mater, its ivy-covered buildings and broad lawns as familiar as his own house. After that, he needed the map to find the way (right on Emerson, three blocks to Maple, and another right).

There, again, nothing stood out. The block featured three-story apartments and low duplexes, cheap housing for students. Old cars lined the curbs, their wheel wells rusting from winter's salt, paint fading in summer's sun. Next to them, the Bug looked fancy. He pulled to the curb and studied the map again, but the circle covered a whole block. Lindsay never mentioned any friends who lived near campus. Then again, she didn't say anything about going to the Botanic Gardens or the beach, either.

The engine noise scuttled his thinking, so he killed it and rolled down the window. Nearby, a stereo wafted a mellow man's voice:

Slip sliding away, slip sliding away

You know the nearer your destination the more you're slip sliding away

Over five minutes, three people walked by. All ignored the man in the orange VW. An El train blotted out the music momentarily, but when it passed the quiet vibe returned. Minutes elapsed. Then a teenaged boy skateboarded toward him and skidded to a halt.

"What's shakin'," he said. "You looking for something?"

He looked no older than Aden, with messy blond hair past his ears, a velour shirt, and cutoffs.

Duncan shook his head, but the boy leaned a slim arm on the windowsill. "Cause if you were, I could take care of you right quick."

The boy sucked on a joint with a sweet, seductive aroma.

"Not something, someone," Duncan said.

"Who's that?"

"My daughter."

"Who?"

"Blond, pretty, a bit older than you?"

The boy straightened, took a final puff, pinched off the flame and pocketed the nub.

"She in trouble?"

"No."

The boy studied him with a squint fitting a cowboy. "I know you."

"I doubt it."

"You been here before?"

"No."

His skeptical look remained. Then recognition streaked across his face. "You're that guy... on TV."

Duncan nodded.

"And your daughter...." He looked down to the pavement, then away, and spoke to himself. "Shit. Smooth play, Shakespeare." When he turned back, he bent to the window and put his face almost inside its frame, inches from Duncan's. "Sorry, man. I didn't know I knew you."

"It's alright. Have you seen her?"

"No, never."

"You're sure?"

"Honest. I'd narc if I did. But why?"

Words eluded him to explain the zaniness of searching for a dead girl.

"She marked this place on a map."

The boy stepped back, glanced up and down the street, then leaned in even closer.

"Here's the lowdown. People come here to turn on, you dig?"

"She didn't do that."

The boy looked down and smiled to himself. "Course not. I should just shut up."

He withdrew and put a foot on his skateboard. "This your flip top?"

"Hers."

"That how you found out?"

Duncan nodded.

They stared at each other an uncomfortable time before the boy spoke again. "Forget what I said. She probably just wanted to get down." He tilted his head toward the music. "Guys in the frat house have more parties than Hugh Hefner."

Duncan glanced toward a brick bungalow set back from the street. He hadn't noticed the Greek symbols above the door, which had faded to the same dingy grey as the rest of the wood porch. In the driveway, an electric yellow muscle car gleamed in the sun.

"Thanks," Duncan said. "You've helped."

He fired up the Bug, which caught loud and rough like a lawn mower engine, but the boy lingered alongside the open window.

"Keep on keepin' on," the boy finally said and rolled away.

From his pocket, Duncan extracted the pin he took earlier from Lindsay's visor. After turning it over several times, he stuck it into his lapel and started for home.

CHAPTER 12

LATER THAT DAY, as he awaited the start of his press conference, Duncan looked over the crowd, which numbered at least triple what he'd attracted for previous rallies or pressers. In the front row a half dozen radio reporters waited, their boom mikes targeting the podium. Behind them stood well-coifed television anchors with burly cameramen, their spotlights cutting through the morning haze. Rumpled scriveners made up the third wave. Interspersed were two dozen still photographers outfitted in jungle vests laden with lenses. All looked ready for combat.

A number of faces Duncan didn't know or had seen only on television. He spotted a press pass for the *Washington Post*, another for the *New York Times*, a third for the *Times of London*. Why would people out of state or overseas care?

The public—hundreds of them—waited in clusters behind the news throng. Businessmen held hot dogs away from their suits, mothers agitated strollers, and a couple ragged men banged cups on the sidewalk to beg for change. On the perimeter, two dozen uniformed police stood at ease.

"What did you tell them?" Duncan asked Kai.

"To expect a major announcement."

"You say I was coming back?"

"I didn't want to steal your lines."

More like waiting to see if Duncan had changed his mind. Still, it worked. They'd need the exposure to push Lindsay's case.

With this many people, they filled Daley Plaza. At first they'd planned to use Kai's office, but Margo wanted to send a message: "We're for real."

Appearing at the center of city government said as much. Behind them rose the county seat, it's flat facade of brown glass and rusted steel blocking out the sky. Across the street, Chicago's City Hall cut a conservative profile, its white stone porch like a Greek temple. In the middle of it all, Picasso's sculpture rose five stories, a geometric bird guarding its nest.

The syncopated beat of a teenager playing a plastic bucket echoed through the plaza. Kai checked his watch and looked to the percussionist, who persisted, eyes closed. Taking this cue, an officer stepped on the drum. The boy stopped, looked up irritated until, seeing the cop, then the podium, he raised his sticks in salute.

Duncan reached for his wife's hand, and as they ascended to the podium the murmuring in the crowd lulled. When he took the lectern, Josie released her grip but remained at his side. Last chance to reconsider. He needed a cigarette, but smoking was off limits here.

"Thanks for coming," he said, his words repeating off the steel and concrete.

He smelled the tang of hot dogs and heard a vendor banging the lid to his cart. Across the plaza, a blue and red striped umbrella offered "Red Hots."

"During the last six months, I've often asked for your support, and you've never failed me. I stood before you certain we would capture the state house." Another pause filled the plaza with echoes. "Then, personal loss forced me to step away. I've taken the last two weeks to reassess my political and personal life, and I've come to a decision."

Wind whistled across the microphone, giving Duncan a final moment of delay. He glanced at Josie who clapped her mittens together to spur him. The crowd stared while the drummer supplied a roll.

"After careful deliberation, I've decided to continue my run for governor."

All around, camera shutters clicked and a strobe of flashbulbs blinded. Duncan looked down, but the letters of his speech spiraled into a white blur. Rather than waste the moment, he continued from memory.

"As you know, last week someone broke into my family's home and stole our most precious possession: our daughter. Now that person walks the streets unfettered, while we live chained to grief."

That last line didn't sound quite right. Duncan remembered Kai's admonition: be strong, not fearful. He was treading close to despair.

"The police tell me they're narrowing their search to a list of known and repeat criminals. These are people who've done... horrible things. Yet they enjoy freedom from prosecution while we suffer the punishment of fear. That can't continue."

A smattering of applause, punctuated by drumbeats, gave him a moment to breathe.

"Bill Stratton made a name for himself going after corrupt politicians. That's a wonderful start, but as long as murderers are free, we all live as captives. We need to shine a light on wickedness, sanitize the city, and cleanse ourselves of the stain left by fear and violence. We must bar the doors to our prisons so that not even the stench of depravity can escape."

"Amen!" said a deep voice, followed by more sturdy applause. Even the police clapped their gloved hands. Where did those last lines come from? Perhaps all his Bible reading. It didn't matter. Inspiration carried him, and he entrusted himself to it.

"This is my pledge, not just as a candidate, but as a man who understands your frustration. Together, we cannot fail. We must not fail. And we will not fail."

What started as polite applause built to a shriek of whistles and a spasm of percussion so loud that even with amplifiers Duncan couldn't have matched it. He stepped back to let the moment settle. Although he could again read his script, he saw no need to continue.

Josie put her arm around his waist, and together they waved to the crowd. When they descended the podium, people converged—a man in stained coveralls and a woman in a fur coat, a teenaged girl on a skateboard and a pretty mother with babe in arms—all wanting to shake his hand. Photographers edged closer with each frame until Duncan felt flesh on all sides.

"Do you believe you can win?" one reporter asked.

"Absolutely," Josie said, faster than he could answer.

"Do you know who killed your daughter?"

"If I did, I'd be after them now," Duncan said.

"Will you make crime fighting part of your campaign?"

"It's part of my life."

"Are you also an environmentalist?"

That last question landed like a sucker punch, leaving him winded. "Excuse me?"

"Your button."

Duncan glanced down at the Theta sign pinned to his collar, then at Josie, whose face showed disapproval.

"It's in honor of my daughter," he said.

"So she believed in environmentalism?"

The question came from a young woman, not much older than Lindsay, with a dress like a potato sack and a press pass from the *Milwaukee Journal*.

"I don't follow you."

"That symbol represents Earth Day, sir. So will you also promote environmentalism?"

"I believe... Lindsay would have wanted that."

Cameras flashed, and Duncan imagined them zooming in to get a clear shot of his lapel. Then the crowd parted, and Kai pushed his way in front of the candidate.

"We'll get you all a copy of our formal statement," he said.

He stepped between Josie and Duncan, placed his hands around their shoulders, and ushered them behind the stage as police pushed back the throng. Under the screen of scaffolding and bunting waited Margo and several other staffers.

"Fantastic," Margo said.

"I got a little off script."

"That's okay," Margo said. "You went with the moment."

Before that day, Duncan never knew what that saying meant.

"That thing about the button...."

"Don't sweat it. No one will remember that part. Just, next time, ask us to accessorize you."

Duncan exhaled and looked around at his staff, who all smiled genuinely. "So, what's next?"

"We've got to meet with the party," Kai said. "We'll need their bread if we're going to play Broadway. The mayor said he'd have a minute later today."

Duncan thought of the city's Democratic Party head, who'd attended the funeral but never any of his campaign events. Mayor Bland, the news hacks dubbed him, but how would he receive this news? Hard to predict.

"Can it wait?" Duncan said.

"Time's against us," Kai said.

"Just till tomorrow."

Josie pinched his arm and said, "Why not now?"

"I've got something to take care of," Duncan said.

Kai looked to Margo, who nodded her approval.

"No longer," Kai said.

"Don't worry," Duncan said. "After this, I'm all yours."

CHAPTER 13

THE WALK TOOK ONLY THREE BLOCKS through a tunnel of Chicago's downtown skyscrapers, which obstructed both wind and sun. Still, Duncan felt renewed at being back in the race officially, as if his own spring had arrived after the long winter of Lindsay's interment.

Inside Berghoff's, an historic German restaurant that proudly displayed the first Chicago liquor license issued after Prohibition, dozens of people wanted to shake Duncan's hand. Quickly, the restaurant's owner stepped in and led him downstairs to the empty basement. Since Cochrane Foods supplied all the restaurant's sausages, Duncan could command a private table anytime.

The interior hadn't changed much since the thirties, with wood paneling, checkerboard floor tiles, brass chandeliers, and black and white photos hanging from the picture rail. In a corner of the Century Room, Ron waited at a solitary table.

"Good speech," Ron said.

"You heard it?" Duncan said.

"WBBM broadcast it live. My staff loved your anti-crime bit."

"I meant it. We're going to stop the mayhem."

Ron smiled indulgently and opened his menu. "Careful with promises like that. People might start believing you."

Duncan let the slight slide and looked over the entrees, although he could recite them from memory: bratwurst and sauerbraten and schnitzel.

"I did some checking," Ron said. "The Kenilworth police haven't shared information with anybody. None of my contacts at the D.O.J., the F.B.I., or the state attorney's office know about the case."

"That unusual?"

Ron turned over his menu and studied the list of home-brewed beers before replying. "In a high profile case like this, yeah. Usually, a bunch of agencies get involved.

"I also talked to a friend down in organized crime. He couldn't recall any recent political killings in Chicago. But—"

Ron paused at the arrival of their waiter—a stooped, greying man who took their order without notes: for Duncan a beef roulade and for Ron a corned beef sandwich. Once he left, Ron continued.

"It's not implausible. The local mob controls a lot of industries."

"Like?"

"Gambling, prostitution, towing."

Duncan shook his head as though these allegations stuck to him personally.

"That's not all," Ron said. "They charge street tax on everything from garbage to dry cleaning."

"I don't know about anything like that," Duncan said.

"Let me run a couple of names past you, just in case."

Ron burrowed into a leather briefcase at his side and extracted a manila folder marked "confidential," then opened it like a menu so Duncan couldn't see the pages.

"Ever heard of Francis John Schweihs?"

Duncan shook his head.

"He goes by 'The German," manages collections and enforcement on the north side. We suspect him of at least five murders including Sam Giancana, who used to be the boss here before he took off to Mexico. He got killed three years back when he returned for a visit."

Neither name meant anything to Duncan, and he said so to redirect his old friend.

"What about Albert Caesar Tocco? We like him for several murders too, including Dino Valente, who owned a vending concession. He mostly deals on the south side below 95th Street, but he's also got a moving van company that's all over town."

Again, Duncan shook his head. These leads pointed far from any world he knew. Yet the killer hid somewhere in the city's cacophonous landscape, and there had to be a path through its crosshatched streets that would connect to him.

"What if we're looking in the wrong places?" Duncan said.

They paused again as the waiter returned with pints of lager bubbling over.

"How do you mean?" Ron said.

"You and the police keep trying to make some connection to my business or my daughter. What if there is no connection? What if some murderer just stumbled on my house?"

Ron set aside his file and sipped his drink before answering. "Unlikely. Despite what the news says, most criminals have a motive besides sheer meanness."

"But it's so far-fetched. I don't deal with the mafia, and my daughter didn't go places where she'd meet... people like that."

"You've got to consider the circumstances though, Dunc. You live in one of the safest towns in the city. Kenilworth's never had a murder in eighty years. Whoever did this not only broke into your house, he went straight to your daughter's bedroom. That's not a crime of opportunity. I hate to say it, but he knew *exactly* who to target. It wouldn't surprise me if he'd spent weeks casing you."

Overhead, the ceiling thumped with the constant shuffle of people and the readjustment of chairs. Duncan listened quietly as the idea trickled down his gullet until it lodged in his gut. "So what would you do?"

"First, I'd ask for help from the state police or the F.B.I. Nothing against your local P.D., but you need someone who's smelled a body before."

"I don't have that kind of power."

"You will, soon."

They paused when the waiter returned with two steaming plates of beef and potatoes. The aroma permeated the empty room, making it too tempting to ignore. After they'd sampled their platters—Duncan's beef fork tender and his potatoes fried to a crispy cake—Ron spoke.

"That reminds me. You may want to increase your security. You have bodyguards?"

Duncan shook his head.

"Hire private ones. I'll give you some names."

"The last thing I want it more people watching me."

"You'll never even notice them."

Duncan forced down some red cabbage soaked in vinegar before answering. "Let me think about it."

"Okay, but promise me one thing. Take this list. See if any of these guys have infiltrated your business. Ask your assistants, the ones you trust. At the least, we might be able to rule out some of them."

He handed over a one-page family tree of grainy mug shots with IDs below. At the top, Joseph "Doves" Auiupa—old enough to be a grandfather, with thinning white hair and glasses—held a prison number under his chin; beneath him waited John Philip "Jackie the Lackey" Cerone—middle-aged, bald, pale, but with a malevolent leer; then James "The Turk" Torrello, who looked like a used car salesman in an ill-fitting suit and grin; Joseph "Little Caesar" DiVarco, and Ken "Tokyo Joe" Ito, the only Asian, looking neat and prim next to the others.

Duncan's eyes raked the paper until one name at the bottom of the pyramid stopped him: Daniel Reid. In a city stuffed with Irish, it didn't stand out, but it did ring familiar. The picture, of a thick-set redhead with an inscrutable frown, didn't help.

"I'll ask my staff," Duncan said. "Maybe they're not telling me something."

CHAPTER 14

AS SOON AS HE REACHED HOME, Duncan headed to his office. Thanks to Josie's reorganization, files covered every part of his desk except the blotter. He moved the piles in a clockwise rotation, uncovering one surface at a time, checking for loose pages, but couldn't find the message he wanted. Finally, he noticed a pink corner of the "While You Were Out" pad protruding from under a phone book.

Calls had come in from the usual suspects: news reporters, reps from the Kiwanis and Rotary clubs, law firms, and the teachers' unions. Not what he wanted. Under a stack of manila folders he found more: his secretary, his dentist, *Newsday* magazine. Not it. By dropping the files on the floor one at a time, he cleared the desk. Still not there. Just as he reared to kick the debris, he lifted the blotter and found it: a message from Joe Sturmer reading "Third call."

He dialed as fast as the rotary would spin.

A husky voice answered, "Yeah?"

"Joe?"

"Who' s this?"

"Duncan Cochrane. Is this Joe?"

"Governor, never thought I'd hear from you."

"I've been... indisposed."

"I heard."

"So you called three times."

"Yeah. I never believed you'd drop out for good."

"What did you want?"

"Like I said at your party, we want to hear about your labor policies."

"Kai could have told you that."

"We want to hear it from your mouth."

The insolence. More than anything, Duncan wanted a cigarette, but with Josie in the house and with the temperatures outside near freezing, he had to abstain.

"I know how much you've given my campaign."

"We thought you'd forgot."

"No, but I've had other things on my mind lately."

"I heard. I'm real sorry about that."

Was that sarcasm? Without seeing his face, Duncan couldn't tell. He pictured Sturmer: thick, immobile, waiting to crush whatever got in his way.

"So you're not involved?"

"In what?"

"What happened."

"I'm not hearing what you're implying."

Duncan inhaled and held his breath for calm. "This has nothing to do with my family?"

"All our members are family."

"I mean *my* family? You haven't...?" How could he say it without being explicit? "You haven't contacted us, *directly*?"

"It's hard enough getting you on the phone."

"So you haven't got any grievance with me?"

"You're asking the wrong guy."

"Who should I ask?"

"Someone higher on the depth chart."

"Such as?"

"Danny. Downtown."

Duncan hung up without saying good-bye.

***

Later that day, Duncan cruised West Devon Avenue, one of many Chicago neighborhoods he barely knew. Even though it lay just across the city border and only five miles from his house, Rogers Park was a world apart. Low-rise apartments, built square like the bricks that made them, alternated with small retail stores—tire companies and family restaurants, a sewing-machine repair shop next to a comic book store—a sector for the other half.

The street numbers rose by single digits—4321, 4323, 4325—stretching his drive to thirty blocks. Finally, he saw the hand-painted sign with ornate, Old West lettering: "Shooter's Showroom." He parked, checked for familiar faces, and entered the store.

Inside, glass counters lined three walls, and behind them peg boards held weapons of every size and description. It reminded him of a hardware store, so packed he didn't know where to begin. At one counter a pair of men fingered a military rifle. Instinctively, Duncan walked away toward a section with shotguns, single and double barrels, different lengths and stocks—at least, that's what he thought the grips were called.

"What can I do for ya?"

Startled, Duncan looked up to see a dark-skinned African with a stringy build who held the entire left side of his body rigid. His accent could have been Southern, though it lacked the proper twang.

"I need a gun."

"You in the right place. What kind ya want?"

"I don't know."

"Well, how ya plannin' to use it? Huntin', target, protection?"

"The last one."

The man turned and ran a hand along the counter as he walked away. "You don't want none of these, then. They'll mess up everything in the room."

Duncan followed him to a section of handguns, arranged parallel in the glass case. The salesman pulled out three and laid them on the counter.

Duncan hadn't fired a gun since basic training, and even then he felt uncomfortable. The noise always startled him, and the recoil hurt his hand. On the range he'd use up his required rounds quickly, knowing that as a college grad he'd never get shipped to Korea or endure combat. While serving stateside as an accountant, he'd rarely even worn his pistol. If the brass visited and wanted everyone on high alert, he'd unearth it from the bottom of his footlocker. Not even they claimed the North would sneak attack the States. Then the thought of shooting someone, even a stranger intent on murder, disgusted him. Now he could imagine it: sighting on Lindsay's killer, watching the man blanche, and then seeing him die, the life leaking from a hole in his neck.

"This first one's a revolver," said the salesman. "Holds six shots. A .357, so it'll stop near anybody you aim at, whether you fire or not."

The silver barrel and wood grip reminded Duncan of Westerns. When he picked it up, the density surprised him. That must be why cowboys always carried theirs in a holster.

"Anything less showy?"

The salesman offered a black shadow. "Nine millimeter, semi-auto. As powerful as that .357, but more compact. Takes an eight-shot clip and fires as fast as you can pull."

It felt small but heavy, with a slick finish. Again Duncan tried to imagine himself with it but couldn't. Only police carried such weapons, and they also wore it on the hip.

"Anything smaller?"

The last disappeared in his palm, with a plastic grip that instantly felt comfortable and reminded Duncan most of the water pistols he'd used as a child.

"A .32, single shot. Not real accurate, but it'll get the job done."

"Would I need a permit?"

"According to the politicians."

The man stared at Duncan defiantly. Was that a dig? Not likely. Kai had forbidden him from mentioning gun control, and he'd always dodged questions about it. He handed back the pistol and drifted toward the other side of the store.

"You mind if I look around a bit more?" Duncan said.

"Of course, Governor."

So the salesman did recognize him. Duncan glanced at the other two men in the shop, but obsessed over a rifle. What would the press do if they found out? Better not to think about it. He should decide and get out before anyone else recognized him.

"Okay," Duncan said. "That'll do it."

* * *

Two hours later, as dusk fell, he drove his Cadillac through a warehouse district near the Clyborn El stop. Although the buildings looked identical, with corrugated sides and flat tar roofs, none of them bore numbers. He flipped on his lights, which showed nothing more. Most companies hadn't even put up a sign to reveal the nature of their business. Just as he neared the end of the cul-de-sac and slowed to turn back, Duncan saw a small plaque for "McCready Imports" and pulled into the vacant parking lot.

From the loading bay emerged a man in a black leather jacket down to his thighs. His red coloring and freckles betrayed Irish roots. He looked older than Duncan by at least a decade, with wrinkles around the eyes and grey peppering his short hair. With a thick knuckle he rapped on the driver's window and waited for Duncan to roll it down.

"Why don't we take a walk?" he said, puffing vapor.

"Are you Danny?"

The man opened the door and waited for Duncan to exit before answering. "I'm not used to meeting the man in charge."

"I've got something personal to discuss."

Danny turned and walked down the empty street slowly, forcing Duncan to follow.

"It's about my family," Duncan said.

"I read about what happened to your daughter," Danny said. "That's a terrible thing. Whoever did that, he's not fit to live."

In the dim evening light, Duncan studied his face for insincerity but found instead the hardened stare of disapproval.

"You're right. He has no place in this society."

"If you don't mind me asking, do the cops know who did it? The newspapers haven't said anything lately."

Duncan reached into the pocket of his wool overcoat to grip his new .32. "That's why I wanted to see you."

"I don't get what you're saying."

Duncan drew the gun and kept it at arm's reach, pointed it toward the man's heavy belly. "I think you do."

Danny stopped and stared impassively at the pistol. "To be blunt, my superiors aren't too happy. They think you're taking our money and ignoring us. This... " he nodded toward the gun "just reinforces that."

"Haven't I always kept our agreements?"

"Lately, you don't act so interested."

"I don't even know what you want. All I know is I used to pay you, and now my campaign gets checks back."

"Nothing about our arrangement has changed."

"Then why come after my Lindsay?" Duncan said.

Danny gave him the same disapproving frown he'd used when speaking of the crime. "We had nothing to do with that."

The Irishman never broke Duncan's gaze, his pupils as still as the rest of his body.

"How do I know you're not just covering yourselves?"

"My superiors are direct. If they had a problem with you, you'd know about it. Right now, they're waiting to see how you do in the election."

Duncan lowered the barrel to his thigh but kept his finger on the trigger, wary of the stranger standing close enough to touch. "I... I'm sorry. The police said.... They led me to believe that some organization—"

"Cops don't understand us. We're not thugs. So long as you deal honest with us, you've got nothing to fear."

"My mistake."

"You've got a lot of stress on you, so I can see how you might of been misled."

Danny turned and walked slowly back to the car. When he lifted the door handle, the latch clicked like a gun being cocked. He watched Duncan step in then left the car door open. His hands dug in his coat pockets, the fists balled.

"This is a dangerous neighborhood for a man like you," Danny said. "I can see why you might want protection. It may not be enough next time, though. Better you don't come back."

CHAPTER 15

"PROTECTION?" JOSIE SAID.

She set a platter of pot roast in front of him and sat at the other end of the dining table. So they wouldn't have to go out in public, Josie home cooked all their dinners, serving them on white linens and bone china.

"Until this ends," Duncan said.

He resisted sharing anything from his meeting with the union.

"Are we in danger?" she said.

"No, nothing like that. It's just, I'm going to be away from home a lot with the campaign, and I'd feel better knowing someone was watching."

Josie paused in the middle of spooning some salad. "Would they live with us?"

Duncan pictured a policeman shacking up in their guest room, his uniforms hanging in the closet, his gun belt slung over the bedpost. Leave it to a woman to hone in on the domestic effects of such a move.

"They could stay in a car."

Glynis looked from her father to her mother and back again in disbelief. "Out in the cold?"

She appeared sullen and groggy, her hair dry and filled with static, her cheek creased from a pillow. Lately, she'd been sleeping at odd hours, with no schedule.

"They can take my office," Duncan said. "It doesn't matter. I just need to know you're safe."

Duncan spooned meat and potatoes onto two plates and passed them to the women, who starting without him.

"What if we just had someone drive by the house?" he said.

Josie dropped her fork and stared at him, her silent message: stop scaring her.

The doorbell rang. Duncan hesitated until Josie dismissed him with a wave. As he passed her chair, he squeezed her neck, but she stiffened at the touch.

In the doorway, Tom Dalyrmple slumped against the jamb, his hair and clothes disheveled. Duncan glanced backward to where the women sat out of sight but probably not earshot.

"Is Glynis here?" he slurred.

"She's not available. Something I can do for you?"

Tom wiped his face roughly with the heel of his hand but said nothing.

"Tom, what's wrong?"

"Glyn... " he said.

Drunk. After the funeral Tom had downed scotch like a frat boy, rushing past the taste toward inebriation. Did he want Glynis or Lindsay? Probably not even *he* knew.

"I understand, Tom. You miss her. We all do. We...."

Words failed him as well. He needed to escape.

"I'll tell her you stopped by. Take care, Tom."

"Yes, sir."

After locking the door, Duncan glanced toward the dining room. He didn't want to confront his family yet, so he skirted them and walked to his office, where he poured himself a scotch and stared out the back window. Bare trees cut silhouettes against a cobalt sky. After downing a tumbler, he closed the door and dialed the police.

"Could I speak to Chief Dunleavy?"

"He's not here."

The voice sounded female, but older, with a nasal quality Duncan found irritating.

"When'll he be back?"

"Tomorrow most likely."

"I need him today. Say it's Duncan Cochrane. Call him at home if you have to, but it needs to be right away."

"Can somebody else help you, sir?"

"No, I want the chief."

"I'll try to find him."

Duncan hung up. Even from his office, the pot roast smelled intoxicating, but he didn't want to leave the table again if the chief called right back. Instead, he looked over the mafia family tree from Ron. He'd practically memorized it, making the foreign names and faces appear familiar.

When the phone rang, Duncan grabbed it as though he could suppress the noise.

"Mr. Cochrane, what can I do for you?"

The chief's calm tone grated but also reminded Duncan of the need for restraint.

"Tom Dalrymple just showed up at my door."

"He shouldn't have contacted you. We've warned him against that."

"Why? What's he done?"

"Earlier tonight, we found his car parked down the street from your house. He was under the influence but with the car parked, so we cited him for drunk in public and took him home."

"Why would he watch us?"

A pause told Duncan the chief was forming his words carefully.

"Guilt."

"If he's guilty, why don't you arrest him?"

"I said guilt, not guilty. His father alibied him for the night of the crime. But if he keeps this up, we'll have to bring him in."

Through the earpiece, Duncan heard voices rising and falling like waves, suggesting the chief had ducked out on a party to make his call.

"Don't do that. He's... not bothering us."

"We'll keep an eye on him then, while we look at other angles."

"So you still think organized crime is involved?"

"That's our primary theory."

"But you've got other suspects?"

"We're considering many theories."

"Care to share any?"

"Maybe tomorrow."

"Fine. Talk to you then."

They hung up. From the dining room, Duncan heard plates clattering as Josie cleared the table. The desktop clock said he'd been away for twenty minutes.

**

The table sat empty when Duncan returned, the women gone with the food, leaving only the smell of pot roast. He found the meat tin foiled in the fridge. When he sliced off a piece, it still felt warm, but he could hardly taste it.

Upstairs, in their bedroom, Josie stood by the window with her back turned, the lights off. The street lamps shined through the sheers. She didn't move, even as the bed springs squeaked under his weight.

"Who was that?" she said.

"Kai. He wanted to talk about tomorrow."

"I mean at the door."

"A reporter."

Duncan loosed his tie and threw it to the floor, then kicked off his wing tips.

"You need a shower," she said.

He unclasped his belt and threw it next to the shoes, then unbuttoned his shirt. His pants proved more difficult, but by leaning side to side he freed them as well.

"Too tired," he said.

He lay back and rested his head in the crook of his arm so he could watch her. In silhouette she looked youthful, her torso still a figure eight, her hair smoothed flat except for a flip at the back.

"What are you scared of?" she said.

"Until the police catch someone—"

"You can't worry about that."

"But I do worry."

He wished she would face him, even though it was too dark to see her expression. At least then he would feel some connection.

"Worry about your campaign then," she said.

"I do that enough."

She turned but remained by the window.

"Lie down," he said, and reached toward her.

"Not when you're like this."

"Like what?"

"Needy."

CHAPTER 16

"DID YOU WATCH THE NEWS LAST NIGHT?" Kai said.

The campaign manager sat on the edge of his desk, a tiger surveying all below. His pointed boots, flared slacks, and open collar shirt looked too mod for Duncan, to say nothing of the buckskin jacket with fringe, aping that TV show about Daniel Boone. Duncan shook his head and glanced around the office at his remaining staff—Margo, Parish, and Carl—who all smiled approvingly.

"I got tied up," Duncan said.

"We led off all three local broadcasts."

"How'd I come off?"

"Terrific. The anchors threw around words like 'courageous' and 'dedicated'."

On the couch opposite, Margo leaned forward from a cross-legged yoga pose. She wore a flower print dress that covered her legs but with a denim vest, an incongruous blend of matron and hippie.

"Your word choice and body language were perfect," she said. "You projected strength and decisiveness, but without the arrogance of power. You just need to be careful about your tonal range. At a couple points your voice cracked. That suggests vulnerability."

"Please, don't try to script my emotions."

Margo leaned back, looking wounded until Kai interceded by handing him a stack of newspapers. On top, the *Sun-Times* blared "Game On" in massive type.

"We made the front page of every sheet in the state," Kai said.

Midway through the pile, the *Tribune* demurred "Campaign Resumes," but a side bar distracted Duncan. "Murder suspect in custody." The first three graphs read:

Police detained a drunken suspect Wednesday lingering outside the home of gubernatorial candidate Duncan Cochrane. Cochrane's daughter, Lindsay Cochrane, was murdered inside the home last month.

Officers cited Tom Dalrymple, 22, of Kenilworth for public intoxication after they found him in a car on Sheridan Road, just outside the Cochrane estate. Police officials declined to comment on the incident.

According to anonymous sources, detectives interviewed Dalrymple following the death of the candidate's daughter, but he has not been charged in the case.

The story continued inside the paper, but Duncan didn't want to make it obvious what he was reading by flipping to the jump. He regretted Tom's public shaming, but the boy had brought it on himself. Instead, Duncan worried that the police were sourcing the press. Evidently, the chief's concern about confidentiality didn't extend to his staff.

When he noticed the silence in the room, Duncan looked up to see Kai smiling at him.

"Enjoy the good publicity," he said. "It won't last."

Kai walked around his desk to a paper blotter with a calendar for the month and pointed to the rest of the week. When Duncan craned his neck, he saw that it overflowed with illegible pencil scratches. "Margo, how are we set for appearances?"

The media rep unfolded her legs and leaned forward, touching fingers to knees with the delicacy of a praying mantis. "Booked solid. We'll start with the inner city, where our polling is weakest, then work our way downstate. Next week, we've got appearances in Springfield, Decatur, Peoria, maybe Bloomington."

"Those are farm towns," Duncan said. "Half the state's democrats live in the city."

Kai palmed the stack of newspapers beside his desk. "We've got the audience's attention. We need to keep it."

Duncan shifted in his egg cup chair, its white, molded plastic an ovoid cocoon. His spine ached from being forced into its unnatural C shape, so he lugged his weight to its lip.

"I'm not giving up on downstate," he said, "but let's keep it to day trips."

Margo folded her hands in a prayer pose, the fingertips barely touching. "The drive takes three and a half hours. We'll spend most of our time getting there and back when we should be making at least five or six stops a day."

"Not if we leave early, get on the road by six. That puts us in town by nine-thirty. Then we'll have the whole day for appearances. You can have me for twelve hours."

Duncan glanced around the room, where the staffers eyed him with confusion and suspicion. He settled on Carl, the veteran of the group, who leaned forward on his cane to triangulate his weight.

"Mr. Cochrane," he said, "we're still behind, and my sources say Bill Stratton's going to resume his campaign this week. We've got a short shelf life and little time to sell our product."

"I understand," Duncan said. "I just don't want to be away from home overnight."

Margo opened her mouth, then looked to Kai for support.

"We'll do what we can," he said.

Duncan escaped the egg cup and walked to the window, though his spine still felt molded to the chair's shape. Below, the cars and people looked small enough to handle, but Duncan's former sense of mastery eluded him.

"That reminds me," Kai said. "Jesse Jackson called. He wants to meet about school desegregation and affirmative action."

"Do *we*?" Duncan said.

"We want his support," Kai said.

"But those aren't our issues."

Duncan glanced self-consciously at Parish, the only black member of the team. "No offense."

Parish held up his hands, palms forward. "I'm hip," he said. "But couldn't the Rainbow Coalition deliver a lot of votes?"

"Don't worry about it," Margo said. "The machine always turns out the black vote."

Parish frowned but said nothing, a minority in more ways than one.

"How's our funding holding up?" Duncan said.

"Better. The party kicked in $100,000."

"How'd we get them to commit that much?"

Kai smiled slyly and looked toward Duncan before answering. "I reminded Mayor Bilandic of all the things Duncan has done for Cook County and the importance of keeping the City of Chicago at the center of the state party."

He paused. "Then I told him that our future support depends greatly on his support now."

"You threatened him?" Duncan said. "You know how City Hall can hold a grudge."

"With our polling numbers, they can't afford to."

"So we're gaining?"

"Two points in the last poll, and that's without the bump from today's headlines."

Outside, clouds slid rapidly toward the lakefront, but inside the building felt warm and still. With so many floors, the Hancock required full climate control. No windows opened, although on sunny days the south side ones let in all the heat. Duncan stretched his stiff back theatrically, arms out, twisting side to side as though he'd just woken from a satisfying nap.

"That's about it, then," he said.

Taking his cue, Parish, Margo, and Carl filed out, leaving him alone with Kai.

"Fancy a walk?" Duncan said.

The campaign manager looked as though he'd suggested a beer run to Wisconsin. "Where?"

* * *

The elevators fell so quickly that by ground level Duncan's head ached. On the street, he looked left toward the white stone steeple of the Water Tower, one of the only buildings downtown to survive the great fire. That way led to the Magnificent Mile of shopping and crowds, no place for a private talk. Across the street, the gothic sanctuary of Fourth Presbyterian Church lay open, but he'd feel sacrilegious plotting there. To his right stood the Drake Hotel, site of his failed fundraiser. Finally he thought of all the walks he took after Lindsay died and knew where to go.

They headed north, bypassing the Drake and taking the pedestrian underpass of Lake Shore Drive until they stood on Oak Street beach. Midweek on a breezy fall day, no one lay in the sand or dipped a tentative toe in the water, where the wind stirred white caps. The skeletal guard towers stood empty along the boardwalk, waiting for next season. Unlike Kenilworth beaches, Chicago's smelled of sewage and exhaust from the adjacent freeway. A concrete path extended to the horizon in both directions, linking the affluent North Shore to the impoverished South Side. They followed its line toward prosperity and past the high rises of the Gold Coast.

"I'm worried," Duncan said.

"About?"

"Losing focus."

"On the campaign?"

"The investigation. The police are hung up on a kid who's clearly innocent. The way they're going, they'll never find who did it. Meanwhile, the reporters are losing interest. Did you see how little ink they gave that article today?"

Kai straggled behind, his platform heels a poor choice for long walks on concrete, so Duncan turned and walked backward to face him.

"How does that relate to the campaign?" Kai said.

"There's no point in me winning the election if Lindsay's killer gets away."

"A couple weeks ago, you had more publicity than you could stand."

"I know, but I won't feel safe until somebody's locked up."

"That's why you don't want to travel?"

"Essentially."

A pair of joggers passed them wrapped in the navy and orange jerseys of the Chicago Bears, sweat vaporizing from their bare heads. Duncan waited until they moved out of earshot before speaking again.

"What about legislation?" he said. "I've been thinking about some parole reforms—"

"We don't want to get too square," Kai said. "Once you're governor, you can write any policy you want."

"Isn't that what people hate about politicians? They're always offering vague promises and no specifics."

"We've got to be careful. You're running as a business-friendly democrat, not a hard line conservative. Let's not stray too far into law and order."

"But you said people are responding to that."

"They're responding to your personal story, not your policies.

A gust threw sand against them, forcing Kai to pause and squint against the hail.

"What we need is money," he said.

"What about the party's donation?"

"It's a start, but the governor's got a huge war chest. Now that we're drawing close, he's not going to conserve any of it."

"Could the Rainbow Coalition help?"

"The reverend has always believed 'tis better to receive than to give."

"I didn't know God was soliciting donations too."

"I don't know about God, but the church is."

"Can we make do?"

Kai looked up the path to where it converged with the lake and sky.

"This is our chance," he said. "We can win this."

"Last week, you said that if I dropped out, I could run again."

"Sure, but you may never get this close."

"So you lied."

"I tried to help."

Although Kai's résumé showed a steady climb, it lacked the breakout win he needed to woo the party power brokers. For him, Duncan was that chance. With a loss, he might spend the rest of his career babysitting corrupt aldermen.

"How?" Duncan said. "How can we win?"

"Exposure. And money. We'll need at least half a million for TV and handbills."

"Another fundraiser?"

Kai frowned. "It's too late in the show for rewrites."

"Have any rich friends or family?"

"That's more your area than mine. The butcher's union has been generous. You think they might kick in some more?"

"I doubt it."

"They seemed pretty keen on us at the last fundraiser."

"Things have changed."

"Things?"

"They're not satisfied with their contract."

"What if you gave them a bump?"

"They'd still be peeved."

They walked on in silence until a shriek broke the standoff and a bicyclist skidded toward them. Duncan sidestepped him like a matador, but Kai tripped over his own boots and caught the handlebars in the gut. As all three men stood panting, Duncan examined the intruder. Despite the cold, he wore tight black shorts, a T-shirt reading "Red Zinger," and a hat with a mini brim like a child's baseball cap.

"You're Duncan Cochrane!" the rider said.

Once he'd regained his composure, Duncan said, "I am."

"From the news!"

He reached for a sweaty handshake, which Duncan accepted.

"We're all with you, man!"

"I appreciate your support."

"I'm not talking about the campaign. Though, I mean, good luck with that, too. I mean your daughter. What happened to her, man, that was whacked!"

"Yes, I agree."

Duncan waited for Kai to intercede, but he eyed the rider as though he coveted his 10-speed.

"Well, thanks for stopping," Duncan said. "I always like to meet supporters."

"You got it!"

The man pedaled away while looking back and waving a two-fingered peace sign.

"About our money problems," Kai said. "You ever watch 'Dialing for Dollars'?"

CHAPTER 17

THE PHONE RANG SOMEWHERE IN THE DARK interval between night and morning.

"Mr. Cochrane?" a man said.

Still half asleep, Duncan struggled to pinpoint the voice.

"Yes."

"Sorry to wake you."

Duncan pushed himself onto one elbow, and the pressure on the joint helped rouse him. Josie rolled away, still dark to the world.

"I didn't want you to hear the news from anyone else."

The voice registered: Chief Dunleavy.

"We have a suspect."

"Who?"

"Can you meet me in Northfield in an hour?"

The bedside clock radio flipped digits to 5:45.

"Why Northfield?"

"I'll explain when you get here."

The chief gave him an address—meaningless—and reiterated the time.

"And bring your daughter," he said. "We might need her."

* * *

With barely time to shower and dress, Duncan grabbed a bathrobe and headed to his office, but when he switched on the light the bulb popped, leaving him again in darkness. He groped to the desk and flipped on his banker's lamp, which helped some, but its green shade funneled light to a narrow arc, and he had to stretch the cord taut to illuminate the middle

106

drawer. He wanted the mafia list Ron had given him. Instead, he found dry Montblanc pens, a silver envelope opener, and a stamp pad for his signature. Before meeting the chief, Duncan planned to memorize all the names and their connections, yet the page eluded him. Next he tried the side compartments, but no light reached their back recesses.

Duncan trod to the kitchen and rifled another drawer by the dishwasher, where he kept a flashlight, but couldn't find it. Instead he grabbed a box of matches and returned to the office, sure that by now he had awoken the entire house with his fumbling. He searched all seven drawers, flaring a new match for each one. Soon the office stank of sulfur, and burnt sticks littered the desktop, yet nowhere in the stacks of campaign literature and financial reports did he see those grim-faced suspects. He persisted until reaching the bottom row, where in place of the list he found his gun. Its silver barrel angled toward him, reflecting the match's orange flame. The house heater hadn't yet kicked on, and he shivered before closing the drawer on the weapon. In time it might be more useful than the list, but not yet.

* * *

The sun tipped the horizon as Duncan stopped on a residential block in Northfield. A half dozen police cars lined the street, one bearing Kenilworth's emblem, but all sat empty. With no one in sight, Duncan paused to survey things. The condo rose two stories with a brick front and shingled roof that wrapped the second floor like a hat pulled low. Sliding doors on the top half made two eyes in the mask, yet both balconies glared back vacant. Not even police tape guarded the entry. When Duncan approached it, with Glynis close behind, a motion detector triggered a light above the door. Quickly, a uniform emerged to stop them on the walkway. He radioed inside to check their credentials.

"He's your next boss," a man replied loudly through the speaker.

Chief Dunleavy met them at the front door and marched them through a vacant living-dining room to a vacant kitchen. He closed its louvered shutters—as though they offered any soundproofing—before speaking.

"We can't disturb the locals," he said, "or they'll get territorial."

The chief explained that a "solo female resident" woke to find a man standing over her bed with a flashlight.

"He tried to sexually assault her," the chief said.

"She was raped?" Duncan said.

"Not raped," the chief said. "She fought him off."

"So why bring us here?"

"We don't get a lot of these crimes on the North Shore, so whenever we do we look for duplicates. The Northfield police knew about yours and called us right away."

The chief glanced toward Glynis, who'd slumped into a chair by the table.

"We'd like your daughter to talk to the victim," Dunleavy said. "See if there are other similarities."

On hearing her name, Glynis held her hand to her throat protectively.

"You up to that?" Duncan said.

It took several seconds before she nodded.

"As soon as the locals are through with her, we'll break in," Dunleavy said.

They waited in silence while Duncan took in the kitchen: flower prints covered the walls and European post cards dotted the fridge, yet he saw no photos of a woman. The rest was impersonal: copper pots above the stove, mason jars of tea and coffee on the counter. Already Duncan felt self-conscious peeping the home of a stranger, let alone a victim. Minutes passed. Just when he could stand the stillness no longer, a beat cop opened the door to say, "She's all yours."

He led them upstairs to a back room lined with bookshelves that over-flowed with hardbacks. At its center sat a woman on a leather lounge chair guarded by three uniforms. She looked closer to Duncan's age than his daughter's, wrapped in a sagging bathrobe, but she'd pulled back her faded hair in a neat bun. Her pale face suggested a weariness beyond the day's events, yet she sat with perfect posture.

"This is Ms. Davis," said one uniform.

After uncomfortable nods all around, the chief kneeled by her and explained their presence, then asked her to repeat what happened. Immediately, the woman looked toward Glynis and spoke only to her.

"I was sleeping," she said, "when I felt something touch my leg. At first I assumed I was dreaming, but then I saw a light. It moved around the walls and ceilings like—what do they call them—god beams? When it got to me, it stopped."

The chief leaned in to catch her eye the same way he had with the Cochrans days before.

"So he was shining it in your face," the chief said.

"Yes," she said, squinting at the memory. "But when I looked up, it moved away."

"Did the man say anything?"

"Something absurd, like 'I'll be out of the way right quick.' "

"How did he sound?"

"At home, like he lived here."

"No, I mean his voice. Did it sound deep, high, thin, heavy?"

Ms. Davis raised her hand to shield her eyes as though reliving the event. "Black. He sounded black. You know that, that, slang they use? He sounded like that."

Duncan glanced to his daughter, who stood with her head lowered so he couldn't read her face, her arms wrapped around each other.

"You didn't see him?" the chief said.

"Not then," Ms. Davis said. "I didn't have my glasses on, but he kept spotlighting things, then touching them—my loom and spinning wheel. He must have stepped on some knitting needles because he started cursing with the foulest language."

They all looked to the bedside, where a spatter of blood stained the shag carpet.

"Did he have shoes on?" said the chief.

"I don't know."

He frowned but said, "Go on."

"When he yelled, I ran."

The chief nodded for her to continue, but Ms. Davis had to visualize it first, holding out her hands as though groping her way through the dark.

"I stumbled down the hallway until I got here and locked myself in."

She looked to the flimsy door made from two thin sheets of plywood, inadequate to keep out a toddler.

"Did he follow you?" the chief said.

"I heard him bumping into more things, so I screamed as loud as I could. 'Get out!' That seemed... it must have frightened him because next thing he was stumbling down the stairs."

The chief looked to Duncan as though this detail confirmed something.

"And after that?" he said.

"The front door slammed, so I ran back to the bedroom to see if he had left. When I got to the window, he looked up."

She studied the ground for several seconds.

"He looked... hideous. He had bushy red hair and blotchy skin and a fat nose. He looked like some sort of, I don't know, half breed."

As she paused, the chief turned to Glynis.

"Does any of that sound like the man you saw?"

Glynis stood still and silent for so long Duncan thought she'd never answer.

"I don't... I can't tell. I never saw him."

Duncan glanced to Ms. Davis, who leaned forward on the couch, chin in hands.

"He made a lot of noise?" Duncan asked.

"I'm a light sleeper. Ever since my husband died. I... I never felt safe being alone."

"But you heard him, in the hall?"

"He kept running into things. He kept cursing so much I thought he was going to...." She clasped her hands to her chest, unable to say the words. After regaining her breath, she turned to Glynis and asked, "This happened to your sister?"

Glynis nodded but offered no explanation.

"Do you think...?" the older woman said. She turned to the uniforms, who refused to speculate, then to the chief.

"You did well to get away," he said.

When Duncan looked again to his daughter, she hugged herself so tight it looked painful.

"I need to go," he said. "I've got appointments."

He took Glynis' hand and led her to the doorway, then remembered his manners and turned to Ms. Davis, who sat immobile on the couch.

"I don't know whether to say I'm sorry or thank you," he said, "but I'm glad you're alright."

"And you," she said.

If only that were true.

They descended the stairs and walked to the door before Chief Dunleavy caught up.

"I thought this might be more definitive," he said.

Duncan looked down on his balding crown and slim shoulders before answering.

"Don't ask us to go through this again," he said.

The chief looked startled and took a half step back.

"I know the only reason we're here is because of my... because I'm running for office, but please don't take us to any more crime scenes. I felt like such a... " he searched for the right word "voyeur back there."

The chief pocketed his hands before speaking. "Alright. I won't call unless it's absolutely necessary. But I still think this is the same man who attacked your daughter, and we need to find him."

"Fine," Duncan said. "Just don't ask us to relive what happened again."

CHAPTER 18

"GOOD MORNING, MR.... KO–PEK–NEE? This is Duncan Cochrane. I'm running for governor, and I need your support."

Duncan leaned back in his desk chair and stared at the ceiling, preferring its blank, white expanse as he repeated the opening salvo he'd used so often in the past week. Since Kai's inspiration on the beach, the candidate spent an hour every morning soliciting donations. First he called friends and family, who'd been generous but hadn't the resources to fund his campaign alone. Then he'd tried business associates and colleagues. When those ran dry, he tried frequent donors to the Democratic Central Committee. Finally, Kai gave him a list from Common Cause, anyone who'd given even $10 in previous elections. The tally ran hundreds of pages, more than the Chicago phone book. Half the entries were dead ends, out-of-date phone numbers or people who didn't want to be bothered.

This man too had the sound of futility, the cautious "hello," the silence after his introduction. Still, Duncan ran down the script, which he'd by then memorized, about making the city safer and restoring justice to the state, then asked for a donation. He expected the click of a hang up, but instead the man said, "How much do you want?"

"No amount is too small."

It sounded weak, uncertain, the opposite of what Duncan hoped for. By the end of the hour he needed $10,000 to reach his daily goal and to compete with Big Bill Stratton and his million-dollar war chest. Like this, he'd never get there.

"Would five thousand dollars do?"

Startled to silence, Duncan glanced again at his list to see who he'd called. His finger traced down the column of crossed out names until he came to the first unblemished one. Harold Kopechne of Highland Park, a Pole from a wealthy suburb along the lakefront.

"That would be more than generous."

Begging for money had always felt awkward for Duncan, an affront to the Protestant work ethic imprinted on him by his parents and grandparents, who refused to take handouts during the Great Depression and instead lived on what they could barter. With such a boost, he could finish his calls early, eat breakfast with Josie and Glynis for the first time in a month.

Before Duncan could thank his new benefactor, Kopechne surprised him again.

"Oh, and Governor, don't worry about what Rica's writing. None of us believe that old communist."

Reflexively, Duncan laughed at the slight of Chicago's most famous columnist. "I won't, sir. We'll all need a second skin before this is over."

With that they hung up, yet Duncan couldn't dismiss the last comment. What column? Duncan hadn't read anything disparaging about himself lately, but he hadn't checked the opinion page in a week either and relied on Kai to update him. Would his campaign manager censor the negative?

From the front of the house, Duncan heard the scrape of a saw. Workers were installing a new alarm system just before the campaign started its push downstate. Even with a suspect identified, he wanted to be cautious, and to feel less guilty about leaving his family alone.

Forty-five minutes remained before the driver would pick him up, so Duncan walked to the kitchen, where Glynis and Josie were sharing coffee and sweet rolls. Josie had already dressed in wool slacks and a silk blouse while Glynis wore her bathrobe. "Either of you seen today's paper?" he said.

Josie handed Duncan the front section of the *Tribune*.

"No, I want the *Sun-Times*."

"Why?"

"I need to check something."

He found Rica's column on page three under the heading "Foul Balls and Foul Tips."

Last week at the Billy Goat Tavern, a man sidled up and took the stool next to me. He ordered an Old Style and sipped the foam off the head before turning to admire mine.

"You read the papers much?" he said.

Assuming that he didn't recognize me, which I counted a good thing, I did admit to some knowledge of the day's news.

"That guy Cochrane's sure turned grape juice into wine. Losing his daughter is the best thing that ever happened to his campaign. Don't get me wrong, I'm not saying he planned it. Just, without that, he'd have nothing to say."

I nodded, sipped my brew, and stared into the distance, keeping my thoughts to myself. While it's true that Duncan Cochrane's polling numbers have risen since his daughter's murder, I wouldn't claim a conspiracy. Dirty politics are standard here in Chicago, but I've never heard of a candidate killing off one of his own for publicity.

"All I'm saying is, her murder's very convenient."

With that wisdom imparted, my neighbor took his beer and wished me a good day.

After he left, my old friend Nits Grabowski took his stool. "I don't like that guy," Nits said as introduction.

"You don't like a lot of people."

"He seemed sideways to me."

I nodded and reached for the bowl of nuts on the bar. The young man didn't come off as especially bent compared to many I've met in the Billy Goat, being well dressed and with a sheen on his hair. Still, I could see what Nits meant.

Some people just have an air of falsity about them, and this young man did, probably because when he's not bar crawling he works for Bill Stratton's reelection. He's one of many well-placed operatives who've started a whisper campaign to discredit the governor's opponent.

Not that his cynicism is totally unfounded. How a man could lose his daughter and then return to the drudgery and degradation of politics a week later is hard for a lot of people to fathom.

Still, I've always thought Mr. Cochrane deserves our sympathy more than our judgment, and I said so to Nits.

"Who's judging?" Nits said, tipping sideways on his barstool to relieve the pressure in his lower intestine. "But we got enough certifiable politicians in this town. Why should we vote in one more?"

I didn't say it, but I've always assumed that anyone who runs for office in this state is certifiable. How much worse could Cochrane be?

Duncan threw the paper, then stared out his back window where a breeze strafed the glass with sand. He couldn't define what upset him more: the whisper campaign, or that people saw something positive in Lindsay's death.

When he looked back to Josie and Glynis, they stared at him with wariness.

"What's wrong, Dad?" Glynis said.

"Dirty politics."

She picked up the ragged papers.

"Don't read it."

She ignored his warning and finished before speaking. "They think you wanted Lindsay dead?"

Duncan walked to the back door and stared out the glass panes, keeping his back turned so he could hide his anger.

"It's just a smear campaign. It has nothing to do with Lindsay."

"How can you say that?" Josie said, and her tone betrayed irritation.

Duncan turned and said, "Kai warned us about these kind of tricks."

Josie walked to the sink, threw in her coffee, rinsed the trough, then looked at him as though he had started the rumor. "Why are they even talking about Lindsay?"

Unable to hold her gaze, Duncan turned back to the window, where the wind bent the trees like sailcloth. "Maybe they think we're vulnerable there."

"I don't care about their strategy. I don't want Lindsay... besmirched."

"They don't even name her in the story."

"Everyone *knows* who they mean. You don't have any other dead daughters, do you?"

Duncan looked to Glynis, who broke off a piece of sweet roll while studying the Datebook section as though deaf to their conversation.

"You can't take this personally," Duncan said. "It's just politics."

"You're supposed to be avenging her, not defending her honor."

Duncan didn't want the alarm installer to hear them, so he lowered his voice in hopes it would calm her. "I know, and I am. I'll talk to Kai today. We'll come up with a response—"

"Don't say anything more," she said and walked down the hallway with a determined lean. Her footsteps creaked up the stairwell, then a door slammed overhead.

Duncan sighed and looked to his oldest daughter, who offered a weak smile. Her face lacked makeup, her hair lay matted, and her bathrobe bore pills along the collar from all its recent use.

"Will people really believe this?" she said.

"The Republicans just want to provoke us."

The clock gave him fifteen minutes until the driver arrived. "You going into work today?" he said.

"I have a headache," Glynis said.

"We'd be happy to have you down at the campaign office."

She lowered her eyes and stared into her empty coffee cup, looking ready to cry. "Is there something else I can do?"

"Your mother's right, the best thing we can do is nothing."

CHAPTER 19

REV. MCLEOD'S SERMON—about the relief that comes with faith and forgiveness—felt endless, so Duncan studied the sanctuary. It looked typically Presbyterian: white walls, clear windows, a bare altar. Like Calvin, the church shunned idolatry. Only the organ pipes stood out, and they were unpolished. The scarcity was supposed to focus listeners on the lessons of Christ, but all Duncan could contemplate was getting out of his hard pew. He shifted his weight, and Josie clenched his thigh to still him. Since declaring his candidacy, he'd attended church religiously, yet after Lindsey's death the lessons no longer salved him.

After the service finally ended, he shook hands and accepted condolences from the small congregation, then lined up for more of the same from the minister. The queue moved slowly—Rev. McLeod liked to talk—and Duncan began overheating in his topcoat. Each step seemed a move to escape, yet at his turn the minister seized his hand and wouldn't let go.

"So glad you came," McLeod said.

"Your sermon was... inspiring," Duncan said.

"Just keep coming back."

Duncan nodded and smiled at the cool air just outside, but when he stepped onto the church lawn, a police car waited by the curb. Chief Dunleavy met him half way down the walk.

"I tried your house, but your daughter said I'd find you here," he said.

Duncan waited silent, conscious of the people passing.

"I need you to look at something," the chief said. "Could you follow me to my office?"

"How long's it going to take?" Duncan said.

"Only a minute."

Duncan looked for an excuse among the bare trees and wide lawns about them until Josie said "of course."

On the short drive, they did not speak, but Duncan sensed her disapproval.

* * *

Inside the chief's office, he sensed something different. The cheap furniture remained, as did the grip-and-grin photos and the civic trophies. Nothing appeared out of place, yet everything looked askew—the drawers, the blotter, the lampshades—as though someone had rifled them. The chief too looked off, his hair mussed, his pants wrinkled at the knee and thigh. His collegiate act had degenerated to drunken professor.

"Take a look at these," he said.

He passed them an album with five black and white mug shots. All showed young men of ambiguous race, scowling with fatigue and irritation as though they'd been woken from a sound sleep.

"Anyone you know?"

Duncan studied them briefly then let the book fall to his lap. "No."

He passed the photos to his wife, who looked harder but came to the same conclusion.

"You should probably ask Glynis," Duncan said.

"I have," said the chief. "She didn't recognize them either."

Irritation swelled in Duncan as he thought of the police interrogating his daughter without him there, but he knew better than to say anything in front of Josie. She still believed the case was progressing, and he didn't want to disillusion her.

"Who are they?" she said.

"One is the Northfield suspect," the chief said.

He pointed to the third of the photos, which showed a man with kinky hair, rough skin, and a broad nose. The face's pits and valleys ran like tire tracks on dirt.

"How'd you find him?" Duncan said.

"The victim," he said. "She picked him out of a lineup like this one."

Duncan thought of Ms. Davis, with her recollection, and imagined her picking one at random to relieve the pressure of interrogation.

"You're sure?" he said.

The chief nodded and leaned the mug shot against a lamp so it faced away from them.

"What about the name Oges Hoxter?" he said. "Mean anything?"

Duncan searched the Rolodex of his memory but found no such entries. Even with all his contacts in business and politics, he'd remember that name, and certainly it belonged to no one he knew socially.

"You think *he* killed my Lindsay?"

"Like I said before, we don't get a lot of these cases around here."

"I still don't see the connection. Why would he choose my house, my daughter? If we've never met, and he didn't know Lindsay...."

"That's what we need to determine. Truth is, he wasn't someone we had on our docket. He's got a lengthy rap sheet but, like you said, no apparent connection to your family."

"So then why —"

Josie put her hand on Duncan's thigh to silence him. "What's your experience tell you?" she said.

"Well, we're following the clues where they lead, and right now they lead to him."

"Have you handled a case like this before?"

"Every one is different."

Duncan covered Josie's hand with his own and spoke. "But why would he do it?"

The chief started tapping his pen against his shoe, only instead of keeping a steady rhythm he let it skip like a stone, the tempo going flat with repetition.

"He's got a long history with state agencies," the chief said, "been institutionalized one way or another since age ten. Eight years in and out of foster care and juvenile hall. At eighteen, he graduated to prison. So far he's done five stints in twelve years."

"How could he commit that many crimes and still be out free?" Duncan said.

"It's a sad fact: a lot of career criminals never get more than a few months in lockup. Back when I worked parole we called it doing life six months at a time. As long as you're not killing people, you'll never get a long sentence. Instead, we'll let you out every year to do the same thing to somebody else."

Twelve hours after his last cigarette, Duncan could still taste its earthiness. All morning his family had been too close, but as soon as he lost Josie he would smoke half a pack.

"Does it hurt your case that we couldn't identify him?" Duncan said.

The chief beat out a few more paradiddles until the pen fell from his fingers. "Probably not."

"Probably?"

"Well... a defense attorney could question it, but that shouldn't matter." He frowned as though unsure whether to go on.

"So what's next?" Duncan said.

"We still need to find him. We know where he lives and frequents, but we haven't caught up with him yet. We will, though. I doubt he even knows we're looking for him. Plus, these guys aren't good at hiding. They travel in narrow orbits. It's only a matter of time till he circles around again."

Duncan stood and put on his coat, then helped Josie into hers. "Thanks for your time, Chief. You've been very enlightening."

The chief rose to shake hands. "I'm sorry someone like this came into your lives. Now that we've IDed him, we'll need to take our time, make sure we put him away for good."

"You catch him," Duncan said, "and I'll make sure he never gets another chance."

* * *

On the trip home, Duncan let the radio do the talking, but once they pulled into the driveway Josie proposed a beach walk.

"In these clothes?" he said.

"Your shoes already need a shine," she said.

So he followed her into the dense sand drifts, feeling the grains pool in his heels and watching them settle into the dimples of his wingtips.

"Why are you so tense?" she said.

"I'm not."

"You all but yelled at Chief Dunleavy."

Duncan sidestepped a rogue wave and paused to let the water absorb back into the beach.

"It's been a month," he said.

"It'll be over soon," she said. "As soon as they catch this... whatever his name is."

"Hoxter," Duncan said.

He steered her away from the water, but every step took them deeper into the sand.

"You sound skeptical," Josie said.

"I just don't get it. Why our house, our family?"

"You have some other theory?" she said.

Duncan stopped to shake out his pant legs before replying "no."

"Then let the police do their jobs."

CHAPTER 20

WITH ONLY A DAY'S WARNING, the Chicago Police Officers Association couldn't book a private room for their meeting with Duncan. Instead, they used the lunch area of the downtown station. A half dozen cops sat around the cleanest of the Formica tables, the one closest to the refrigerator and coffee maker, which hummed and dripped in unison.

Though off the clock, the officers remained dressed for work, half in their street blues, the others wearing tweed blazers and wide ties. They kept their masks on too, dead eyeing each other and him. From all his recent contact with cops, Duncan had learned not to take their coldness personally. These men stalked the grimmest corners of the city and wore the fatigue on their faces.

"You supported my opponent in the primary," Duncan said, "and I know you're still loyal to him."

"You mean to the party," said the oldest of the officers, whose grey hair and weathered skin contradicted the bulk in his shoulders and chest.

"Right. But their man lost, so there's no reason your union can't endorse me now."

"We always vote the ticket," said a captain badged Wilson, whose dark hair lay slicked back like a Raven's wings.

"Nonetheless," Duncan said, and wavered, thinking the word made him sound too patrician. Too late now. "I'd like to earn your official backing. I know how hard the last few months have been for you."

Three months ago, six uniforms got caught looting TVs, stereos, and jewels from an apartment on the Gold Coast. Since then, local politicos had denounced the department, demanded its reform, even threatened to have the chief fired, all with typical bombast.

"That's all posturing," the captain said.

"Still, I'm committed to making your jobs easier. I'll increase sentences and strengthen our parole system so criminals get no more second chances."

Silence followed. Typically, the cops betrayed nothing, leaving Duncan to build a holding cell out of his own words. While he searched for better ones, the coffee maker overflowed with a hiss, off-gassing burnt Joe. A uniform flipped off the machine, though it continued to sizzle.

"I don't get what you want from us," said the captain. "Like I said, we vote the party line. Beyond that, there's not much we can offer you without the party's blessing."

"Hear me out," Duncan said. "This legislation will make all your jobs easier. I know you must tire of arresting the same people over and over again, only to see them let out a week or a month or a year later to commit the same crimes. We're all tired of that cycle."

"The soup line," said the old captain.

"Beg your pardon?"

The phrase escaped before Duncan had time to think about it, a gentleman's excuse. He should have said "what" or "sorry" or even "huh." Margo had warned him to watch his diction, and instead he sounded like some formal English governor.

"We call it the soup line, when guys keep coming back for more."

"Exactly. That's a great way to put it."

Detective Gino Peruzzi, a union shop steward who'd arranged the meeting, leaned forward to clear a space in the conversation. Small and lean, the detective still knew how to intimidate, with a tilt of the head that provoked confrontation. "Look, Mr. Cochrane, I'm not aiming to be rude here. I appreciate you coming down. But I heard it all before. Every guy running for office says the same thing. 'I'm gonna get tough on crime.' What makes you different?"

"They haven't lost a child."

It strayed from the script, but when Peruzzi glanced down Duncan knew his counterpunch had knocked the wind out of the detective.

"My daughter's killer is a career criminal."

Again he heard the pained breathing of the wounded. Only now the cops glanced sidelong at each other, their first signs of indecision.

"It's not public yet," Duncan said, "but the Kenilworth police know who did it. He's been arrested a dozen times and served more than ten years in jail but never longer than a year.

"Why a man like that is allowed to get out over and over again to find new victims...."

Duncan felt his throat go dry and reached for a water glass. The pause let him figure out what to say next. He'd all but ignored Margo's counsel, but nothing that he'd planned to say felt relevant anymore.

"Last week he broke into another woman's house. He's a predator who belongs in jail. Whether or not I win this election, I'm going to make sure he doesn't hurt anyone the way he's hurt me and my family."

Detective Peruzzi leaned forward again. "You should tell people that."

The other officers shifted in their seats and stared at him.

"Go easy on him, Gino," said the oldest of the bunch.

"No, I'm not being hostile here, but you need to tell people what's going on. People like you, people with money, who live in nice neighborhoods think it can't happen to them. Till it does. Then they're asking 'Where's the police? Why didn't the police protect me?' They don't get it, that it's not up to us. No matter how many times I arrest a guy, the judges and the lawyers always go easy on him, like all he's got to do is apologize and everything's gonna be okay."

"Mind your manners," the old cop said. He turned to Duncan with an indulgent smile. "Gino just lost a big case. What he's trying to say is, *we* know what you mean, but until the politicians in Springfield figure it out they're going to keep letting guys out early. Rehabilitation doesn't work, Mr. Cochrane. Incarceration does."

"That's why he's got to tell them," Peruzzi said.

The detective pivoted for anyone who'd contradict him. "Without a real person behind it, the politicians aren't getting it. But if one of their own was to explain it, they'd pay attention. You do that, you can count on us to work for you."

"I can do that," Duncan said.

CHAPTER 21

THE DOORBELL RANG AT 6:30 as Duncan vacillated between a blue and grey suit. Back when he worked in meat processing, suits meant somber occasions like church or board meetings. However, for the campaign he'd worn a three-piece every day, had developed a personal relationship with the overnight dry cleaner, had bought two more get ups from Brooks Brothers after staining one with coffee, and still struggled to find enough dark socks and fresh ties. Every morning he had to recall which color shirts he'd worn already that week (two white, one blue, and a salmon, which he'd never repeat).

Duncan's first instinct said to ignore the bell. His driver wasn't due for another thirty minutes, and that left the news bugs as the likely ringers. Yet predawn felt too early for mosquitos. On the second chime he reconsidered and jogged down the stairs in his stockings, sliding on the living room hardwoods and nearly ramming the heavy front door. He opened it to see Chief Dunleavy looking cold but triumphant.

"We got him," the chief said.

He wore only a thin blazer, and his hair danced in the wind as if staticked.

"Hoxter?"

"The Chicago police picked him up an hour ago at his house. He had his bags packed and his car loaded. It's a good thing they got him now, otherwise we'd be in a manhunt."

"Was it... did he say anything?"

"Not yet, but we haven't talked to him. He's downtown at the city jail. Later today he'll be transferred to Northfield. Once they're through with him, we'll have our chance."

"But you're *sure* it's him?"

"We'll be more sure after we prod him a bit, but all the evidence is pointing that way."

Duncan stood immobile until a gust of wind chilled his midriff. He glanced down to find half his shirttail untucked. Even with years of practice, he still needed a mirror to get dressed. Were the police the same way? Did they need repetition before getting all the clues to line up?

"When'll you be sure?" he said.

"There's no hurry. He'll be charged for the other break-in, and his bail will be so high there's no chance of his getting out. We want to check him out thoroughly before proceeding. Right now we can quiz him as much as we want, but as soon as we file charges, lawyers will arrive to protect him."

The chief smiled as though expecting a tip, but Duncan felt little generosity toward him. The explanation made sense, but his first words still rankled. 'There's no hurry.' Not for others. The case would be resolved in time, or not. Either way, their lives would continue. Meanwhile, his hung in suspended animation.

"It'll be soon, though? I need... I want to know everything. I still don't understand...."

"I'll keep you appraised," the chief said. "I may need you to confirm or refute some of what he says. So you'll be hearing from me again soon. Only...."

"What?"

The chief crossed his arms and shivered against the cold. "We're entering a new phase, one that'll move much slower. Murder cases can take months or years if the defense wants to play games. You'll need to prepare yourselves for a long wait. We may not get much useful info from him. Interrogating suspects doesn't work like in detective novels. They don't just confess as soon as they're caught and explain themselves. Your patience may be tested."

Duncan frowned, looked to the horizon, and tucked in his shirttail against further drafts.

"It already has been," he said.

* * *

Green Acres, a retirement home in suburban Oak Park, marked the campaign's first stop of the day. As his Lincoln Town Car passed through a pair of rolling iron gates, Duncan thought of Hemingway's famous descriptor of the town as holding "wide lawns and narrow minds." The first part certainly fit. A grass span larger than a football field surrounded a Victorian mansion. He hoped the second part proved false. Though usually Republican leaning, seniors often swung statewide races because they voted in such numbers.

Kai met him on the gravel drive wearing a splotchy Hawaiian shirt and form-fitting bell-bottoms. Later, they'd have to discuss his flower power attire.

"You see this schedule?" Kai said, extending a clipboard with papers an inch thick. The first page blocked the day into ten-minute time slots until eight p.m.

"Looks busy," Duncan said.

"Yeah, and we're already behind."

"I had a few personal things to take care of."

"Well, now you have twenty minutes to shake as many hands as you can."

They walked up the steps and through a heavy, wood door into a foyer with period floral wallpaper and a tile mosaic on the floor.

"Good day, Mr. Cochrane," said a trim Asian woman. "I'm Ms. Hwang."

As they shook, she leaned forward in a near bow, embarrassingly formal.

"Please, call me Duncan."

"Our residents are all excited to meet you."

She led them down a narrow hallway, which disgorged into a large solarium streaked by sunlight from a wall of east windows. The room grew a faux garden of grass-green carpet and floral wallpaper, but it smelled of damp wool and cough drops. At least a hundred people sat in clusters of four or five around card tables and sofa sets. Some turned as Duncan approached, but most remained engrossed in their games.

Ms. Hwang steered them to a quadrangle of women playing bridge, who on his arrival placed their hands face down. The next moment a spotlight hit Duncan. He turned to see a camera's lens pointed at him.

Ms. Hwang brought him back by touching his arm. "Mr. Cochrane, I'd like you to meet Mrs. Linklater, Miss. Sophie, Miss. Burnett, and Mrs. Aptow."

The four smiled as though Duncan stood in for their closest surviving relative. He squeezed each of their hands gently.

"Very kind of you to come," said one woman with apple blossom painted on her cheeks and an expensive silk blouse.

"It's kind of you to stop your game for me," he said. "You all probably know I'm running for governor, and I want to ask for your support."

"Oh, you had it from the moment you walked in," said Miss Burnett, whose strawberry hair stood up in a beehive. "How could we not vote for you after all you've been through?"

"I don't want to talk about my struggles, I want to hear about yours. How's the economy affecting you all?"

He expected to hear them grouse about inflation or the Cost-of-Living Adjustment to social security.

"Oh, they provide for us very well here," Mrs. Linklater said.

In her cable knit sweater and flower print skirt, she embodied domesticity. Still, the answer sounded canned, as though she'd been fed the line ahead of time. Would she have said the same without their governess looming?

"I'm pleased to hear it, but I'm more interested in how the *government* has treated you all. Have things been difficult for you lately?"

"We don't need to worry," Miss Linklater said. "Everything we need is right here." She patted her hands on the table three times, then gave a meaningful look to Mrs. Aptow, who sat opposite.

"Still, I know how difficult this economy must be for people on a fixed income."

"Heavens, he thinks we're dependent on a government check," Mrs. Aptow said, and leaned back in her chair. She shook her head as though erasing the question but kept her eyes fixed on Mrs. Linklater opposite.

Miss Burnett leaned forward and said in a conspiratorial voice, "Everyone here has other income. This place doesn't come cheap."

Since he couldn't coax from them the quote he wanted, Duncan straightened. "Well, I've interrupted your game long enough."

He turned to walk away until Miss Sophie's voice halted him. "Did they ever catch the man who did it?"

As he paused, her eyes misted. Duncan glanced toward the camera, which stared brightly back. "There's a man in custody now," he said.

"I haven't heard a thing about it," said Mrs. Linklater. "Why hasn't it been on the news?"

"Well, the police arrested him just yesterday."

The four nodded sympathetically, and Miss Sophie grasped Duncan's hand. "You take good care of your family," she said.

"I will ma'am, thank you."

Another hand grasped his opposite arm and gave a gentle squeeze. "Mr. Cochrane," said Ms. Hwang, "many of other residents would like to meet you."

"Of course."

She led them, tailed by the camera's light, to a trio of men on old velvet couches. "This is Mr. Cochrane," the hostess said. "He's running for governor."

"Pleased to meet you, Governor," said one with the accent of the English working class.

"I won't have that title for several months yet."

"Right you are, Governor."

Duncan wondered if the staff had warned people he was coming. Not that it mattered. With the spotlight still on him, he needed a few good one-liners.

"Tell me, how has the economy affected you?"

"Oh, it's no problem at all," said one.

* * *

An hour later, as their limousine drove toward the city, Duncan asked Kai all the questions he'd suppressed in front of the pensioners.

"Why didn't you tell me there'd be media?"

"Didn't know till this morning. The station needed footage of you, and we need the publicity."

"Can't you give me a little more warning? I felt like a criminal on the witness stand."

"We can't turn down any media. That's what's got us back in the race."

"At least let me figure out what to say first."

"They're not recording your whole speech. At most they'll show two sentences, and the rest will be a news anchor talking over footage of you shaking hands."

"What's newsworthy about that?"

"Reporters are insatiable. Every day we've got to feed them something."

"Or else?"

"They'll turn on us like lions."

Deep potholes announced they'd entered the city limits, and Duncan gripped the armrest against the lurches and dips of the road. The pause let him rehash what he'd heard.

"*Are* we back in the race?"

"In the party's latest canvass, the gap had closed to five percent."

"All based on a few stump speeches," Duncan said. "How's the governor reacting?"

"That's the thing. He's not. He's doing the usual county fairs and charity golf gigs but no campaigning. I'm not sure if we've caught him off guard or if he's saving up for something."

Duncan didn't know Bill Stratton personally—had only seen the man once live at the St. Patty's day parade—but he doubted the governor would lay low. Big Bill projected power, in his thick mid-section, his wide-legged stance, and his booming courtroom voice. His style didn't allow him to be quieted or to go easy on a competitor.

"So what's next?"

Kai glanced at the clipboard and checked his watch. "A confab with the Manufacturers Industrial Union, then an interview on WGN, a fundraiser with the Kiwanis Club of Lincoln Park, a meet and greet with the students at DePaul, and a restaurant opening in Wrigleyville."

"No, I mean overall."

They rounded a corner fast, and Kai grabbed the "Oh my God" handle before answering.

"Now that we've got the debate scheduled, it's just staying on script."

"I can't keep repeating the same slogans."

"Margo will coach you. Basically, keep hitting them with what we've got. People are really responding to your tough on crime spiel, so forget about the economy. Focus on penalty reform. Get people to talk about how scared they are."

Duncan thought of the tag line to *Saturday Night Live*. "Live from New York, the most dangerous city in America." If you could make fun of crime, could you inspire people with it?

"You don't think we need something more concrete, a plan, a law, something?"

"Did you see how those geriatrics reacted? You've got their empathy, take advantage."

"I don't want pity."

"Not pity, empathy."

"What's the difference?"

"Identification. They feel for you because they can relate, and Big Bill Stratton can't match that. It's the one thing we've got over him, and we've got to use it. Once you've found a wedge issue you keep hammering it until either it breaks the election open or your leverage gives out. The *worst* thing we could do now is stop."

The limousine accelerated up an onramp, pressing Duncan into the leather seats so hard he couldn't right himself until they'd reached freeway speed.

"Are we that late?" Duncan said.

"I asked our driver to keep us on schedule."

Duncan shook his head to clear the distraction and stared out the window at the skyscrapers of downtown, which enclosed them in towers of power.

"I don't want people feeling sorry for me," Duncan said.

"Look, I understand how sensitive this is. I don't want you lapsing into soliloquy either, but right now crime *is* our issue. *Don't* talk about the details, if you don't want to, but remind people that you've suffered too."

"They already know that. Christ, the papers have run our story every day since."

"People have short memories. You can't trust them to make the connection. And you hit all the right notes back at the old folks' home. Just say the police have got a suspect, and you want to make sure he never gets out of jail. Act determined."

Not long ago, he didn't have to act. Evermore in this campaign, the line between sincerity and posturing was blurring so much that Duncan couldn't tell his true feelings from the manufactured.

All for Lindsay, he thought. This is all for Lindsay.

* * *

By the time he returned home, Duncan fell hoarse from blaring his message. Josie had saved him a large bowl of veal stew, which he planned to eat in silence. As the thick gravy soothed his throat, she tried to start a conversation.

"I saw you on the news tonight," she said.

"Mmmmgh?"

"Twice. First, they had you campaigning, then for a story about that murderer."

He imagined the two of them framed in mug shots like conspirators.

"Maybe now they'll focus on the campaign," he said, softly.

Even those few words stung, so Duncan sipped his red wine, but it burned going down. He pushed aside the glass.

"You can't allow that," Josie said.

Duncan let his hands fall to the table and stared at her, awaiting an explanation. She leaned forward across the long oval and stretched her hand toward him, but she could not reach.

"As crude as it sounds, Rica is right. It's the best thing we have going. If you forget about Lindsay, you'll be forgotten too."

"I won't forget," he said.

"Dammit, you know what I mean. You're too close now to let up. You have to chant her name until everyone is chanting it with you. She's your reason for staying in the race."

He reached for a roll, buttered it, and thoroughly chewed a bite before answering. "But she's not," he said. "I'm in this because of you."

She withdrew her hand and sat up straight. "No," she said, "you wanted this too. You never stopped complaining about meatpacking. You could have kept at it another ten years and retired like all the other titans of the North Shore, but you wanted something different."

"To satisfy you."

"It's nothing to do with satisfaction."

"Then what? Power? Fame? Why is this more important than our daughter's memory?"

She stood and walked around the table to kneel beside him so she could grip his arm. "Because I can't run. No woman in this state can get elected as long as the Bridgeport mob run things. The Machine won't let us. Look what they've done with the E.R.A. A meaningless resolution to confirm what we already know — that women are every bit as worthy as men — and our legislature won't pass it. Six years they've been dallying. With that kind of obstruction, a woman couldn't get on the library board here.

"This will be Lindsay's legacy: that you get elected."

"So Lindsay is leverage."

"She's the only leverage we have."

She remained kneeling beside him, so he felt compelling to say something.

"You remember her first day at college?" he said.

They'd all driven a thousand miles from Chicago to Poughkeepsie to drop her off at Vassar, though flying would have saved three days.

"Of course."

"You remember what she told us before we left?" On the steps of her new dorm, she'd hugged them both and smiled at their parting tears. "I'll always be with you."

"Which is why she needs your focus now."

He nodded and looked at the empty place mat diagonal from him. "Where's Glynis?"

"Upstairs."

"Doing what?"

"Sleeping, I expect."

His watch read 8:45. "This early?"

"She's feeling ill."

Duncan nodded and ate a spoonful of stew with a large potato piece, scalding his tongue. "Flu?"

"I don't know."

"Fever?"

"I don't know, Duncan. She's old enough to tend her own colds."

The doorbell rang. Couldn't he get half an hour unmolested? By the third chime, Duncan worried it would wake his daughter and strode angrily over. To his surprise, Chief Dunleavy again stood on the stoop, but compared to the morning, his face looked dejected.

"There's something we need to discuss," he said.

"Okay."

Duncan stood aside to admit him into the hallway but stopped there. Nowhere on his priority list had he written finishing the day as he'd started it: with another visit from the cops.

"It's about that announcement you made tonight. We're at a delicate point, and disclosures can only hurt us."

"Disclosures?"

The chief studied the ceiling as if seeking a politic response. "It's Hoxter. Apparently he heard you on TV. As soon as we asked him about Lindsay's death, he shut us down. Wouldn't say a thing other than 'Don't finger me for that'."

Duncan swallowed hard, and his throat pinched with the effort. What exactly had he said? Just that the police had a suspect in custody.

"God... dammit!"

The words escaped before he could stop them, a month's worth of caged emotions, and echoed through the hallway. He didn't care about offending the chief, but he didn't want Josie or Glynis to overhear.

"I'm sorry," the chief said. "You couldn't have known."

Duncan's throat burned from the outburst, so he said quietly, "What now?"

"Up until then Hoxter was pretty cooperative, so we're going to have another go tomorrow, try to convince him that if he talks we'll cut him a deal. In the meantime, we don't want to give him any more reasons to mistrust us, so please don't discuss him publicly. I know you're in the middle of a campaign, but our case may depend on it."

"Alright, I'll give you a couple days."

"I can't promise that he won't hold out longer."

"And I can't promise that my patience will hold out, either."

CHAPTER 22

THE BIGGEST STAGE YOU'VE EVER PLAYED. That was how Kai described the Madison Theater, site of the one and only gubernatorial debate. Or perhaps he meant the live television audience, estimated at a couple hundred thousand, far above normal due to the close margin and the horse-race coverage in the media. Either way, the old movie house looked huge with sixteen-hundred people packed in the main floor and balcony.

The governor had insisted on holding the debate in Peoria. By Illinois' standards it qualified as a major city, but go a couple miles past downtown and you ran into cornfields or the worldwide headquarters of Caterpillar. Earlier, as he entered the auditorium, Duncan saw men in overalls and baseball hats, as though they'd just come in from the plowing the fields. The women arrived more done up in house dresses and makeup, but even they looked country. This guaranteed Stratton a hospitable audience of white, rural, conservative voters. For Duncan, it represented an acid test of his platform with mainstream votes. As in vaudeville, where performers asked, "Will it play in Peoria?" an act that succeeded there could succeed anywhere.

The spotlights burned like a heating element set to slow roast. Sweat made the pancake makeup around Duncan's eyes and nose congeal into a batter that hardened then cracked and froze his face. In the orchestra pit, three cameras targeted Duncan's podium. With seconds before broadcast, the TV producer gave him a five finger countdown. He again felt like an outfielder watching a pop fly accelerate toward him, trying not to close his glove too soon. Margo's last-minute advice repeated in his head.

"Don't get hypnotized by the camera's red eye."

Where *was* she, or Kai, or Josie? He strained to see past the spotlight but could make out only silhouettes of heads and shoulders in the audience.

"Governor, you have three minutes for your opening statement," said Katie Sizemore.

Homey, plump, non-threatening, and not terribly bright, Katie represented one of Duncan's many concessions. As the co-anchor of the Springfield nightly news cast, she offered up the kind of softball pitches that the governor needed.

"Thank you," the governor began. "Recently, at the Columbus Day parade in DeKalb County, I met a volunteer firefighter named Roy Steele...."

While his opponent blathered, Duncan studied. Bill Stratton stretched wider than his podium and nearly twice as tall. Margo had insisted that the two men be separated by at least ten feet. Voters favored bigger men, she said, even oversized ones; or in Kai's words, "We can't let that corn-fed farm boy upstage you."

Stratton's blue suit, black tie, and white shirt looked classy but not expensive, suggesting a down home sensibility and a Sunday services formality. His face softened the effect: doughy, jowly, with gold-rimmed glasses and a receding hairline. He could have been a kindly but strict grandfather lecturing about civic duty, except for the volume of his voice.

"Recently, I met James Monroe, a farmer in Arcata whose family has owned the same plot for ten generations," the governor boomed.

Typical of his folksy style, Big Bill's speech lacked specifics or meaning except for creating a mood of domestic comfort, exactly as Carl had predicted.

"The governor wants to stay in character," he'd said. "You've got to expose the blue blood under his red neck."

For the moment, all Duncan could do was stand and wait.

The vibrations started in his chest, a warming that rose toward his throat, then radiated to all his limbs, not fear but energy, sucked from the lights, absorbed from the murmurs of the audience, charging his nerves with an electric buzz. Before that day, the closest he'd come to the feeling was the tipsiness after a concussion. To steady himself, Duncan leaned on the podium and pretended to take notes. When this failed, he looked up to the great dome in the ceiling, its plaster work ornate as a wedding cake, and tried to look contemplative.

A lull brought him back. Stratton had finally stopped, and Katie was repeating her instructions. One last breath, a look to the blacked-out audience, a smile to the cameras, and he began.

"Since Bill Stratton took office, crime has proliferated. A few weeks ago, a man broke into my family's home and killed our daughter as she slept. I've continued my campaign because I don't want any of you have to suffer such a devastating loss. Tonight, I'm proposing a three strikes policy. In baseball, you only get three chances, but in Illinois you get limitless swings. If I'm elected, anyone who tallies three convictions will get a life sentence. We don't need to keep letting out career criminals."

It was his big reveal, scripted during the opening statement for maximum impact. At Duncan's insistence, the campaign finally committed to specifics, but with all the lights out he couldn't see how people reacted. Even after he finished, the audience stayed docile except for muted applause, and when Duncan allowed himself a sidelong look, Big Bill looked serene.

After checking that the cameras had panned back to his opponent, Duncan glanced stage right for Kai but couldn't spot him. In the corners, thick piles of sawdust and straw hid behind a heavy gold curtain, awaiting the return of the circus or the Wild West show. That explained the barny musk.

Meanwhile, the governor responded, "My opponent has made much of the dangers of society, but outside of the mean streets of Chicago, crime rates in this state are low."

In the wings, Duncan finally spotted Kai, hands behind his back like a proud father at a school play. When he whirled a finger next to his head, Duncan had to suppress a smirk.

"He's also been cozying up with the labor unions," Stratton said, "whose ties to organized crime are well established. When the time comes to collect, who knows what the price will be."

What did he say? "Organized crime"? Was he talking about Lindsay? No one had speculated so except the police, and they hadn't even shared it with prosecutors. More than just name calling, Stratton was sending him a message without putting it into words. It was a brushback pitch, a warning saying, "Don't think you're using crime against me here." How dare he. Two weeks before balloting, and the governor was resorting to street fighting tactics. More than ever, Duncan wanted to punish Big Bill for his impudence. He had one minute to adjust his swing, so he set aside his notes and let passion carry him.

"If the mafia has infiltrated labor unions, it happened on your watch, Bill," he said.

Compared to the polite clapping following his opening statement, the auditorium sounded like an empty cave, with only shuffling feet and stray coughs. Too hard. He'd swung too hard and missed completely. Offstage he spotted Kai pointing furiously to his palm as if to say get back on message, so Duncan returned to his notes.

"The only people Bill Stratton has ever prosecuted are politicians. I don't believe the average person fears their elected officials will break into their homes and assassinate them. He wants to know he's safe in his house at night. That's why I'll be introducing new measures that stiffen sentences for all crimes, limit parole, and build new prisons. The permissive attitude of this state government has to stop."

When he finished, the applause resumed, but backstage Kai slumped, head down.

* * *

As their final gesture on camera the opponents shook hands, but Stratton broke his grip as soon as the red light dimmed and turned without a word of congratulations. To a former athlete, the parting felt unsportsmanlike.

For five minutes after, Duncan exchanged pleasantries with Katie and the organizers. Then, anxious to debrief, he excused himself and pushed offstage. There Kai grazed on a buffet of cornbread, baked beans, tuna casserole, and lemon bars, all in the mismatched cookware of a potluck by the local 4-Hers.

"Where'd the Governor get that claptrap about organized crime?" Duncan said.

Kai glanced to the stage, where a dozen paces away Stratton chatted with the moderator as if they were old friends. He set down his overflowing plate and probed his molars with a pinkie before answering.

"All our donations are public record," Kai said. "I'm sure the governor knows to the penny how much we got from the unions."

"But he said organized crime."

"It's a typical smear tactic," Kai said, "Democrats being in the pocket of unions."

"No," Duncan said. "Didn't you hear the innuendo? He was talking about Lindsay."

"I doubt that, but if he was then it probably came from Kenilworth."

Duncan recalled the chief on TV next to the governor apologizing for his failures. "I don't believe it. He wouldn't."

"The governor is his boss. He controls a lot of money. With a word he can get any department more beat cops or a new station."

Duncan looked toward Stratton, who ignored his stare, but whose smile betrayed that he claimed the victory.

"So how badly will this hurt us?" Duncan said.

"Won't know for sure till tomorrow," Kai said, "but Carl said the focus groups came back pretty favorable."

Kai nodded noncommittally as Margo joined them, then put his hand just above the belt of her denim skirt.

"You were watching on screen," Kai said. "How'd we handle that crack about unions?"

"Great," she said. "You didn't look at all upset."

"It felt weak," Duncan said, "like I was just fighting off his pitch."

Before she could reply, Josie clicked up to them with quick, mincing steps. She wore a form-fitting chocolate dress from Saks and had combed her hair into a flip, dressed to impress not the sponsoring matrons but the television audience.

"So this is where you're hiding," she said.

Duncan put his hand on her lower back, but got only a malevolent smile in return.

"How's the buffet?" she said.

"Great comfort food," Kai said, and lifted a fried chicken wing.

"Let's make sure to thank the cooks," Josie said.

Then she turned her back toward them and said only to Duncan, "I need a moment."

She led him backstage to the converted janitor's closet that served as his dressing room, furnished with only a vanity, a mirror, and a coat rack. A bare bulb overhead gave it the ambiance of an interrogation room. As soon as the door closed, she whirled at Duncan like a knife fighter.

"Why would he say that?"

"About the buffet?"

"Don't be daft."

He stared mute until she explained, "That nonsense about organized crime."

"It's a standard conservative jab," Duncan said. "Big, bad, labor, and all that."

"No," Josie said. "He meant more than that, and you know it."

Duncan turned and saw his reflection in the mirror, but the face looked foreign, its hooded eyes and grim mouth a stranger's. The dissociation forced him to look away. God, what he wouldn't do for a cigarette. Only nicotine could release this much tension, but that was impossible, so he breathed deep and turned back to her. "I think it came from the police. The chief's been sharing his conjectures with the governor."

"About organized crime?"

"That was one of his theories, but before the arrest. Now, it's just Bill's gamesmanship."

"That's why you acted so bent on getting us protection?"

"One reason."

"And you didn't tell me?"

"I didn't want you to worry."

She shoved his chest with both hands, but he moved only inches before hitting a wall.

"Tell me there's nothing more to this," she said.

"Don't read too much into it."

"Like what? That we put up our daughter's life as collateral?"

She raised her hands to push him again, then turned to restrain herself. "What kind of people are these?"

"The butchers' union? What do you want me to say? They're dirty? We don't know that for a fact."

"Yes, we do."

"It's part of the business. If you work in meat packing, you have to deal with them."

"So we traded their support for Lindsay."

"No! That's absurd."

She turned to inspect him. Since he couldn't escape her stare, Duncan sat at the vanity and began removing his makeup. Even its immobility couldn't hide the sadness in his eyes.

"What else will they take as payment?" she said.

"Stop! This has nothing to do with Lindsay."

"You're sure?"

She placed a hand on his shoulder and stared into the mirror, her eyes locked with his, imploring for the truth.

"As sure as I can be," he said.

CHAPTER 23

NOW THAT PEOPLE RECOGNIZED HIM, Duncan hated to use public phones, so he'd begged the concierge at the Palmer House for a favor and found himself in the manager's office with the door closed. It felt cramped and cluttered with papers, carts, filing cabinets, and a mini fridge, but it did offer privacy. He dialed from memory.

"Detective Peruzzi, it's Duncan Cochrane. I need a favor."

"Sure thing, Governor," the detective said.

"Please, don't call me that yet."

"You got to act as if, Governor."

"Excuse me?"

"It's what they say in recovery. Act as if you wasn't a drunk, so you can think like a normal guy. It's a way to get your head around the way you want to be."

"Good motto. Alright, then I need you to do something for me."

"That's more like it. What'ya'need?"

Efficient, the way the detective compressed three words into one.

"A few days ago your department arrested a man named Oges Hoxter."

"Good name for a crook. What specifically do-you-want-to-know?"

Again the last five words blurred.

"Where you arrested him."

The desk clock ticked five times before Peruzzi answered. "How come?"

"You mean why did you arrest him?"

"How come you want to know?"

"I think... the Kenilworth police think he killed my daughter."

143

Another uncomfortable pause. Had he asked too much?

"Look, Governor, I want to help, but I don't want to give you information and then find out you went after the guy or something crazy like that. Whether he gets hurt or you do, somebody's going to trace it back to me."

"It's nothing like that. He's already in custody. I just need to speak to his relatives. I'm... I need to know if he killed my daughter, and he's not talking to the police. So I thought... I'm hoping they'll be more cooperative."

"Hold on."

Peruzzi's tone gave away nothing. If he'd gone to his supervisor then next on the line could be some lieutenant or captain asking Duncan to justify himself. That'd be tough, but if he "acted as if," he might get away with it. Still, he felt relieved when Peruzzi spoke again.

"Okay, governor, I've got it, but I can't let you go there by yourself."

"I promise, I'm not going to hurt anyone."

"No, I believe you. It's the neighborhood. Nobody should go into Woodlawn alone. You gotta let me take you."

In ten minutes he'd be speaking to a Chamber of Commerce committee. From there, every moment was scheduled until nine o'clock except for an hour break at noon when he'd probably be talking strategy with Kai.

"You have any plans for lunch?" he said.

* * *

Peruzzi idled outside the hotel in an unmarked burgundy Pontiac LeMans. When Duncan reached for the passenger door, another man lowered the window and said, "In back, please, sir." Duncan sank into the rear seat, knees to chest, and stayed silent while Peruzzi drove to Lake Shore Drive and turned south.

"I didn't expect an escort," he finally said.

"Like I said, no white man goes into Woodlawn solo, not even a cop. Meet my partner, Frank Field."

"How do, sir?"

Field turned—big and black and strong—straining against the material of his suit coat as he reached to shake hands.

"I don't mean to sound naive," Duncan said, "but what's so terrible about Woodlawn?"

"You ever heard of Jeff Fort?" Field said, looking back over his shoulder.

"Is he the one accused of misusing federal funds?"

The two cops exchanged smirks.

"That's what he'd say," Peruzzi said.

"How would you describe it?"

Peruzzi glanced at him in the rearview mirror before answering. "He started the Blackstone Rangers."

"No, remember, he converted," Field said. "They're the El Rukns now."

"Yeah, right. He found religion in prison."

"How's that bad?" Duncan said.

"They can call themselves whatever they want, they're still sheisty."

They passed the Robert Taylor homes—block after block of tenement towers—then exited the outer drive at Jackson Park and headed east along 63rd where the streetscape changed to dilapidated warehouses, vacant store fronts, and abandoned cars.

Field turned around, mashing the front seat into Duncan's knees.

"The Rangers are one of the biggest and most violent gangs we've got. They control everything criminal south of the Loop: drugs, prostitution, weapons. I don't know what you're doing here, but whoever you're going to see, they know Jeff Fort. Either they're with him or they're afraid of him, and that should go for you, too."

Peruzzi turned onto a street of slender shacks squeezed into a unified wall. He stopped in front of a one-story brick bungalow with a narrow dirt lawn accented by weeds. Burglar bars decorated the front door and windows.

"Out here, even the lowlifes need protection," Peruzzi said.

Field popped the door and moved to step out when Duncan touched his shoulder.

"I'd rather go alone," he said.

"You sure?"

"They're more likely to talk to me without a police escort."

"Looks like they already made us."

In the front window, lace curtains fluttered closed. Easy to see why they'd been spotted: their car was the only one on the street with a recent paint job and all four hubcaps.

"Still, let me try."

"Just stay in sight, okay?" Peruzzi said.

The block stank of wild onion and stale beer. Duncan stepped over a shattered six pack and walked up the front steps, which creaked under his weight. He looked for a doorbell and, finding none, banged on the metal screen. When a dark face observed him through a small diamond window, he smiled. Funny, he'd never felt as awkward canvassing. Half a minute passed. As he turned to go, the door opened on a chain and a woman asked, "Yes?"

Through the thin crack, Duncan couldn't see anything, but her high, frail voice suggested someone ready for retirement. He gave her his candidate's grin and moved to block her view of the undercovers.

"I'd like to ask you about your son."

"Who?"

"Oges."

"What about him?"

Duncan shifted his weight until he could see both her eyes, which glared still and dark. "May I come in? This isn't something I want to share with your neighbors."

"You with the police?"

"No."

She closed the door, and for a long moment Duncan thought that he'd blown it. Stupid to deny the obvious. Then three locks clicked open. The voice belonged to a woman with brown skin more polished than his Oxfords and hair spun into a bun. In a floral housedress and a single gold cross, she looked demure but too young to be Oges' mother.

"The police is like vampires," she said. "They only come in if you invite them."

Duncan smiled and followed her to the living room, which offered a stained velour sofa, a pair of rickety wooden chairs, and an imitation walnut coffee table with a vase of plastic flowers. The couch looked sturdiest, so he sat there while she perched on the edge of a chair diagonal.

"Thank you, Miss...."

"Hoxter, same as Oges. Never been married. Don't intend to neither. You can call me Florence, though."

From the set of her mouth, she meant it. Duncan studied her for a resemblance to Oges. The arch of her eyebrows looked similar, but she lacked the weathering of hard living.

"So you're his sister?"

"Umm hum."

"When did you last see him?"

"Must of been six months. We don't talk much. If you know Oges, you know why."

"But the police arrested him here."

"Not with me at home. He must of let hisself in."

Strange that Oges would have a key if he didn't live there, but Duncan let it pass.

"So you don't know anything about his arrest?"

"I heard. A lady down the block read about it. I don't touch the papers myself, they so full of lies."

"Then you think he's innocent?"

"Nobody knows my brother would say that. He's no innocent, but that don't mean he done the things they say."

Outside, a car horn wailed long and loud. Duncan glanced toward the front window, where the patrol car hid below the high sill. The detectives couldn't see him either, so he stood and walked to the large pane, turning his back so he could watch Miss Hoxter.

"You mean the burglary?" he said.

"Like I say, Oges done a lot of things, but one thing he never done was rape."

"How can you be so sure if you two aren't close?"

"Same way you know your own kin. You know what they capable of and what they not, and he's not that way."

All the time he'd spent with cops was swaying how Duncan read people. Instinctively, he disbelieved everything she told him but didn't want to confront her with the inconsistencies until they were played out.

"What is he then?" he said.

"He just struggling to get by, like everyone. You a rich man, so you don't know how it is when you not sure where your next meal's coming from. That man got three kids and a woman to take care of. He got a little business fixing cars, but in between he got to support hisself."

"Is that why he broke into that woman's bedroom?"

She looked down at her hands, which worked the hem of her dress. "He a desperate man. I don't know how much experience you have with them drugs, but they change a person. They changed him. Growing up he fell into trouble like any other boy, always getting into things he weren't supposed to, but not a bad child, not mean. Then he found that cocaine. That's when I cut him off. When he start stealing from me and our mama, rest her soul, I know I have to cut him off."

She nodded to herself but continued to finger the fabric as though his shame stained her.

"So he's a thief?"

"I can't deny that," she said. "Oges stole and cheated everybody he know. But he's no killer, Mr. Cochrane. I know that for a fact. And he's not the one killed your daughter."

She dropped the frayed edge to stare at him steadily.

"How can you be so sure?" he said.

"Because I saw him after. He couldn't hide a thing like that from me. Oges, he a terrible liar, always has been. Every time he lie, he gets this little smile like he think it's funny. It were a game between us growing up. He'd tell a lie and wait for me to call him on it. If he'd of killed your daughter, I'd know. I'm real sorry about what happened, but Oges not the one you want."

During this defense, her eyes never wavered, and her mouth drew in a thin line. Either she lied far better than her brother, or she believed everything she'd said, which gave Duncan plenty of cause for doubt.

"Thank you for speaking with me," he said. "I'm sorry to ask about such a thing."

"I know how you must be feeling. I seen too many people killed before they time. You always want to know who done it and why."

As he moved toward the door, she pursued him, still apologizing.

"Don't hate my brother for how he is. He can't help hisself."

After he stepped onto the front porch, Duncan turned to say goodbye, but something distracted him: a mat in the hallway held a large pair of black lace ups.

"Bye, Governor. I hope you find who you looking for."

Before he could reply, she slammed the door and slid home the locks. Sweet talked by a killer's kin. How gullible could he be?

When he returned to their car, the two detectives stared like schoolboys curious about a friend's date.

"You get the confession?" Peruzzi said.

"Not yet, but I will."

CHAPTER 24

SPRINGFIELD, ILLINOIS' CAPITAL CITY, was a hamlet compared to Chicago, with barely a hundred thousand people and an economy that depended wholly on state jobs. Take away them and it would be nothing but a train stop for farmers to load their crops. At its center stood the Capitol building, three hundred and sixty feet tall, shaped like a Greek Temple, its dome the highest point in town. It was the only feature that mattered on the flat prairie.

In a hotel room several blocks away, Duncan felt the great building looming over him as he paced through yet another meeting.

"How're we doing?" Duncan said.

"The latest *Tribune* polls have us in a dead heat," Kai said. "There's still fourteen percent undecided, but the rest split evenly."

Carl leaned forward on his cane as though about to stand but instead adjusted his wide hips as though settling in for a long stay. "It's the damnedest break down I've ever seen," he said. "Everyone's voting against type. We're up ten percent with registered Republicans and down an equal number in our party. Probably our focus on crime. People don't know how to peg us."

Kai flipped open his clipboard and scanned the agenda. "I just got the skinny from the *Sun-Times*. They're backing us on the editorial page tomorrow. We've also picked up endorsements from the *Champaign News-Gazette* and the *St. Louis Post-Dispatch*."

"What about the *Tribune*?" Duncan said.

"They haven't backed a Democrat since... when, Carl?"

"Ever," the veteran said.

"Forget about the arch conservatives. We're aiming for the moderates."

Duncan walked toward the picture window where the zinc dome gleamed in the twilight. "So what's our strategy?"

Margo squirmed in her swivel chair with the enthusiasm of a kindergartener, her strawberry blond ponytail swinging behind her.

"All we've got to do is tone down on the anti-crime rhetoric," she said.

"Isn't that what got us here?" Duncan said.

"I hear you," Margo said, holding up her hands in protest. "But we've already got that voting block locked in. Now we have to fine-tune your image, make you appear more fatherly."

"Being a father is what inspired the message."

She sat back as though chastised.

"What about our mailers," Duncan said. "Won't those pull in some votes?"

"Of course," she said.

"That's not enough," Carl said.

Duncan turned to the old Republican, who scowled in disapproval. "My sources tell me the governor has a cache of negative TV ads."

"What's the skinny?" Kai said.

"He calls Duncan 'a closet liberal.' Supposedly he has footage of us at a soup kitchen. A spot like that could really hurt us with centrist voters."

"They're not going to be fooled by that bunk," Margo said.

"I once lost a race because the candidate wouldn't eat an ice cream sundae," Carl said.

Outside, the yellow beams of four spotlights turned the capital's dome to gold.

"Even if I'm wrong," Carl said, "Big Bill Stratton has resources we don't. He could call in a hundred thousand favors at the last minute. For us, a tie is a loss. We've got to pull ahead and hope we can hold out."

"What if we went back to the economy?" Parish said. "Inflation is up two percentage points in the last two years and is heading toward double digits."

"We already tried that," Carl said. "People can't see or feel inflation, and unemployment has been steady. No one's going to get excited about statistical fluctuations."

"Aren't we alienating minority voters by carping on punishment?" Parish said.

In the room's yellow light, his skin looked even darker than usual.

"We've lost some support among the Blacks and Hispanics," Kai said, "but those are more than offset by gains among the independents."

Parish nodded once but looked unconvinced.

"Shouldn't we be talking about the energy crisis?" Margo said.

"I've still got my Earth Day button," Duncan said.

"We don't want to get too tight with Carter," Kai said. "Don't forget the sweater speech."

Duncan pictured President Carter in the Oval Office with his cardigan, preaching about conservation. His career might never recover.

"If we say nothing, it's another issue the governor can claim," Carl said.

"Even if I'm elected, what can I do about gas prices?" Duncan said.

"Nothing," Margo said. "Just show that you know what a drag it is."

A knock startled them. With all the campaign staff present, Duncan couldn't think who would disturb them. Parish walked to the door, peered through the peephole, and turned back.

"No one's there," he said.

A tension at the base of Duncan's skull wound tighter. Instinctively he reached for his gun, but it lay useless in his suitcase. A moment later, the knock came again, this time followed by feet shuffling.

Parish looked all directions through the viewer, then asked, "Who is it?" without reaching to undo the locks.

"Trick or treat" came a chorus of voices.

He opened the door on a half dozen children no higher than his waist waiting with bags extended. One boy wore his hair greased back with a white T-shirt and black leather jacket, aping *Grease* or *Happy Days*; another had on the red cape and blue jumpsuit of *Superman*; a third recycled last year's favorite costume, the black mask and cape of Darth Vader.

"Trick or treat, I am sweet, give me something good to eat." The smallest boy — who wore rainbow suspenders with a clashing orange and blue striped shirt — twisted his ears. Was he the scarecrow from *The Wiz*, or the alien in that new TV show?

"Anyone have candy?" Duncan asked.

The adults looked at each other to inaudibly shift the blame for forgetting Halloween. Still, who expected to be hit up in a hotel? When no one else stepped forward, Margo grabbed a plate of animal cookies from the coffee table and processed to the door as though she bore the offering in church. With her ponytail and plaid flannel shirt, she looked as done up as the trick-or-treaters, who happily cleaned the platter and disappeared down the hallway.

"You shouldn't have done that," Duncan said.

"We can get more."

"Children aren't supposed to accept unwrapped candy."

She looked stricken, but Kai waved away the tension.

"It's cool," he said, "they're too young to vote."

Duncan checked his watch: only six hours before his next appearance, a spot on one of the morning talk shows.

"What about the governor's hit piece?" he said.

The staffers all looked to Carl for insight. "It's going to focus on your lack of political experience."

"We could appeal to civil servants," Margo said. "Big Bill's done everything he can to shrink the state rolls. There's got to be a lot of people still pissed off that they can't get their sisters and daughters hired into a state sinecure."

"Not enough," Carl said. "Most of them will vote for us already, and the rest are loyal to the governor for personal reasons."

"If we suggest he planned to take away farm subsidies, it would tick off a lot of rural voters," Kai said.

The others looked at him with puzzlement.

"The governor hasn't said anything like that," Carl said.

"He doesn't have to. We will."

Duncan stared out the window at the shimmering dome of power. "I won't lie. Big Bill's committed plenty of sins. We don't need to invent any."

The phone interrupted, and Duncan answered, thinking it might be his wife.

"I have a call from Mr. Ron Turner," the hotel's operator said.

"Put him through."

He placed a hand over the receiver and looked to Margo. "I need to take this in private."

She held the line until Duncan picked up in the bedroom and closed the door.

"Hey, boss, hope I didn't wake you."

"Corruption never sleeps, Ron."

"So you're in Springfield?"

"The lair of the enemy."

"How are things in that great cesspool?"

"It's starting to feel like home."

Ron laughed and waited, but Duncan had nothing else clever to fill the silence. With a moment of privacy, he dug in his suitcase for a cigarette.

"So," Ron said, "I know you didn't call me for advice about politics."

"I don't think the Kenilworth cops know what they're doing."

"Why's that?"

"They're afraid to arrest anyone. There's a man in custody for another break-in, and they keep talking to him, but he's not saying anything, and without a confession they won't act."

"Mafia guys don't give us a lot of help."

"He's not in the mafia. He's just some guy who rips people off."

"That's how a lot of them make a living."

"I had some friends with the Chicago police check it out. There's no evidence he's into organized crime."

"Some soldiers hide their affiliations."

Unable to find his smokes, Duncan looked around the hotel room. On one wall hung a portrait of Abe Lincoln, the state's first and only president, his bow tie and half beard undermining a serious expression. His political career had begun in Springfield as well, but Duncan couldn't imagine the victor of the Civil War being so hampered.

"He's black," Duncan said.

"As in Afro-American?"

"Yes. He's a middle-aged black man from Woodlawn."

"Well... what's his name?"

"Oges. Oges Hoxter."

"Never heard of him."

"There's no reason you would have."

"You're sure he's unaligned?"

"He's only been arrested for burglary and drugs."

The bureau. Duncan had stuffed the last pack there so the staff wouldn't see it. He opened the top drawer, then a window, and inhaled the cool night air along with the nicotine.

"How long since the police hooked him up?" Ron asked.

"A week."

"Most murder suspects confess within twenty-four hours. The longer it takes...."

"So they're not going to get him?"

"You need to jump start the case."

"How?"

"A reward. It'll draw lots of media attention and maybe attract someone who knows something."

"You really think a reward will goad someone to do the right thing?"

"Money is a strong motivator."

Duncan let the idea percolate through him with the smoke. "How much?"

"Enough to animate some son of a bitch who's down on his luck."

"Ten thousand?"

"That's plenty."

Half satisfied, Duncan took a final drag and laid the butt on the edge of a nightstand.

"Thanks, Ron. I'll let you know if anything comes of it."

"Something will. The question is if it'll be any good."

"We live in hope."

They hung up, and Duncan checked the clock: nearly midnight. Late, but not too late. He lit a new cigarette off the old one, then dialed. After a half dozen rings, Josie answered.

"It's me," Duncan said. "I need to ask your permission on something."

"What's that?"

Her voice betrayed the fatigue of the hour but something else too: mistrust.

"I just talked to Ron. He suggested we offer a reward."

"Why?"

"We need something to get the police moving on Hoxter."

"Fine. Is that all?"

With honest Abe staring down at him, Duncan couldn't hide his true motives. "There's no way I can separate it from the campaign."

"No. Not after what that bastard implied during the debate."

"It was just rhetoric."

Even to him the reasoning sounded flawed, but Duncan wouldn't concede to her anxieties. He waited half a minute, but Josie refused to answer. With the conflict still stiff between them, he hated to hang up, yet he needed to get back to the campaign staff.

"Only a week left," he said.

"What? You're mumbling. Are you eating something?"

Duncan stubbed out his cigarette before answering. "Halloween candy. You'll see. It's all going to work out. A year from now, Hoxter will be in prison and you'll be in the governor's mansion at the signing ceremony for the E.R.A."

"Is that the candidate Cochrane talking or my husband?"

"Both. See you soon."

They hung up. Through the fog of his smoke and framed by his narrow bedroom window, the Capital's metal dome looked far less imposing. Duncan fanned the air clear and closed the casement before he returned to the sitting room. Seeing him, the staff fell silent.

"I've got an idea," he said. "A reward for my daughter's killer. We could make an announcement in the morning."

The staffers looked to each other, nodded, and smiled, silently calculating the impact.

"I'll get a news release together," Kai said.

"And I'll call a press conference," Margo said. "Ten o'clock."

"You think that'll be enough?" Duncan said.

In the pause that followed, the staff individually turned to Carl for the last word. "If it isn't, I hate to see what the governor has planned."

CHAPTER 25

THE VISITOR'S ROOM AT THE COOK COUNTY JAIL offered few distractions. Its walls and ceilings shone pure white, its stools and benches gleamed solid steel, its only adornment a "No Smoking" sign. With the space subdivided into carrels like in a library, Duncan couldn't even see the visitors adjacent, but he could eavesdrop.

To his left, a husky contralto said, "Well if your dumb ass hadn't got caught in that man's house, it wouldn't be like this."

Did the voice belong to the same woman whose rose perfume overpowered even the bleach that purified the room?

On Duncan's other side, a young man said, "You right, you right, I feel you, but it ain't like that."

From the sounds of it, all visitors felt the same tension. The entire setting—from the metal detectors, to the guards, to the signs prohibiting contraband—cast those on the free side of the room as suspects. Even Duncan's celebrity earned no special treatment. The guards subjected him to the same searches and delays as everyone else.

After many minutes, a door opened across the glass partition, and Oges Hoxter emerged wearing a jumpsuit in monastic red. Between his cuffed fists he held a plastic cup as though it were a chalice. When Oges extended his hands to his guard like an offering, the uniform loosed him and left.

Up close, his face eluded categorization. The broad nose and chin suggested a black man, but the pale, freckled skin and the light hair contradicted that. Maybe his mother switched lovers after Florence. As he reached for the phone, Oges revealed a hand with only four fingers and a stub where a wedding ring would rest.

"Ain't I see you on TV?" Oges said.

"Possibly. My name's Duncan Cochrane."

Oges jerked back his head. Then he spun on his stool, stood, walked a lap around the cubicle, and returned to grab the phone again.

"I knew it. You the man running for... what's that... mayor?"

"Governor."

"That's right. How you like that. I got the governor here for a confab. Nobody going to believe this shit. I mean, excuse my language, but this is too much."

He threw up his hands as if he were a supplicant before an altar, and his limbs moved with the fluidity of the double jointed, his gangly arms cross cut with veins and tendons.

"Wait till I tell my sister. She not going to believe this."

Duncan forced a smile and nodded. "I already spoke to her."

Oges' head snapped back again as though he'd been struck. "What she say?"

"That she doesn't believe you're guilty."

"Of what?"

"Attacking Ms. Davis."

Oges shook his head in disbelief. "Then why she ain't been to see me?"

To stall, Duncan rearranged himself on the stool. "Probably because the guards treat everyone here with suspicion."

Oges let out a long whistle so loud that even through the phone it made Duncan wince. The inmate didn't seem to notice, though, and proceeded to more head shaking. "You got that right," he said.

Aside from his jittery energy, Oges showed no evidence of guilt or remorse or even recognition why Duncan had visited him. The man persisted in casting himself as a victim.

"You know, someone broke into my house as well," Duncan said.

Oges took a large swig from his mug, which held at least a quart of coffee so viscous it clung to the rim after he finished drinking. "Yeah, I heard about that," he finally said, in a voice softer than before.

"Around the same time they caught you."

"There's some messed up people in this town. In here, too. People that don't care about nobody but theyselves."

"That's why I'm here," Duncan said. "I want to hear what you know about that."

The inmate transferred the phone to his other ear before answering. "Well, you know, I hear that somebody strangle your little girl."

Duncan churned his phrasing. That he called Lindsay a "little girl" sounded odd. Even in the dark, it would be hard to mistake her for a child. And had the media reported that she'd been strangled? He couldn't recall.

"I'm not asking what you heard. I'm asking what you know."

Oges took another swig of coffee before answering. "Well, as of now nothing, but I can get you the dope right quick. With all the hoodlums up in this cooler, must be somebody know who did it."

Duncan noted his phrasing "right quick." Hadn't the burglar at Ms. Davis' house used those same words?

"I think you know already."

Duncan caught his dilated eyes and attempted to look through them to the memories caged behind. Instead he saw only vacancy and deceit.

"I don't know why you giving me the hairy eyeball, but you got ahold of some bad information."

Duncan studied his adversary and waited. He displayed nothing but misdirection. His eyes wandered aimlessly and his mouth ground invisible food as though he were masticating the truth into unrecognizable pieces. His body too stayed in constant motion: his feet tapped, his hands shifted, his head swiveled. He aped a spastic child whose energy couldn't be restrained.

"Your sister called you a bad liar, and she called it right. I can read it in your face, hear it in your voice, and smell it on your breath."

"Jump back! You don't know what you saying."

"I do."

"You can't believe what the man tell you. They besmirch me with lies of every kind."

"I don't think so."

"You wait. You see. I had nothing to do with that."

"With what? Breaking into my house? Killing my daughter?"

Oges dropped the phone, let out a low, sad whistle, and shook his hands as though they'd been burned, then picked up the receiver delicately.

"With that neither. You talk to my sister, so you know. I never hurt no woman."

While they locked eyes, Duncan reached into his coat pocket for his revolver but found it empty. "So you're not a cocaine addict and a serial burglar who's been arrested a dozen times already? And don't bother lying, I've already seen your résumé."

"I don't deny I had some trouble with that cocaine, but that don't make me a killer. Probably you don't understand because you never associate with people like me, but not everybody up in here is a killer. Some people got that in them, true that, but not all of us. A lot of people are just regular folk."

"Then why are you here?"

"Why am I... why am I here? You don't understand what it's like out there trying to main-tain." He stretched the word into two long syllables. "A man's got to feed his family some way. Now for a man like you it ain't a struggle, but for the rest of us...."

Instead of finishing, he shook his head in disgust.

"You never supported your family. Even your sister told me so. You're here because you broke into a woman's apartment and attacked her, the same way you did to my daughter. You're a predator and a threat to everyone you cross."

Oges dipped his head and raised his hands in prayer toward some god of the wicked who would deliver him from his punishment. After a moment of silence, he finally stopped fidgeting, cupped the phone, and leaned forward until his lips almost touched the plastic divider.

"You upset. I understand, with what happened to your daughter. If I was you, I'd be mad too. I'd be out in the street looking for the man that done it, so I could punish him worse than any police ever could. I understand that."

"Don't you patronize me. You don't know about grief. You've never cared enough to know what loss is."

Without thinking, Duncan slapped the barrier between them. The thick plastic dulled the thud, but it still echoed throughout the room. At the sound, all conversation stopped in the adjacent booths. Oges leaned back on his stool and fixed Duncan with a stare before speaking.

"You the one persecuting me. You trying to yank my chain, but you got no evidence against me, nothing. You in here talking about how I killed this person and raped that person. Now you want to lock me up before I even get tried. You like the lynch mobs down south, want to hang a man just for being black."

Duncan reached to set down the phone, convinced that Oges and his sister were playing with him. Then he thought better. "You're right," he said. "I'd hang you if I could, but the state won't allow it. I'll have to settle for keeping you here forever."

Oges stared at him and slowly grinned. "You can't. That's why you here. If you could, you'd have the fuzz do it for you."

"In a few weeks, I'll be governor, and I'll do whatever I want with you."

"Then you never know who kill your little girl."

"I know already. I'm looking at him."

"You think so, but you wrong. You don't know enough about how things is to judge."

Oges nodded contentedly to himself and took another huge swig of his liquid tar.

"You think I'd trust you?" Duncan said. "A thief and a liar?"

"Only a thief know another thief when he see him."

"I don't have to be one to recognize one right in front of me."

"Then you never know who kill your little girl."

CHAPTER 26

IN A DOWNSTATE DINER, the campaign staff squeezed into a narrow booth for their penultimate breakfast. Duncan and Kai took up one side while Carl, Parish, and Margo held in their elbows opposite. The place mimicked the fifties: black and white floor tiles, a chrome bar with spinning stools, and red vinyl on all the seats.

The diner also played up the sex appeal of its waitresses, putting them in pink mini dresses, yet the one who arrived balancing five breakfast plates had legs too slim to pull it off. She looked even younger than Duncan's girls, with brown hair in a ponytail and blotchy skin that she tried to cover with too much makeup.

First she set down Duncan's "Hung Over Easy," a platter overflowing with two eggs, four slices of toast, sausage links, biscuits, hash browns, and a side of ketchup. While his staffers had ordered modest breakfasts like granola, fruit cups, and oatmeal, Duncan had opted for the house special.

"How's our schedule today?" he asked Kai.

"Full. We've got a speech in the students' union at nine, a grip and grin with the mayor at half past ten, interviews with the local scribes at quarter to twelve, another speech at one to the teachers' union, and then... hmmm, a private session with someone named Rose Marie at two thirty. She must be a big contributor, but I'll have to check. Why?"

Duncan waited until the waitress stepped out of earshot. "I'm calculating how much to eat. What are my chances at a real lunch?"

"Clean your plate, boss. We're not stopping until the show's over."

For efficiency, Duncan piled the eggs on the toast and smeared both with ketchup, a mix both rough and runny. During the lull that came

162

with eating, he took in the other patrons: mostly students making do with coffee or a Danish. Without exception they ignored him.

"You think anyone here knows me?" he said.

"They will after this morning," Margo said.

"But will the students vote?"

Carl leaned over his toast and juice to speak. "U of I makes this a Democratic bastion in a Republican empire."

Before cutting into his sausages, Duncan poked at their dry skin, which released no juices, so he forked in a mouthful of potatoes, which broke crisp outside but chewy in.

"Any change in the polls?" he said.

"Still too close to call," Kai said.

The waitress returned to ask how everything tasted. Before Duncan could compliment the potatoes, a television above the counter distracted him. Governor Stratton appeared on screen looking more somber than usual, his skin grey and his eyes dull behind gold-rimmed glasses. Even his hair looked aged, growing dry and brittle. Below his face, a text banner incongruously read "Cochrane's Daughter."

"Could you turn up the sound?" Duncan said.

" ...contrary to the charges made by my opponent, this administration has given all of its resources to investigating the person or persons who so viciously attacked Lindsay Cochrane five weeks ago."

Parish dropped his fork with a clank. "We never called him derelict."

"It's misdirection," Margo said. "Make yourself look like the victim of a smear campaign that you fabricate."

"Shhhh," Duncan said.

The diner had quieted, and everyone watched the grainy, black-and-white TV as the governor continued: "Despite our best efforts, the killer or killers remain at large. My opponent has announced a reward for information as to their whereabouts. While I appreciate his desperation, I cannot justify paying off those who would harbor fugitives. We must find other ways to prosecute the guilty."

"*Desperation*," Kai said too loudly. "Clever way to smear us."

"For these reasons," the governor read, "I have asked the state police to assume responsibility. This in no way reflects dissatisfaction on my part with the efforts of the Kenilworth police. They have exhibited dedication and diligence and will continue to play a key role, but the state police possess staff and technology not available to civic agencies and will bring to bear a fresh set of eyes.

"Mark my words," the governor said, and looked into the camera, "we will not stop until the persons responsible are locked away for good. As long as I am in charge, there will be no place in this state for lawlessness."

Parish shook his head and said, "He sounds like a sheriff in the Wild West."

"Which is exactly what he wants," Margo said. "Keep up his law and order image."

The governor stepped aside, and Chief Dunleavy moved before the camera. Odd to have him appear at a news conference for his firing, and more proof of his complicity with Stratton.

"We have investigated over a thousand leads," the chief said. "We have talked to eight thousand persons in forty-eight states and five foreign countries. We have taken four hundred thirty-nine finger and palm prints and polygraphed forty-one subjects. We have followed every lead to its conclusion. And while we have yet to arrest a suspect, I'm sure we've already identified the responsible parties."

He appeared as disconsolate as any criminal facing execution. No matter what the governor said, the veteran officer took this as repudiation. He didn't understand the politics, that his department amounted to nothing but a red herring.

After the network switched to its anchor, Duncan looked to the waitress and mimed turning down the volume. With the TV silenced, the diner's low hum of conversation returned.

"The media are repeating his shtick like a chorus," Kai said.

"It's the network," Margo said. "They've always been his doo-wop girls. Most reporters won't be so slavish."

"You think it's just a publicity stunt?" Duncan said.

"Of course," Margo said. "Big Bill's desperate."

Duncan couldn't share her glee. His tactics had backfired. Rather than igniting the police, the reward had politicized the case even more. Once the election passed there'd be no pressure to pursue it. A silence fell over the table as the others realized the import of Margo's words.

"Don't worry," Kai said. "As soon as you're governor, the state police will be your handmaidens."

The others nodded. Duncan tried to smile but lacked the confidence. Every one of his efforts had failed. He felt as helpless as on night of Lindsay's murder.

"The good thing is we know how the governor's going to respond," Margo said.

"I wouldn't count on this being all he's got planned," Carl said. "I've hear rumors he has a hit piece coming out tomorrow."

Duncan's breakfast sat half finished. Unconsciously, he grabbed a cigarette. As he reached to light it, Kai stopped his hand.

"Not in public," he said.

Duncan frowned but complied. Another day of forced abstinence.

"So what should we do?" Duncan said.

"We can't let him have the last word," Kai said. "How much mulah do we have, Parish?"

"We're already in deficit, and the printers won't give us any more credit."

"What if we held a news conference," Margo said, "thanked the governor for his work but called him crass for waiting until two days before the election?"

"Not dramatic enough," Kai said. "We need to embarrass him, let people see how plastic he's being."

Duncan disliked their direction and held up his fork to interrupt. "I don't want to alienate the state troopers. We can be gracious and still attack the governor for his shortcomings."

The others turned silent. In this lull, Duncan realized Carl hadn't spoken. "What do you think?" he said to his Republican adviser.

The older man made a tent of his hands and stared down them as though through the sight of a gun. He let the others wait an uncomfortable time before answering.

"He's scared," Carl said, "otherwise he wouldn't be saying a thing."

"So he thinks this will save him?" Duncan said.

"He thinks," Carl said, "that he's going to lose."

CHAPTER 27

AT MOST, DUNCAN INVITED a dozen people to his home for holidays and dinner parties, but on election night, at least a hundred crowded the downstairs, sitting on the steps, blocking the halls, even standing in the back yard. With the campaign out of funds, the staff had nowhere else to gather. It would be their last night together, so they ate, drank, and conversed like spectators awaiting their home team's comeback.

Duncan circulated but found nowhere for a solo cigarette break. He felt like a stranger in his own house, surrounded by acquaintances who all hoped he'd recognize them personally. After he finished his third scotch, Josie grabbed the crystal tumbler.

"It's early," he said.

"And you're going to be up late," she said.

Duncan looked to Kai, who sat back in the thick cushions of the couch cradling his own whiskey and talking inaudibly on the phone. The campaign manager cupped the mouthpiece and whispered, "She's right."

Feeling chastised, Duncan followed Josie to the kitchen and watched her arrange shrimp and mushroom canapés on a silver platter. She wore a cowl neck sweater that hugged her breasts and brown trousers that did the same to her thighs. From behind, Duncan wrapped one arm around her shoulders and placed the other on her hip.

"Not now," she said and pushed him away.

Two months since they'd been intimate. Though Duncan understood why, he still felt punished.

"What else do we have to drink?" he said and opened the refrigerator.

"I told you, no more alcohol."

"I need something to keep my hands busy."

"Then have some cranberry juice."

He poured three fingers into his tumbler, where the ice cubes crackled and popped.

"You don't have to play hostess," he said. "Try to relax."

"Says the black teapot."

"I've got nothing to do."

"Talk to the guests."

Out the back window, the lake disappeared into the blackness of night. The polls had closed an hour before, but the counting had just begun.

"I can't—"

"Then go find out how you're doing. Just don't get tipsy. This should be your most serious moment."

"You're no fun," he said and kissed her cheek.

In the living room, smoke drifted into every corner. How badly he wanted to bum a cigarette, but he had to content himself with a vicarious high.

As distraction, he studied the television, which showed reporters highlighted against a dark backdrop. Something familiar about the scene stopped Duncan, and after squinting he realized what: in the background stood his home. Out the front window, three news vans idled by the curb. The spotlight of a camera blinded him to everything but the silhouette of a man. He walked to the front door, flipped on the porch light, and returned to the living room to see it glowing on TV.

"When can I swat those insects away?" he asked Kai.

"Never. Get used to it."

Duncan shook his head and turned back to the television. With the end so close, he felt unprepared to assume office and make good on all his promises. Early on, he'd never questioned his readiness. Leading the state would be like leading a company, with more employees and customers but the same challenges. These last six months had convinced him otherwise. Governing was nothing like running a business. There was no bottom line, no quarterly report, only polls, and they changed daily. In business, when he made a decision, others followed. Here, no matter what he said, others second-guessed. How could he lead a chorus of doubters? His only answer came from Kai: "It's all part of the act."

On the TV, utility workers in cherry pickers were tearing down Stratton posters from lamp poles and buildings. The crawler read "Illegal Postings?" Duncan turned up the sound.

" ...from the Mayor's Office said maintenance workers were re-moving the Republican incumbent's campaign signs during routine maintenance. A spokesman for the governor called the cleanup 'vot-ing fraud'."

"What's this?" Duncan said.

Kai shrugged and said, "Looks like the mayor finally came through for us."

Before Duncan could object, he recalled a mailer from earlier that day. The state's Republican caucus accused him of "mafia ties" based on his support from "organized labor." Though he immediately de-nied the charge, none of the networks covered it or the hit piece. As usual, voters had to sort through the propaganda on their own.

The television flashed some numbers in bands of blue and red: exit polls gave Duncan a twenty percent lead in Cook County, which took in all of Chicago and its suburbs but not the rural south where Republicans held sway. The camera flashed to an old Asian man in a blue suit. The banner below his name read "pollster."

" ...and our experts are saying it could be days before the contest is officially decided..." a female voice said.

Duncan muted the volume and spun to see Kai still on the phone. Nearby, Carl stood idle, so he asked the old Republican, "Is that right?"

Before Carl could answer, Kai held up a finger of patience.

"Who's he talking to?" Duncan said.

"Friends in the state elections office," Carl whispered.

"Isn't that tampering?"

The veteran pol leaned forward on his cane and shook his head. "Everybody does it. Otherwise, we'd be waiting on our morning papers."

Feeling shut out, Duncan walked to the dining room, where Josie was refilling the bread and vegetables for fondue. He dipped a carrot, extracted as much viscous cheese as the stick could hold, and shoved it in his mouth, then repeated the process with celery and broccoli.

"Careful you don't make yourself sick," Josie said.

Hands on hips, Duncan stared at her with mock frustration. "If I can't eat or drink, what can I do?"

"Govern."

He grabbed a long fork, stabbed a piece of bread and twirled it in stringy cheese.

"Where's Glynis?" he said.

"Upstairs."

"Why?"

"She isn't feeling well."

In the living room, he'd seen three of her high school friends, now his volunteers.

"She should at least make an appearance," he said.

"You want me to tell her?"

Josie's tone betrayed her impatience with Duncan's impatience.

"I'll get her," he said. "At least it'll keep me from eating."

Upstairs the only light came from underneath Lindsay's door. Duncan listened outside her room but couldn't hear anything above the conversations below. Inside he found only her bed-side lamp for company. They had not changed her room since that night. Even the bedspread remained, reminding him of finding her wrapped in it. He extinguished the bulb, closed the door, walked to Glynis' room, then knocked heavily.

"Who is it?"

She sounded groggy. When Duncan looked in, she lay in bed silhouetted by moonlight through the shears.

"Your next governor wondering why his daughter isn't at the party."

"I've got a headache."

He flipped on the light, making her squint, and walked to her. Her forehead felt cool and dry. The gesture reminded him of when the girls were little, and he had to check if they were lying about illness to avoid school.

"Could you at least say hello to your friends?"

"I'm not dressed."

She lifted the front of her flannel nightgown as evidence.

"So, pull yourself together."

She sighed and lay motionless.

"It'd mean a lot to me."

"In a minute."

On the bedside table sat a container of Slumber Time pills. When he shook the bottle, only a couple rattled inside.

"Have you taken any of these?" he said.

"One."

"Go easy on them. We need you awake tonight."

When she sat up, her nightdress hung like a curtain. How could she be thinner than just a month ago?

"Wear something nice," he said. "You may be needed on camera."

She sighed and dismissed him with her turned back.

Back downstairs, Duncan found Josie again in the kitchen, putting ice in a silver bucket.

"How long has she been like this?" he said.

"Like what?"

"So lethargic."

Josie pursed her lips and thought. "A few weeks."

"Why didn't you say something?"

She smashed a bottle of champagne into the chiller and said, "You weren't here."

"But I always called."

She shrugged and wrapped a towel around the cork.

"I could have done something," he said.

"Like?"

"Like what I'm going to do tomorrow: call Dr. Baumgartner."

"Glynis won't see him."

"What do you mean?"

"I asked. She refused. She said it's just fatigue."

"Well, if Glynis won't go the doctor, I'll bring him here."

"Fine, invite him. We'll serve leftover fondue."

Duncan ignored her sarcasm and returned to the living room. On TV, rows of people were sorting paper ballots. Below the image crawled the words "Heavy turnout forecast."

Duncan looked to Kai, who sat motionless, the phone pressed to his ear.

"What are they saying?" he mouthed.

Kai held up a finger for patience, then nodded as though the person on the other end could discern the movement.

Close by Duncan found Margo, who held a sheaf of papers to her chest secretively. She'd let down her red hair and wore a plaid wool dress to make herself look of legal age to vote.

"You have a minute?" she said.

"From what the news is saying, I should have hours."

"I want to go over your acceptance speech."

"Isn't that like an actor uttering *Macbeth* on opening night?"

Margo squinched her eyebrows questioningly, but Kai snorted his appreciation.

"Isn't that bad luck?" Duncan explained, "planning a victory statement before you know the outcome?"

"When else could we do it?"

"We," she'd said. To his staff the campaign constituted a group project, not the election of one person but many. In any speech, he'd have to thank them all.

A click distracted him. Kai had finally hung up and was looking at Duncan with ambiguous judgment.

"So what are your sources saying?"

"They're saying..." Kai paused, chewing his words "...that we have a small lead, but it's too soon to call it."

A murmur passed over the room, and one woman asked, "We won?"

"Not yet, everyone," Duncan said. "Let's not celebrate yet."

A moment later, the bell of the phone cut through all other sounds. Kai picked up, listened, then said, "We don't have a statement yet." He hung up before cracking a half smile.

"The press. Apparently word is out that you're ahead."

"What should I say?" Duncan said.

"Nothing until we're sure. We don't want any 'Dewey Defeats Truman' headlines in the *Trib* tomorrow."

"Then what should we do?"

"Margo's right. Start practicing your acceptance speech."

"And if your forecast is wrong?"

"Carl can write something in concession, but move to different rooms. I don't want him bleeding defeat into our victory."

* * *

The next two hours passed with the intolerable gait of a funeral march. Duncan and Margo sequestered themselves in his office to rewrite thank yous half a dozen times, seeking an elusive tone that mixed jubilation with sobriety. He favored a call upon the legislature to immediately pass his anti-crime bill, while she resisted details. As Kai suggested, they had no contact with Carl, and Duncan pushed aside his worries about losing. If anything, he hoped his suffering was nearing an end. No god could be cruel enough to take away his only avenue for revenge.

Josie interrupted them once, bringing mushroom cap hors d'oeuvres and a refreshed cranberry juice for Duncan (though she permitted Margo another class of chablis, he noted), while outside the talk and laughter crescendoed. By the time they finished, the party had reached a pitch far above any campaign rally. The volunteers, and even some staffers, laughed as though the race had ended, but Duncan felt only anxiety coiling in his stomach. Unlike him, they hadn't been limited on drinks.

Kai remained in the same position on the couch, the phone pressed to his ear, the image of studiousness.

"So where are we?" Duncan said.

When Kai held up a finger to mute him, Duncan looked around until he saw Parish.

"Nothing official yet," Parish said, "but all the networks say you're in the lead."

"What about Kai's source?"

They looked to the campaign leader, who jingled the ice in his empty glass. "Nothing yet."

Duncan searched for distractions and found his wife's bemused smile.

"You ready?" she said.

"For what?"

She extended a hand toward the front window, where headlights shone through like search lamps.

"Where's Glynis?" he said.

Her pause told him all he needed to know.

"Could you please tell her that she's needed downstairs immediately?"

In the hallway, the grandfather clock struck ten times, so Duncan turned up the volume on the news.

"Good evening," said Bill Curtis, the WASP anchorman of the local CBS affiliate. "Our top story is the close race for the governor's mansion. Standing by in Springfield is Vallis Mainger."

A pretty, young blonde appeared in front of the golden dome of the state Capitol. Despite a grey wool coat, she hunched her shoulders to her ears.

"With almost ninety percent of the returns counted, Duncan Cochrane holds an edge of almost fifty thousand votes. We've had no word from the campaigns, but insiders predict his lead is too great for the governor to overcome with so few ballots remaining."

Cheers drowned out the rest of her report. People Duncan hardly recognized embraced him. Someone put a glass of Champagne in his hand, and without thinking he raised it in a toast.

"It's been a long six months," he said, "but we made it."

Another cheer cut him off, and by the time he'd drunk once, wiped the run off from his chin, and raised his glass again, a hand caught his arm.

"Governor," Margo said.

"Too soon to celebrate?" Duncan asked.

He looked to Kai just as a man's voice shouted, "The governor's conceding."

All eyes turned to the television, where the camera zoomed in on Bill Stratton standing at a podium. The state flag stretched behind him, its eagle emblem looking fierce. Stratton adjusted his glasses before looking into the camera.

"First off, it's been a tremendous four years in office, and I want to thank all the people who've made it possible."

He named a dozen of his inner circle as well as Republican legislative leaders and family members. Soon his speech degenerated to an award acceptance. Duncan's neck tensed as he waited the official word.

"Lastly," the governor said, "I want to congratulate my opponent. We can only hope he's as skilled at governing as he is at campaigning."

"Even on his way out, he can't resist one last dig," Margo said.

"It doesn't matter," Kai said.

Duncan turned to him. "Are we declaring victory?"

"We are."

More cheers echoed through the room until a loud knock startled everyone.

"Governor," Margo said. "You should meet the press before the evening news ends."

"I want Josie and Glynis with me."

When he found his wife in the crowd, her expression betrayed more dread than triumph. It confused him until he saw Glynis, who wore a limp powder blue turtleneck that had been a perfect fit. Her hair, though wet brushed, lay lopsided and unkempt, with loose flyaways like new grass from muddy ground. Worst, her eyes sank into swollen cheeks, and her lips quivered like an alcoholic waiting her first drink.

"Everyone get behind me," Duncan said.

Together they walked to the front door, which Duncan threw open like an actor parting the curtains. He stepped forward into a blinding spotlight, cleared his throat, then recited the monologue penned an hour before into the waiting mics.

"First of all, I want to thank all the people who made this possible...."

He thought of the light on upstairs in Lindsay's room and suddenly felt her presence all around him.

CHAPTER 28

DUNCAN WOKE FIRST TO THE FALLOUT. Everywhere in his house lay used plates, cups, napkins, and streamers. On the floor sat deflating balloons, miniature state flags, and overturned goblets. In the hall the grandfather clock wore a cone hat, and in the dining room the sheet cake bore two candles melted to nubs. The carpet remained wet in three places, a new ring shone like a black eye on the walnut coffee table, and a strange purse lay by the sofa. The smell of sweat and smoke and alcohol hung in every room, bringing back the sweetness of cake and champagne.

Before he began cleaning, Duncan walked to the porch and unraveled the newspaper, which blared "COMEBACK" above a picture of him standing on the very same spot. In the bright flash, he looked startled, like a lottery winner accepting an oversized check.

Behind him, footsteps descended the stairs. He turned to see Josie squinting against the morning light, then held up the paper to her.

"When does your staff arrive to clean up?" she said.

"You're it," he said. "We're on the public dole now."

They processed into the kitchen, fixed coffee and breakfast—currant scones with raspberry jam, plus strong coffee—and shared reminiscences from the night before until the telephone rang. Josie looked at him expectantly, but he waived it off.

"It'll wait," he said. "Is Glynis up?"

"I haven't heard her."

"We need to talk about what's next."

He took the stairs two at a time and pounded loudly on her door, then again, and after receiving no reply, peeked inside. She lay motionless in bed, one arm thrown out casually, the other covering her eyes. The sheets bunched around her, and both pillows rested on the floor.

"Glynis?"

He walked to her bedside and nudged her shoulder gently. She remained inert. Again he shook her but with more force.

"Dooohnnn," she said.

"Time to get up."

He lifted the covers to reveal her tartan nightshirt, but she didn't move or respond.

"Honey, wake up."

With one hand on her wrist and the other behind her back, he pulled her upright, but she could not sustain her own weight, leaning against his shoulder and slumping in the middle.

In an instant, he pictured the last time he'd found one of his daughters in bed, but when he checked, Glynis' throat remained white and smooth. He lay her down again to listen to her chest and found her heart beating slowly but clearly. Her forehead felt clammy and warm. Once more he tried to sit her up, but she fell back on the bed as soon as he stopped supporting her.

On the night stand, he saw the Slumber Time pills and shook the bottle. Empty.

He scooped her into his arms, walked to the head of the stairs, and yelled down. "Josie! Get the car."

She appeared in the hallway below still clutching her napkin. "What's the matter?"

"Glynis is sick."

"I'll call an ambulance."

"NO," he said. "Driving is faster."

The closest hospital waited in Evanston, two miles away and a straight shot south along the lakefront. Even at seven a.m., traffic backed up at every traffic light. Mostly, Duncan kept his eyes forward, but at lulls he glanced into the back seat, where Josie sat with Glynis laid in her lap. His daughter gave no response beyond a few grunts when Josie stroked her forehead. After ten agonizing minutes of swerving through traffic, he screeched into the roundabout for the emergency room and left the car running as he carried his limp bundle inside.

A nurse appeared with a gurney, and he laid Glynis on it like a child prepped for bedtime.

"What's wrong?" the nurse said.

"She won't wake up," Duncan said.

They race-walked down a hall and into an examining room while all around them people appeared. A man in scrubs cuffed Glynis' arm to check her blood pressure while a woman shoved a thermometer in her mouth and another man listened to her chest with a stethoscope.

"Has she eaten anything?" the nurse said.

"Not today."

"Is she taking any medications?"

The nurse stared as Duncan chewed the question.

"I found some sleeping pills by her bed," he said.

"Do you know how many she's taken in the past twenty-four hours?"

Behind them, the medical staff were stripping her clothes and palpating every part of her.

"What are they doing?" Duncan said.

"Do you know how many pills she took?" the nurse said.

"No. Several?"

"Has she consumed any alcohol?"

"Some champagne last night. Why?"

"It can intensify the effects of the barbiturates."

At the party, Duncan had forced a glass into her hand to toast his victory. She'd only sipped it, but he'd lost sight of her in the hubbub after his acceptance speech.

Behind him, the doctors were shoving a tube down Glynis' delicate throat. They must have been listening to his interrogation, although none were looking at him.

"What are they doing?" Duncan said.

"Emptying her stomach," the nurse said. She placed a hand on his back and steered him to the door. "Let's talk in the lobby."

"Do you have a private room?" Josie said.

Duncan hadn't noticed her at his side, although she must have been there the whole time.

"This way," the nurse said.

She led them back down the hall and into a tight room, empty except for a conference table and chairs. As they entered, Duncan remembered his car sat idling in the driveway.

"I've got to park," he said.

Outside, the Cadillac looked violated, with three doors thrown up and the engine coughing exhaust. He rounded the driveway slowly, then spiraled through the parking garage until he found a space three floors up. All the while, he asked himself how much did they need to know? He'd already explained the pills and the wine. He had little else to say, yet he feared more questions.

To begin, the doctor handed them forms for her name, address, insurance, painless enough, then studied their answers as though suspicious. Then she reviewed everything they'd said before, plus more questions. ("Was she taking any other drugs?" "You're sure?" "That includes illegal substances?" "You're sure?")

After, the nurse left Duncan and Josie alone in the conference room, where a single vent blew on them warm and dry.

"Why didn't you tell me she passed out?" Josie said, calm but stern.

"I wasn't sure."

"We should have called an ambulance."

"It was faster without."

"You didn't want anyone to know."

The accusation hung between them, confirmed by his silence.

"All you care about is your image," she said.

"She'll be fine. It was just an accident."

Josie stared at a blank wall silently until another woman entered the room. She looked funereal in a black suit jacket and skirt, her grey hair pinned into a bun. After pulling a chair close to them, she sat immobile, hands folded in her lap, no clipboard or paper for notes.

"I'm Dr. Livna Wolf with the psychiatry department," she said. "I understand your daughter overdosed last night."

"It was an accident," Duncan said.

"Do you know how many pills she took?"

"A few."

"And she was drinking?"

"We were celebrating."

The doctor nodded and stared at them expectantly, but Duncan couldn't explain.

"Has your daughter been depressed recently?"

Though he wanted to, Duncan couldn't answer the question, so he hung fire, waiting on Josie. She'd recovered herself enough to relax her frown and soften her eyes. After an interminable pause, she replied: "She's had trouble sleeping."

"Is she under a doctor's care?"

Both parents shook their heads in unison.

"So you both believe this was an accident?"

As the doctor stared, Duncan felt himself overheat beneath the vent's blast.

Finally, Josie answered, "Yes."

The doctor shifted her weight, but her expression remained neutral. "I understand you've suffered a recent death in your family."

"Her sister," Duncan said.

"And your daughter found her?"

"Yes."

The doctor nodded and withdrew a pack of Dunhills from her coat pocket. She offered the cigarettes to Duncan, but he shook his head. Instead of taking one herself, she pocketed them like lollipops at a dentist's.

"Do you believe that is the cause of her sleep difficulties?"

Duncan nodded and looked to his wife, who'd glanced away. The heater kept up its slow roast.

"How is she?" Josie said.

"Stable. There doesn't appear to be any immediate danger."

The parents exchanged a look of reconciliation before she spoke again.

"However, we'd like to keep her overnight."

"Why?" Duncan said.

"Given the likelihood of a suicide attempt, I need to speak to her before she's discharged, and I don't expect she'll awake for some hours."

"We just said it was an accident."

"Accidents are not always unintentional."

"What does that mean?" Josie said.

"Sometimes people overdose because they're in distress. Even if she didn't intend to kill herself, disturbed sleep and a death in the family all put her at great risk."

"Of?"

"Withdrawal, depression, self-injury. Without speaking to her, I can't offer a diagnosis," she said. "But I can tell you that her symptoms are all consistent with acute depression. That's common for people who've experienced a sudden shock such as losing a loved one or witnessing a violent crime. In your daughter's case, both."

Unable to stand the heater's intensity, Duncan stood and walked to the door, where a narrow window gave a view on the empty hall. From there he couldn't see into the emergency room, only a brightly lit corridor leading indefinitely in both directions. He turned and studied the doctor before answering. From afar she looked small and compact, hardly intimidating, yet her words sounded threatening.

"We can't risk leaving her here," he said.

"Risk what?"

"Publicity."

"I can assure you, your daughter's status is confidential."

"What if someone saw us? Driving here, in the waiting room? If you know who I am, you know how much attention this could generate. I don't want to read about my daughter's accident on tomorrow's front page."

"Governor, I can assure you...."

"I've heard that promise before but never seen it kept."

If his position intimidated her, it didn't show in her face except for a slight frown. "Please understand," she said, "we only want to protect your daughter."

"I've heard that before, too."

"Enough," Josie said.

Duncan turned, surprised at her stern tone. She wouldn't look at either of them, but sat with her body coiled into itself, ready to spring.

"I've already lost one daughter," she said. "I'm not risking another."

She looked at the doctor, ignoring Duncan's silent message to stop. "You want to ask her about last night?"

The doctor nodded.

"Nothing else?"

"I can't predict where that discussion will lead."

"I don't want you prying into our lives. She's had enough inter-rogation as is."

"It may be that she needs someone to talk to."

"She has us for that."

Her tone jabbed angrily, although she stayed seated, her eyes fixed on the doctor.

"I'll try to confine my questions to the overdose."

"Don't try, do," Duncan said.

"However," the doctor said and paused. "I'd recommend that you enroll her in some sort of ongoing counseling. Whether this was an accident or not, she'll need to manage her sleep without drugs or alcohol."

"Let's talk about that after she's released," Duncan said.

The doctor stood and straightened her skirt before moving to the door. Duncan held his ground there, forcing her to pass only a foot away. With one hand on the knob, she paused and turned to face them again.

"Congratulations," she said. "On your victory, I mean. It must be very gratifying."

***

While Josie remained at the hospital, Duncan returned home. As soon as he walked in, the phone rang. He tried to ignore it, fearing another attack of the press, but after the tenth bell he strode to his office. Below the campaign literature and posters piled on his desk, he unearthed the phone. A woman's voice asked him to hold for Capt. Simpson, so he sat on the one empty surface, his antique oak chair, and waited. When the state policeman picked up with a jovial "Good morning, Governor," Duncan said wearily, "What can I do for you?"

"Our director asked me to review your daughter's case with you."

"When?"

"Whenever's convenient."

"Where are you, Springfield?"

"Yes sir."

"Next week?"

The other man's hesitation implied his displeasure.

"Please speak plainly, Captain."

"Your family members are still our best witnesses."

Eight weeks and the Kenilworth cops hadn't found any substantive evidence. Incredible. Duncan's irritation demanded a nicotine release. But no, he'd pledged to quit after the election. Why make the promise and break it the next day?

"Give me a minute."

He shoved aside a box of bumper stickers to uncover the blotter of his desk calendar, where scribbled appointments abruptly stopped after Election Day.

"How's the day after tomorrow?"

"Good enough. I'd like to speak to your daughter, too."

"She's... not feeling well."

"I understand, sir, but she's the only person to see the assailant."

"I don't want to stress her."

"I promise we'll be delicate."

"Maybe in a few days."

The captain allowed a lengthy silence to convey his disapproval.

"Has the reward generated any leads?" Duncan said.

"Many. We're following up as quick as we can, but...."

"What?"

"Rewards attract a lot of publicity seekers. It's taking time to weed out the wackos."

Duncan looked away from the captain's disapproving stare. "Anyone else you're planning to interview?" He thought of Oges, gulping down coffee at state expense, probably gloating to the other inmates about how he'd evaded the police and the governor.

"Your son."

"He's not home." The statement came out more strident than he intended, so Duncan added, "He's been back East for the past four months."

The captain cleared his throat, forming his words carefully. "A phone interview will do."

Given his evasions about Glynis, Duncan didn't want to be difficult. "I'll set up something in a few days, but I'll see you the day after tomorrow."

"I'll have my men ready for you."

CHAPTER 29

THE CONFERENCE ROOM at the state police headquarters barely fit four chairs. Moving boxes flanked every wall, stacked three high, all with Cochrane written in red on the side. On a round table sat files labeled with the names of Duncan's family, friends, and business contacts. At least the Springfield cops had contained the information to this single room, which offered no windows and a locked door.

For the meeting with his new boss, Captain Simpson wore dress blues—more fitting than Chief Dunleavy's academic outfits, though too formal. His buzz cut couldn't hide grey hair, including a neat mustache, nor his uniform a sagging chest. Still, he possessed the bulk to subdue people and an expression that never wavered from military sternness. He could have been a grandfather, but one who could still take his grandson in wrestling.

"Governor," Simpson said, "meet Dr. Serafina Durazo."

The doctor couldn't have stood more than five feet or weighed over one hundred and ten, but she wore a black business suit that rounded her hips and breasts. Although probably fifty, her hair remained uniform black, and her cocoa skin showed no wrinkles. Her perfume—Chanel No. 5—suffused the small office. In its television commercial, a woman lay by a pool as the shadow of a plane passed over. "Share the fantasy," it invited. Duncan glanced at Josie, who wore no makeup, loose-fitting pants, and a bulky sweater. Expecting her to play the temptress felt unfair, but he couldn't help sharing the fantasy that the doctor offered.

"What's your role?" Duncan said.

"I'm a criminal psychologist."

Though her diction chipped every word to perfection, she spoke with a slow, strained pronunciation that failed to hide her Spanish accent.

"She's creating a profile of the suspect," Simpson explained.

"We appreciate your help," Josie said.

The doctor nodded and smiled, trying for ingratiation.

Before their meeting, the Cochranes had toured the governor's mansion and the executive offices, eaten at Maldaner's, the preferred restaurant of local politicians, even set up a calendar with the social secretary. Moving promised a change for the better, yet in this narrow room it felt as if nothing had changed. The state police offered sturdier chairs and a table of real wood, but the manila folders, the photos, and the frustration had not changed.

"Are you going to charge Hoxter?" Duncan said.

"Like I said last week, we're starting from day one," Simpson said. "We want to analyze everything and see where it points."

"And where does it?"

"We're not convinced Hoxter's a match."

"Why?" Duncan said.

Simpson looked to the psychologist, who twisted to face Duncan and Josie head on. "The facts suggest the killer knew Lindsay and wanted to harm her specifically. You testified that he left a pillow over her face. That's typical of a person motivated by anger or retaliation. Plus, the intruder climbed the stairs, sought out her bedroom, and attacked only her. That's not the act of a stranger. We'd typically see this from a husband or jilted lover."

"Lindsay didn't have any of those," Josie said. She shook her head but kept her eyes steady. "The few boys she dated all came from good families, and the Kenilworth police already ruled out Tom Dalrymple."

The captain reached across the table to retrieve a file. "His father alibied him, but we don't put a lot of stock in family as character witnesses."

"Look," Duncan said, "I interviewed him myself, and nothing about his... demeanor suggested... *anything* to me."

Since words failed him, he looked to the doctor for help.

"The Kenilworth police investigated the case as a burglary that turned violent," she said. "They were looking for serial criminals who stumbled on your house."

"You don't buy that?" Duncan said.

"Nothing was stolen, though the killer walked past many items that are easy to resell. And burglars generally break in when no one is home. They want to go undetected. Yet your car sat in the driveway, clearly signaling someone was present."

Duncan sat back and inhaled deeply the chemical tang of the doctor's perfume. "I can't believe this," he said. "For two months, the Kenilworth police have been saying they know who did it, and they just needed more evidence. Now you're saying he's innocent?"

The interviews with Hoxter and his sister repeated on Duncan. Both had acted so adamant, yet he'd caught both lying. How could he believe their versions of events when their versions overflowed with untruths?

"Where are you looking then?" Duncan said.

"We're reviewing everything," the captain said.

Duncan sat back and folded his arms across his chest. "So we're back to where we started."

"Not at all," the doctor said.

She picked a sketch of the killer. The rough charcoal lines depicted a round face without distinction, a match to half the male population.

"If you don't mind, I'd like to review with your daughter what she saw. I believe she has the information we need. Odds are we're looking for someone who Lindsay knew, and perhaps someone who is known to you all."

"That's not possible," Duncan said. "Glynis isn't well right now. She and her sister were close, and ever since her death she's... depressed."

The psychologist nodded but kept a neutral expression that betrayed no empathy. "It's quite possible she blames herself."

"Why would she?"

"Survivor's guilt. The fact that she lived through the attack and her sister didn't is enough to trigger a depressive response."

"Then wouldn't rehashing things make that worse?"

"Perhaps not. In the therapeutic model, reliving the experience allows for the assuaging of guilt. With guidance, she can reinterpret events in a more impartial way."

"So you could treat my daughter while you're interrogating her?"

"Certainly not. Any therapeutic effect would be incidental, but helping to identify the suspect would give her a sense of agency."

Duncan looked to Josie and raised his eyebrows to ask, "What do you think?"

"What do you want to ask her about?" she said.

The doctor looked to Capt. Simpson.

"Everything, from the moment she awoke."

"What good will that do?" Duncan said. "She already told the Kenilworth police everything."

"There may be something they've missed."

"Like?"

"Your son," Simpson said.

"What about him?"

"He never gave a statement."

"He slept through everything."

"But he identified Tom Dalrympe as a suspect."

"Based on a phone call he overheard."

"He might know more."

"Such as?"

The captain rattled through some boxes and retrieved another file. "Officers questioned him three times in the last two years."

Duncan shook his head and inhaled, only to choke on the doctor's fragrance. The only outside air came from a vent above them, but strips hung from it lifelessly. He looked to the door and saw a red handled smoke alarm. How badly he wanted a smoke now.

"Those were... petty things," he said. "Drinking and the like. Things a lot of teenagers do."

"Last year he was detained for auto theft and reckless driving. The year before, fighting in public. Other charges of truancy and underage drinking were dismissed."

"Aden was... immature. That's why we sent him to military school."

"We'd still like to interview him."

"You've already interrogated our entire family," Josie said. The despair in her voice shamed Duncan to silence.

"Don't you see how we've suffered?" she said, looking between the doctor and the captain. "One of my daughters is dead, the other is depressed, my son is away, and you act like we're all suspects."

The captain sat back in his chair and chewed his mustache before answering. "It isn't an indictment. We only want to speak with them."

"I'll make the arrangements," Duncan said.

"No," Simpson said. "With your family's cooperation, we should make quick progress."

Duncan stood and moved toward the door, but its small window of frosted glass offered no outlet. "What about organized crime?"

The captain watched him impassively except for a downturn of his mouth. "Why would you think that?"

"Early on, Chief Dunleavy talked about a mafia link."

"I don't see any evidence of that in the file. Is there something we should know?"

Duncan glanced to Josie, who stared at him with passive intensity. Just from the set of her jaw, he read he anger. "This has to stay in this room," he said.

"Of course."

"You say that casually, but everything the Kenilworth cops did hit the papers."

"We'll be discrete," the captain said. He kept a military posture, back erect, hands clasped, but his eyes accused Duncan of informing on himself.

Duncan walked to Josie and put his hands on her shoulders so that he did not have to see her eyes. "In the meat packing business, I have to deal with a lot of... unpleasant people. Unions and the like. Some of them have... questionable connections."

The captain reached for a pen sitting in the middle of the table.

"Please, keep this off the record," Duncan said.

The captain leaned back and crossed his arms, his eyes saying that he would record every word mentally.

"When I contacted one of them, he denied any involvement, but..." Duncan glanced between his two underlings, who didn't dare press him. " ...he threatened me."

"How?" Simpson said.

"He told me not to contact him again."

"Or else?"

"He didn't specify."

"You never mentioned this to the police?"

"It happened during the campaign, and I didn't want it getting out."

The captain nodded and glanced away from his new boss obliquely.

"Why haven't I heard this before?" Josie said.

"I didn't want to scare you."

Duncan squeezed his wife's shoulders, which tensed under the pressure.

"I'll need his name and affiliation," Simpson said.

"He can't know it came from me."

"You have nothing to fear now, sir. You've got the entire state police to protect you."

Duncan inhaled the hot, dry, suffocating air of the room. "Danny, from the American Brotherhood of Laborers."

The captain reached for the pen, wrote quickly, then looked at Duncan again, using his interrogator's stare. "No last name?"

"That's all I know."

"Description?"

"An Irishman with red hair and freckles."

"We'll find him."

He stood, spurring the others to do the same. Once the door opened, Duncan enjoyed how cool and fresh the air tasted in comparison to that little cell. He shook hands with the captain and the doctor, then turned to go, but Josie already strode three paces ahead, giving him her back.

CHAPTER 30

THANKSGIVING OFFERED THE ONLY RESPITE since the campaign began, yet when Josie backed out of the kitchen carrying a platter of lamb, Duncan couldn't summon any appetite. Even with Aden back from school and Glynis from the hospital, he felt Lindsay's absence more than ever. He paused with his carving knife and fork poised.

"What are you waiting for, Dad?" Aden said. "Let's scarf!"

He wore civilian clothes again—a black mock turtleneck and a plaid scarf—blending the better parts of his old wardrobe with the military haircut and clean shave required for school.

"Let's pray first," Duncan said.

He set down the cutlery and leaned forward to clasp hands with his children.

"Some hae meat and canna eat,

And some wad eat that want it;"

He paused, trying to recall the rest of the poem.

"But we hae meat, and we can eat,"

Another pause, this one longer than the first. Duncan felt Aden's restlessness in his squirming fingers but kept his grip firm.

"And sae the Lord be thankit."

"Amen," Josie said.

Duncan pierced the lamb skin, and the juices ran down, pooling on the carving platter.

"Looks great," he said.

As the family passed their plates, Duncan looked to his wife. She wore a new, red dress that scooped to a V on her breast bone and had wrapped her hair in a French twist. She looked the most beautiful and the most natural he'd seen her since they became public figures.

"Aden, I want you to try the neeps," he said.

"Why can't we have turkey and potatoes like everyone else?"

"This is our heritage."

"But Thanksgiving is American, Dad. Nobody here digs what neeps are."

"It's rutabaga. You know that," Josie said.

The boy twirled to face her. "But nobody else does. My friends won't even come over when they hear what we're having."

Duncan spooned mint sauce over the lamb and inhaled its earthy scent. "Holidays are better with just family," he said.

He scanned the table for confirmation, but only Josie would return his gaze. Aden smirked to himself, and Glynis stared into her lap.

Duncan passed the boy his plate and grimaced as Aden started eating before the others had been served.

"Could you wait?"

The boy set down his silverware, sighed, and stared at the ceiling.

Glynis too sat immobile. She'd returned from the hospital only a day before and had spent most of the time since in her room. Still, she looked more put together, her hair blown straight and foundation on her cheeks. She just needed to get the pills out of her system.

"Do we have to call you governor now?" Aden said.

"Sir will do."

"Just like at school."

"How's that?"

"We call everyone sir."

The image of Aden saluting the staff with "yes, sir" and "good morning, sir" made Duncan smile. Before his son came home for the holiday, Duncan decided to use the weekend as a gauge of Aden's progress. When he told Josie as much, she practically jumped on him.

"So you'd consider letting him move back?" she'd said.

"Not mid-year."

"Then what are you measuring?"

"What my $10,000 in tuition is buying."

With all the plates filled, Duncan nodded for his son to begin. What to eat first? The lamb was still steaming, and the cabbage looked tempting. He tried the boiled green leaves, but the vinegar tasted acidic, so he swallowed some chardonnay and turned again to his son.

"What are they teaching you?" he said.

"Marching."

"What else?"

"Cleaning."

The boy chewed with his mouth open, making loud smacks and slurps.

"What kind?"

"Polishing boots, making beds, washing dishes."

"They've got you on k.p.?" Josie said with mock surprise.

"Twice a week."

"Then you can help me after dinner."

Duncan forked the neeps and blew steam off them until he couldn't wait any longer. They went down silky smooth with just the right amount of salt. Hard to believe such a rough vegetable as rutabaga could be creamed so well.

"Anything else?" he said.

"Killing people."

Glynis looked at Aden with hatred, threw down her fork, and ran from the room. Her shoes clattered up the stairs, then a door slammed.

The boy looked between his parents in mock innocence. "What? It's true. I know like ten different ways to kill somebody without a weapon."

Without a word, Josie stood and followed Glynis upstairs.

"Careful what you say around your sister. She's... sensitive right now."

"She's always like that."

"This is... different. Ever since Lindsay died, she's been depressed."

The boy shook his head and bit off a carrot. "What are you doing with Lindsay's car?" he said.

"What?"

"The Bug. I need some wheels."

Duncan set down his fork and finished chewing a mouthful of lamb before responding. "You're not allowed to have a car on campus."

"I mean for summer break."

"We'll see."

"Mom said you want to sell it."

"It's in the way."

"Not if I've got it. You'll never even see me."

"That's what worries me."

The boy reached across the table to help himself to more lamb, pinching three pieces between his fingers and dripping the juices on the white tablecloth.

"Next time, ask," Duncan said.

"I did! You said 'We'll see,' like I don't know what that means."

"I'm talking about your table manners."

"So you'll give me the car?"

"We'll see."

Upstairs, a door closed softly, then Josie returned alone.

"How's Glynis?" Duncan said.

"Resting."

Aden turned to his mother and stabbed his dinner roll, sawing it open. "Dad said I can have Lindsay's car."

Josie looked at her husband in silent surprise.

"I said we'll see," Duncan said.

"I don't think that's appropriate," she said.

"What do you mean?" Aden said.

"It's Lindsay's."

"Every time I used it, it'd remind me of her."

Silently, Josie spooned more salad into her bowl.

"Then can I buy one?" Aden said.

"You can use mine," Josie said.

"The wood wagon? That thing handles like a hammock."

"What would you propose?" Duncan said.

"Something bangin'."

"Such as?"

"A Corvette or Mustang."

"We couldn't afford the tickets," Josie said.

"You bought cars for Glynis and Lindsay when they turned sixteen."

"They didn't wreck one before they passed their driver's test," Duncan said.

"Me neither!"

Rather than rehash old family disputes, Duncan turned to his wife. "What's for dessert?"

"Fruitcake."

"Oh, man," Aden said.

"You'll like it," she said. "It has raisins and brandy."

"At least I can get a buzz off it."

Not ready, Duncan thought. The boy was not ready yet.

CHAPTER 31

BEFORE HIS FIRST MEETING with the state's legislative leaders, Kai told Duncan that they conducted most of their business in restaurants. Private meeting rooms kept secrets in house while food and alcohol leavened talks. He recommended Saputo's, a windowless Italian eatery with extra large pasta plates, but Duncan wanted something more formal. Instead, he chose a room on the Capitol's first floor, where he wouldn't have to pass the governor's suite upstairs.

Entombed in its dim cavity, he understood why Kai counseled for cuisine. Everything glowered dark and ornate: the stained wood pillars, the burgundy wallpaper, the velvet drapes, the box beam ceiling, the money green frieze. The ambiance aped a museum more than a back room, and it bore as much gold leaf as the tomb of King Tut. Even the chairs felt too formal: high backed and hard. Duncan squirmed to find a comfortable posture then turned to his guests.

"Before I'm sworn in, I want to brief you on my agenda."

State Sen. Timothy Struthers, a rotund man with a brown hairpiece that failed to match the ring of grey around his ears, smiled like a proud father at his son's graduation. During the campaign, the Speaker of the Illinois State Senate hadn't come to even one of Duncan's rallies. Now that he'd be working down the hall, Struthers acted happy to clear his schedule.

"The office will belong to you soon enough," Struthers said.

"I don't think Bill Stratton would appreciate me moving in early," Duncan said.

Struthers broke out another horse trader's smile. "The governor is a very reasonable man when he's backed into a corner."

Rep. Hillary Groves, the Republican Speaker of the House and a close ally of the governor's, replied with a tsk tsk. "Let's not speak ill of the dead before they're buried," she said.

Her dress mimicked a librarian's—a long grey skirt and jacket, hair held back by a tortoise shell clip, and glasses to match—but her expression had hardened into an iron worker's. In an assembly where Democrats outnumbered the GOP two to one, her only power lay in disapproval, so she exercised it with maximal vigor.

Duncan looked to the other legislative leaders for encouragement: Senate minority leader Justin Danberry, whose somber suit and tie reminded him of a televangelist, and Rep. Celio Rossi, a youthful Italian with slick, black hair.

"You all know why I made sentencing reform the center of my campaign," Duncan said. "Obviously, I have personal motives, but it's just as important to me politically."

The two Democrats nodded, but the Republicans stared immobile.

"The man who killed my daughter bounced in and out of jail ten times. Why he got so many chances I'll never understand, but I want to make sure that no one like him ever..." his words failed him "does something..." how to finish it "...like this again."

Struthers clasped Duncan's forearm reassuringly, a gesture that explained how this gross man had survived twenty-six years in elected office.

"It'll be the top of my agenda," Struthers said. "Provided we get some help from our friends across the aisle..." he looked to the two Republicans "...we can get something done."

Sitting erect as a bird on a wire, Groves surveyed them with detachment. "We've pushed sentencing reform for the last five years," she said, "only to have the bills stalled in committee or filibustered on the floor. Now that a Democrat's in the governor's office, I don't see why it's a priority."

"I can't help what's happened before," Duncan said, "but I can promise I'll support any measure that increases public safety."

"What about funding?" Groves said. "We need more prisons. Where will you get the money?"

Duncan decided to shift her pronouns from "you" to "we."

"I'm sure we can shift funds from less important things."

"I'm curious to hear what those are."

Duncan shifted in his chair as he tried to recall the specifics. "The list is with my staff, but I'll get you a copy. For the moment, I only want your agreement on the intent of the bill, not the details."

"The devil is always in the details," Danberry said. From his grim expression, Duncan couldn't tell if he meant the comment literally.

"We're planning a public vetting so everyone can read the proposals," Duncan said.

"For a righteous bill, we'd put aside politics." The senator twisted a silver ring on his left hand. Duncan expected a wedding band, yet it looked too bulbous, more like a class ring with a gold decoration at the center.

"Will you consider our bill on prayer in school?" he said.

Duncan spoke before anyone else had the chance. "Any legislation with merit will get my signature, regardless of party origins. But before that, I want to shut the prison doors for good. If I have to, I'll replace the entire parole board."

"That power rests with the legislature," Groves said.

Struthers smiled and leaned his massive torso forward, nearly tipping over his chair. "We'll have your support on the crime bill, then?"

When she stood, Groves' oval shape evoked a carrion bird with its wings collapsed. "I look forward to your proposal, Mr. Cochrane," she said.

"As do I," Danberry said.

He extended a hand, giving Duncan a glimpse of his ring. Its gold leaf depicted the Savior tied down on a cross. While Duncan stood to shake, his democratic colleagues stayed seated. They remained silent until their opponents had left the room.

"That went better than I expected," Duncan said. "How soon do you think you can get something to me?"

Struthers settled his great bulk and glanced at his colleague before answering. "Let's not be overanxious," he said. "These things take time. Even after we have a bill drafted, we need to put it through committee and both houses, then there'll be a conference to iron out the differences. The soonest we could hope for is by summer recess."

"But with Republican support we could fast track it," Duncan said. "I'd like to have something by the start of next year."

"Don't count on any support from their side," Struthers said. "They want credit for sentencing reform, and they're not about to give you a victory your first week."

"But they wouldn't oppose a bill just because I proposed it?"

"They'll oppose it *because* you proposed it."

Duncan looked to Rossi, who raised his bushy black eyebrows in agreement.

"I have to be honest," Rossi said, "this is going to be a hard sell to my coalition."

"Why?"

"Crime doesn't pay. Who's going to contribute? Prison guards?"

Before the meeting, Kai had run down each of the participants. Of Rossi, he said only "ambitious." Rumor held that the pol had planned a run at the governor's mansion in the next election. Duncan's residence in the office represented a major obstacle.

The governor-elect looked to Struthers for affirmation.

"We're not opposed," the veteran said. "None of us get votes from prisoners. It's just, you're new to Springfield, and the old guard needs to get to know you before they'll follow your lead. Now, if you could offer them something in exchange, that might be persuasive."

"Such as?"

"For the last three years, we've passed a package of capital improvements, only to have the governor veto it. Now, we can get it through another vote, but we need your backing."

"What kind of improvements?"

"Roads, bridges, libraries—essentials like that."

Intuitively, Duncan mistrusted the request. Springfield was notorious for pork barrel spending that benefitted legislators more than taxpayers. Members would barter votes for each other's pet projects while kowtowing to their biggest donors. As a businessman, he'd always found such logrolling offensive.

Duncan looked around the dark, cold room for inspiration. He found it only a few feet away, hanging on the newspaper rack. "Look at this," he said, rising to retrieve that day's *Tribune*.

He held up the front page, which read, "U.S. Congressman, 4 Shot Dead in Guyana."

"Look what's happening around us," Duncan said. "There's violence everywhere."

"I understand," Struthers said, "but that's thousands of miles away. Before yesterday, who'd even heard of Guyana?"

Duncan looked at Rossi, who nodded ambiguously.

"American citizens died," Duncan said. "And a congressman. It could have been one of us down there, if those people had come from Illinois instead of California."

"All I'm saying is be patient," Struthers said. "Have faith, and we'll get it done."

"What if I added more torque?" Duncan said.

The two legislators exchanged a nervous glance.

"How do you mean?" Struthers said.

"If I exert enough public pressure, the members will have no choice but to vote for the bill. No one wants to be seen as favoring criminals."

"Of course, you could try," Rossi said. "But what'll you use as a lever?"

"I'll find something," Duncan said.

CHAPTER 32

MOVING BROUGHT MORE UNREST. Initially it sounded logical to relocate to Springfield: as governor, Duncan would spend most of his time at the capital. Plus every chief executive for a century had lived in the mansion. Since only Glynis stayed with them full time, Duncan saw no reason to hang onto the Kenilworth home. Except while packing, the Cochranes rediscovered things that had been permanently closeted. Josie began in the dining room, kneeling before the buffet as she dug into its lower shelves.

"What about these?" She held up a pair of silver trivets tarnished to bronze.

"Keep them."

"When's the last time we used them?"

"We inherited them from my grandmother."

"That's why we haven't used them?"

"They're an heirloom," he said. "I promised my mother we'd keep them."

Josie sighed but wrapped the trivets in newspaper. The excuse sounded silly to Duncan too but came as close to the truth as he could muster. He stood, brushed off his cords, and started toward the stairs.

"Oh, no," Josie said. "You're not leaving all this to me."

"I'm just checking on Glynis. I'll be back in a minute."

"I'll time you."

Outside, a foot of new snow covered everything. The city had plowed the streets overnight, but most sidewalks remained impassible. The storm had prompted the movers to reschedule for the next day. Lucky thing, since sorting through the house proved to be a bigger job than any of them anticipated. At best they'd finish by nightfall.

Duncan stomped up the stairwell so Glynis would know he was coming. Since the incident at Thanksgiving, he'd been monitoring her. She'd stayed in her room for nearly two days after, eating nothing and talking little. Her therapist had made an emergency house call but said she just needed time.

"Holidays are difficult," the shrink said. "That's when the absence is most acute."

But in two weeks, little had changed.

He knocked lightly, then opened the door without waiting. Glynis sat on the carpet, folding sweaters.

"How's it coming?" Duncan said.

"Fine."

He stepped forward two paces. Behind the bed hid a large steamer trunk nearly full of clothing. Another suitcase stood next to it, and just inside the closet sat four boxes overflowing with books, pictures, and mementos. Only the bed had not been deconstructed.

"You're doing better than we are," Duncan said.

Glynis offered only a polite smile.

In the background, a woman sang high in her register over a synthesized beat.

"Once I had a love and it was a gas

Soon turned out I had a heart of glass"

"What's the music?" he said.

She held up an album cover showing a platinum blonde in a white dress surrounded by five men in black suits on a background of black and white stripes. From a distance, the woman could have been Marilyn Monroe, her hair obviously bleached, her stance defiant, hands on hips. At the top, the album read, appropriately, "Blondie."

"Sounds... different."

Glynis frowned in mock exasperation. "You don't like any new music."

"What about John Denver?"

She rolled her eyes.

"Never mind, just keep packing."

He turned down the hallway with every intention of joining Josie downstairs but paused at Lindsay's room. He'd almost forgotten it.

Inside, they'd preserved everything as was, including a dresser full of her clothes, a bookshelf packed with photos and memorabilia, and walls covered in impressionist prints. The smell had evolved though, from perfume and skin cream to dust and mildew. The week before, he and Josie had debated what to do with Lindsay's things.

"We're not going to just box up our daughter for storage," Josie said.

"Even if we recreate her room in the new house, it won't be the same. She never lived there."

"You might as well say she never existed."

Duncan let the matter drop unresolved, hoping Josie might forget her plan.

How much remained? Inside the closet, the curtain rod bulged with dresses, pants, and skirts. Above them sat her sweaters, stacked in color-coded piles. Hanging from the door, a compartmentalized bag held two-dozen shoes. In her wicker clothes hamper he found jeans, a black bra, and a pink T-shirt. He held it up to read the front's silk screen:

NEVER MIND

THE BOLLOCKS

On the back it continued:

HERE'S THE

Sex Pistols

The size looked too large by half for Lindsay, and he'd never seen her wear anything like it. He weighed the shirt for several seconds before returning to Glynis' room.

"Do you recognize this?" he said. He held it by the corners as though it might be tainted.

"No. Where'd you get it?"

"Buried in the laundry. Could it have been Lindsay's?"

Glynis squinched her nose and shook her head. "She was into folk. CSN, Dylan, Joni Mitchell, people like that."

"So it's a band?"

"Sort of. They're punks."

The term meant nothing to Duncan, though her expression said it was derogatory.

"Where'd she get a thing like this?" Duncan said to himself.

* * *

As he descended the stairs, Duncan recalled another item that needed tending. The .32 lay dormant in his bottom drawer. He could easily leave it and let the movers transport the desk en masse. Only why bother with Hoxter already in custody and the mansion guarded by state policemen?

Then he uncovered a new problem: how to dispose of it. He couldn't just throw it out—in case Josie or Glynis looked in the trash—nor drop it in a public dumpster, where anyone could find it. Even unloaded, the weapon still felt powerful and dangerous, its silver barrel cold and slick. He'd never registered it—for fear the media would hear—which technically made it illegal. That also meant it couldn't be traced to him.

"Duncan," Josie called from the dining room.

"Coming," he said.

He stepped to the hallway and sought inspiration, somewhere only he would look but where he could retrieve it later. The fuse box. It sat outside at the back of the house, where no one would look. But when he squeaked open its rusty hinges, inside he found a flashlight, the same one that had gone missing from the kitchen months before. Why would someone else inspect his fuse box?

"Where are you?" Josie yelled from inside.

Without time to think, Duncan stashed the gun and returned to the house with the torch, exchanging one secret for another.

CHAPTER 33

THE GREAT HALL of the state's General Assembly shone like the nave of a cathedral: three stories high, with four massive chandeliers, floor to ceiling windows, a colonnade, an intricately carved ceiling, and burnished wood everywhere. Standing at the pulpit, Duncan felt like a minister, with a long wooden bench serving as his altar, and a choir loft behind filled with reporters ready to repeat his every word. In front waited his congregation, arrayed in a semi-circle. Of the one hundred and eighteen seats for house members, none sat empty, and senators took up most of the rear balcony. Apparently legislators wanted to hear from their new governor, even if it delayed their holiday getaway. Except instead of pews, the pols sat at wood-topped desks, making him more a teacher than a preacher, leading his students to a logical conclusion.

"Even though I won't be sworn in for another two weeks, I couldn't wait until after Christmas to start on our agenda," Duncan started.

His speech touched on all his campaign themes—closing the revolving door of prisons, stiffer penalties for offenders, the permissive parole terms—and with all the usual guilt trips. Then came his personal appeal, still emphasizing Lindsay's murder but putting more on Hoxter's criminal history. Throughout, the audience sat quiet and respectful, forgoing pro forma applause.

Just before the finish, Duncan paused to catch his breath. The desktop smelled of linseed oil, which made his throat constrict and his nose itch.

"Now, I know there will be significant costs. We'll need to make sacrifices elsewhere."

He omitted the specifics: a twenty-five percent increase in the state corrections budget and the creation of two more prisons, never easy to place since nobody wanted inmates as neighbors.

"You'll all agree, these compromises are a small price for public safety."

Polite applause stopped him, so he used the moment to survey the room. Several members jotted notes; he couldn't imagine about what. Many stared out the windows or toward the ceiling. One read a book hidden under his desktop. Boredom paralyzed many faces. They showed none of the voters' passion. Accustomed to long, aimless speeches, these men and women were treating his talk like a filibuster, waiting until he ran out of breath.

Outside, a train whistle faded into the distance. As it died away, Duncan heard the silence of a chamber waiting on him. Their message reverberated. To hold up all the state's biggest pols two days before Christmas, he better have a good reason.

"I trust you've all seen today's headlines."

He held up the *Chicago Tribune* whose banner read, "4 Slaying Victims Found."

"Yesterday, Des Plaines police found four young boys buried in the home of a man named John Gacy. This degenerate says there are sixteen more bodies under his property and another five nearby. Mr. Gacy also said he molested at least thirty-two boys and young men."

"And this isn't the first time he has victimized our youth. Previously, he sodomized two teenagers. Even though a judge sentenced him to ten years, his Iowa jailers released him after only eighteen months and allowed him to move to Illinois and live with his mother. That was in 1970. A little arithmetic will tell you that if Mr. Gacy had served his entire sentence, he'd still be locked up today."

The audience revived, all eyes fixed on their new leader.

"Surely, we can agree that men such as John Gacy and Oges Hoxter do not belong anywhere but in a prison cell. Surely we can set aside party differences to keep parolees locked up."

"I challenge this assembly to pass a bill by my inauguration. Nothing would make me prouder than to have my first act as governor be signing the warrant that will take away the rights of criminals to continue terrorizing us. Together, we can do this."

At last, the legislators erupted into raucous applause, with cheers of "here, here" and "we will." Once Duncan stepped back from the podium, they rose as one, serenading him like the star tenor at the Chicago Opera. To his left, Senate President Timothy Struthers stood to shake his hand and crushed his palm with enthusiasm.

"Great speech," the Senate President yelled. "Just what I need to prod the herd."

Duncan waved, then noticed Rep. Hillary Groves clapping politely. Her slate grey suit made her look even more like a vulture than usual. Though unsmiling, she nodded once solemnly.

The applause continued for a good minute until Rep. Rossi touched Duncan's arm and led him off the stage. In the aisle, legislators delayed him with handshakes and back slaps while cameras flashed from all directions. The audience acted with the enthusiasm of those on the campaign trail, except now Duncan couldn't tell whether to believe the adulation.

CHAPTER 34

AMIDST DUNCAN'S FINAL WALK-THROUGH, the rooms of his Kenilworth house felt foreign, his family's decor drab and impersonal, with cobwebs in the corners, scuffs on the footpaths, and stains where pictures once hung. Had the home really been so shabby? Maybe these remnants bore false evidence, the skeleton of a body no longer infused with life. Maybe they revealed mere aging, the sagging of the belly, the loosening of the skin, the decay of the posture. Stripped, his body would look no better.

"We'll need the alarm code," said Amity Faux.

The realtor tried to hide her age — which he pegged in the fifties — with hair too blond to be natural and a rosy smear that exceeded her lips. Despite the garish makeup, her uniform looked polished and professional: a plaid, wool skirt below the knees and a gold jacket from her employer.

She'd been a family friend going back to when her children played with Lindsay and Glynis in elementary school. Duncan expected his old acquaintance to be discreet, but notice of the home's final price had still made the gossip section of *North Shore* magazine. He couldn't fault her for the leak — the papers ran what they liked — but it still felt like a breach of promise.

The alarm panel hid behind the closet door — hundreds to install and rarely activated. The salesman called it a small price for peace of mind, but still it offered little reassurance when the killer remained unnamed and Duncan's only defense was legislation.

"Nine, nineteen, seventy-eight."

"A date?"

"The day Lindsay died."

"Oh. Well. Someday you may want to forget that date."

"I'd like to forget that we need such things."

"Sadly, we do. I don't even feel safe leaving my house. Why should I feel like a target because I've been blessed with money? Our parents' generation always thought that prosperity would bring security, but it doesn't. It just doesn't."

Duncan smiled at the sentiment, one he'd heard often in recent weeks. The North Shore felt proud to have one of its own in power, convinced that he shared their concerns for the conservation of property and wealth. Whenever someone alluded to it, he nodded. How could he explain that once you lost something truly precious, material things didn't matter?

"Let's head upstairs," he said.

In Aden's bedroom, the walls shone electric yellow and red, but otherwise the space betrayed no hints of its last inhabitant.

"Our cleaners will prime the walls," he said.

"It's always best to leave a clean slate."

If she only knew. A week ago, Duncan found pizza boxes hidden under the bed, porn mags below the mattress, hash pipes in the dresser drawers. In the desk waited obscene lyrics to a dozen songs, some penned by his son. In the nightstand hid a box of condoms—wishful thinking, most likely, since it remained full and near expiring. The boy had learned to disguise his sins but not renounce them. Defenseless against such disorder, Duncan threw everything in boxes. Let its creator rearrange it.

Inside Lindsay's room dust shimmered in the sunlight with a celestial glow. Duncan had finally convinced Josie to store all Lindsay's things. Now, he felt a pang of regret. The emptiness fed his doubt that moving constituted an escape, but not a change.

"I told the buyers... what happened here," Amity said. "Out of respect, they'll use this room as storage."

"There's no need," he said. "Any ghosts will follow us."

As he closed the closet door, a glint stopped him. High on the top shelf sat a reflective box that he'd missed during the clean up. He had to stand on tip-toe and grope along the shelf to reach it: an eight-track cassette of "Saturday Night Fever," dusty and damaged, its black tape twisted and unplayable.

"Anything important?" Amity said.

"Just trash."

What kind of music did Lindsay like? Glynis didn't mention the Bee Gees. Then again, most of his children's musical tastes felt foreign. Still, the name nagged at him until another memory sparked a connection.

* * *

In an hour Duncan had to be downtown, but the Kenilworth p.d. lay only five minutes away. After handing over the keys to the house, he drove one last time down Kenilworth Avenue and parked opposite the station. For five minutes he sat in the car, debating with himself. Did he really want to know? He had no intention of returning to town again, ever. He could toss the shirt and forget it all.

Chief Dunleavy saw him promptly, though only in the vestibule, where three flies carved circles overhead.

"I didn't expect to see you again," the chief said.

"It's my last day in town, and I wanted to thank you. Even though things didn't exactly work out, I appreciate all the work you did."

"We did our best. The state police have resources we never will. I just hope they can turn over enough evidence to charge Hoxter."

"I've no doubt."

In the pause that followed, Duncan noted how thin and pale the chief's face looked despite a full beard as camouflage.

"They have everything, all our files," the chief said.

"Actually, I wanted to ask about something else. My son has a probation hearing next week, and our lawyer misplaced his files. Would you still have the original report?"

"We should."

They passed through a steel door and walked down a long corridor of humming fluorescent lights to a bank of filing cabinets. Dunleavy flipped through a drawer packed tight with manila folders until he found the right one.

"My secretary will make you a copy," he said.

While they waited, the chief talked up the legislation Duncan had introduced. "I've heard plenty of good proposals before, but defense attorneys and lobbyists always killed them. You think you have the votes to get it passed?"

Duncan smiled, then felt guilty for it. Over the past three weeks, police had pulled twenty-nine bodies, many still unidentified, from John Wayne Gacy's crawl space and the nearby Des Plaines River. Every day the newspapers unearthed some new secret about his depravity: he lured his victims with the promise of a job, he worked as a clown at children's birthday parties. During Duncan's victory tour of the state, someone at every stop mentioned the killer. The story couldn't have been worse, but its timing couldn't have been better.

"With what's been happening," Duncan said, "no one could vote against it."

The chief's secretary returned with two manila folders and handed one to each man. As Duncan turned to leave, the young woman touched his arm.

"Governor, could you sign here?" she said. She pointed to the front cover of the folder where a page bore two other signatures: his own from months earlier, and another he couldn't make out. He turned the file to the light and squinted until he recognized the looping script: Lindsay Cochrane. The date next to his daughter's signature read 9/2/78, two weeks before she died.

"Is this everyone who's received a copy?"

The secretary nodded and stared at him quizzically, so he signed carelessly and left.

Outside, he strode calmly to his Cadillac and drove a block away before parking and opening the file. There he found a photo of Aden looking chagrined and slovenly, his hair falling to his shoulders. The opposite page held a cover sheet with shorthand describing the crime:

Grand theft auto: 1970 Oldsmobile Cutlass S Rallye.

Victim: Mr. Consuelo Gracas, 1805 Maple Ave., Evanston, IL.

Narrative: Mr. Gracas awoke at about midnight on May 24, 1978 to a slamming door. He moved to his bedroom window and saw his car missing, then called 911. At 12:21 a.m. patrol officers found the car crashed into a curb in the 200 block of Green Bay Road, the front tire flat, one axle broken, the ignition stripped. Two blocks away they stopped Aden

Cochrane, 15, of Kenilworth walking north. He was limping and had a bruised forearm. During a pat search they found a flat head screwdriver in his jacket pocket. Because he was a minor, officers drove him home.

The rest Duncan remembered.

With his parents flanking him on one couch and two Kenilworth cops sitting opposite, Aden wasted twenty minutes proclaiming his innocence. He said he'd gone to a party and a fight had broken out. Pressed about how he'd travelled there and why he'd walked home with such an injury, Aden only shrugged. He didn't know the boy who'd driven him there or the girl who hosted it. By the time the police left, Duncan knew his son was guilty; however, the family's prominence convinced prosecutors not to file charges. Instead, they diverted Aden to a probationary court on a charge of disorderly conduct for the "fight" he admitted.

At the bottom of the page, Duncan found the section he wanted.

Items reported missing: an 8-track of "Saturday Night Fever."

Duncan closed the file and stared at the bare trees and the grey sky. It couldn't be. He couldn't bear to think that his son... For many minutes, he tried to rearrange the facts to reach some other conclusion, but failed. His dashboard clock read 3:30, an hour before sunset and the onset of the weekend cattle drive heading downtown. At four he had to meet Kai to review his inauguration speech. That gave him barely enough time to stop at the hotel.

***

Conventioneers in matching blue blazers crowded the lobby of the Drake Hotel. Pushing through them, Duncan kept his fedora lowered, but several still recognized him. By the time he'd finished shaking hands, five minutes remained before his appointment. The elevator trip wasted one. As he entered his suite, Duncan called out "anybody here" but heard only the tick of a clock on the mantle. His family must have been shopping on Michigan Avenue. Glynis needed a dress for the inauguration, and Josie loved any excuse to stop in Chanel and Saks. His own blue suit hung on a dresser's dummy in the bedroom. For now, he didn't need anything that formal; a dress shirt and slacks would do. He sniffed at his musky sweater and decided to invest two minutes in a shower.

When he emerged from the bathroom, a towel wrapped around his waist, hair uncombed, Aden lay on the king-size mattress. He'd returned home for Christmas only the day before and had appeared only for meals. Reclining there, he looked more like the son Duncan recalled than the young cadet he'd expected, having ditched his uniform and spiked the inch of hair left on his crown.

"My bed's half this big," Aden said.

Duncan walked past him to the closet and pulled out a set of white boxers. He kept the towel over him and dressed surfer style, back turned to his son.

"I didn't think you and Glynis wanted to share a room."

"You could have rented us a suite too."

In the closet mirror, Duncan saw Aden sit up and examine his father's naked torso as though sizing him up before a fight. Duncan glimpsed his reflection too—his middle three inches larger than before the campaign—and looked away.

"We'll be on the state payroll soon," he said. "We need to adopt a modest lifestyle."

"Yeah, I see how much you've sacrificed."

Duncan ignored the jibe and threw on a pale blue oxford shirt, then moved to his dresser for a sweater.

"I've got something for you," Duncan said.

From the bottom drawer he extracted the T-shirt reading, "Never Mind the Bollocks."

The boy looked surprised, as though he'd received a Christmas gift.

"Damn, where'd you find that?"

"The laundry at our old place."

Aden stripped off his cashmere sweater and replaced his white T with the logoed one.

"So it's yours?" Duncan said as casually as he could.

"My best threads. I've been looking for this thing for forever."

The boy examined himself in the mirror, his wool slacks contrasting with the slogan "Here's the Sex Pistols" on the shirt back. Even dressed in his killing costume, Duncan still couldn't imagine the boy.... He looked away and stooped to put on shoes and socks.

"When'd you lose it?" he said.

"Probably Thanksgiving."

Duncan did not reply to the obvious lie, instead throwing on a sweater and fleeing the room as quickly as he could, leaving Aden to admire his own aspect.

CHAPTER 35

SNOW WAS FORECAST but not the heavy confetti that fell all around Duncan like ticker tape at a parade. The wind swirled it into tornadoes of white that rose and spread more than they fell. At times it blinded, at others it deafened, and always it chilled.

Duncan's face felt numb and his skin turned pink despite his heaviest wool coat and leather gloves. On Kai's advice the new governor had left off his hat to avoid looking too official. Now the pale flakes on his hair and shoulders undercut that authority. Why had he agreed to hold a press conference outdoors?

Nostalgia. His staff had debated other sites with more history: Haymarket Square, site of the famous union riot, or the Biograph Theater where John Dillinger died. Yet he'd kick-started his campaign at Daley Plaza four months before, so it fit to host his first major announcement there.

Behind the platform stood the steel and glass skyscraper of the Cook County Courthouse and Picasso's giant bird-like sculpture, yet they disappeared in the dense flakes and a monochrome grey haze. With so little visible, the site could have been any place.

"Ready?" Kai asked.

Since his promotion to chief of staff, Kai dressed more formally in blue suits and black wingtips, but due to the storm he wore a red, down coat that squeezed him from chin to thigh. Only his head moved, its ponytail protruding like a handle.

Duncan ascended the podium and surveyed the crowd below him. Only journalists waited — no mothers with strollers, no businessman with

214

hot dogs, not even the homeless with sleeping bags—and they looked resentful. The scribes closed their pads against the snow, the TV anchors held umbrellas to keep their hair from wilting, their cameras shrink wrapped like vegetables, and radio voices shielded microphones under down gloves.

"Friends," Duncan said. "Thanks for coming out on this splendid day."

While the swarm agitating for warmth, Duncan scanned Margo's text, which read: "This historic measure, passed with near unanimous votes in both houses, will not only protect the citizenry from predators in our midst but will send a message to criminals everywhere that the era of free passes is over." The tone sounded too self-congratulatory. He was talking about people's lives, not poker chips wagered at the table of political favor.

A sneeze from one of the newsmen brought Duncan back.

"I have a speech prepared," he said, "but I'd rather speak from the heart."

He glanced behind him to where his family sat, equally uncomfortable. Josie hunched her shoulders despite a black, wool coat and matching beret. Glynis looked maudlin, compressing her white lips in a frown. Only Aden appeared happy in his academy's olive green pea coat—complete with awards stitched to the lapels—and a matching overseas cap. His smile bore a knowing contempt, as though he sensed Duncan's uncertainty.

Duncan began, "If this bill can save anyone from the anguish that my family and I have endured, I will consider it a success. No one who hasn't experienced it can know the emptiness of losing a child. No law can fill that. No punishment can relieve it.

"The man who killed my Lindsay has a long criminal history. If the system worked, my daughter would still be alive today. Whether we'll ever convict him, I don't know, but I promise men like him will never get early parole again."

The wind whistling in Duncan's ears and the snow accumulating on his head, so he scanned several paragraphs and skipped to the last, which he'd written himself.

"From now on, violent criminals will serve every day of their terms, and non-violent offenders will serve at least eighty percent. Three strikes will result in a life term. We'll bring an end to the violence of the wicked and make the righteous secure."

Kai waddled to him with a blank sheet of paper — in so much snow, any signature would smear, so they used a mock bill. Duncan removed one glove, uncapped the pen, scrawled his first name, and stamped his official seal. By the time he finished, Duncan's bare hand cramped with cold.

"I'll take questions," he said.

From somewhere in the honeycomb of journalists, a deep voice called, "Governor, isn't this just a politician's way to salvage some good publicity after the horrors of John Wayne Gacy?"

Duncan strained to see the speaker, whose voice sounded unfamiliar, but a gust blew snow into his eyes. "Under this plan, Gacy would never have gotten out early."

A reporter he couldn't see, but whose baritone he knew from public radio, shouted, "What about good behavior?"

"What about it?"

"The correctional officers' union said your bill will increase prison violence because inmates will have no hope of an early release."

"They should be grateful that we let them out at all."

Duncan tried not to frown against all the negative questions, imagining his dour face on the front page of tomorrow's papers, but the wind and cold made it difficult not to squint.

The deep voice called, "What about the disproportionate effect this will have on young black men?"

The baritone's owner hid in the center of the colony, an anonymous pest who'd dart out and attack when Duncan's blinked.

"What does being black have to do with it?" Duncan said, and immediately regretted his word choice.

"Their sentences are already twice that of whites for the same crimes."

"I can't confirm that statistic," Duncan said.

He hadn't expected this at all. The bill's passage should have been his proudest moment, but the press was attacking from all angles, seeking any exposed flesh.

A young, blond woman in an impractically short coat and skirt spoke from the front row. "Governor, given that the man suspected of your daughter's murder hasn't been charged, will this measure have any effect on his case?"

"When charges are brought, this will ensure he's never free again."

Duncan glanced to the side, where Kai twirled his puffy arm to say, "Wrap it up."

"I'll take one more question," he said.

Martin Gubzik, a schlumpy, middle-aged reporter for the *Sun-Times*, spoke quickly. "Isn't the case against your suspect weak?"

"The police have the right man."

"Then why hasn't he been charged?"

A gust of wind disarranged Duncan's hair, and he paused to push it back into place. "That decision belongs to the U.S. attorney, but he's assured me charges are pending. Thank you all for coming. I look forward to seeing the good news in your stories."

He turned to join his family, but the deep voice followed him. "What do you say to people who think this bill is racist?"

Kai tried to steer him off stage, but Duncan broke free and returned to the mic. "I'm sorry, but how is punishing criminals racist?"

From the midst of the hive, a short, slim man pushed forward. He wore the black suit, white shirt, and horn-rimmed glasses of Malcolm X. His grey fedora had a business card in it, like the old time journalists, which read *Chicago Champion*.

"You're aware that Oges Hoxter is an Afro-American from a poor community."

"That's no excuse for lawlessness."

"What if he were someone from your family?"

"No one from my family could commit such an act!"

The public address system screeched back Duncan's last words as he breathed in short huffs. Too late he realized that he was scowling as more camera shutters clicked.

He stepped back from the lectern and glanced at his family: the women sat with their heads lowered against the wind, but Aden looked more alert than ever.

CHAPTER 36

THE BLIZZARD CONTINUED through the night, adding six powdery inches to the foot already fallen. Downtown, snow blocked all the sidewalks, and street cleaners could not clear even Michigan Avenue, so the Cochrane family breakfasted in the bar of the Drake Hotel. They talked of trivialities — baseball trades and museum exhibits — but never what came next. It would be their last meal together. In a few hours, Duncan and Josie would fly to Springfield, while Aden would jet back to prep school in New Hampshire. Glynis planned to linger in Chicago with friends, though Duncan still hoped she'd change her mind and follow them to the state capital, where he could watch over her.

After eating, Duncan returned to his room to find the phone's red light blinking. The hotel's receptionist read him a clipped message like a telegram. "Both airports closed. Can't return Springfield until afternoon at soonest. Will keep checking forecast. Let you know. Kai."

Duncan turned to his family, who lay on the beds and chaise lounges like listless cats. "We're stuck in town, and the hotel needs the room."

"Who's more important than the governor?" Aden said.

"Lots of people. What do you say we drive up to the old house?"

"Why?" Aden said.

"It's our last chance to see it."

Josie looked out the window where snowflakes clouded the glass with abstract clumps. "Is the outer drive clear?" she said.

"Of course," Duncan said. "Chicago knows how to manage winter."

Without debate, the three gathered their bags and watched as the bellboy shuttled them down the elevator and loaded them into the trunk of their rented Pontiac.

* * *

The trip started slow and slippery, with traffic along Lake Shore Drive sliding around corners and spinning out on straight aways despite creeping at half the speed limit. The landscape faded to silhouettes of grey and white, the buildings discolored squares, the road a tunnel of static. Farther north, Sheridan Road lay empty except for parked cars now landlocked by a snow berm left by the plows. The few people who had dug out their vehicles left behind lawn chairs to stake their claims.

"Good thing we've got snow tires," Duncan said.

Josie scowled at him and said, "Plus free towing."

At their house, eight inches covered the driveway, so Duncan parked along the sidewalk, then clambered through knee-high drifts to reach the porch.

"Anyone have a key?" Duncan said.

"We gave them to you," Glynis said.

"I'll get the spare," Aden said.

He high stepped across the front yard and disappeared around the side to the electrical panel, where they hid the extra key. When he returned, the moisture weighed down his pants and encrusted his shoes.

Inside, the house waited silent. They tamped the snow from their feet, but still left a trail on the hardwoods. Only the curtains hinted at the previous owners. Cleaners had swept away their dust, painters covered their colors in primer white, and disinfectant hid any human smells.

"It's like we never lived here," Glynis said.

Aden traced the walls with his fingers. "Except we've all left behind prints."

Duncan allowed them a minute to survey the downstairs before heading to the stairwell. "I've got something to show you," he said.

They climbed to the second floor landing, where new shag absorbed the sound of their steps, and Duncan led them to Lindsay's room, where only her argyle drapes remained. He walked to her empty closet, then turned to Aden.

"How did your T-shirt land in Lindsay's things?" Duncan said.

"Say what?"

"I found it in the hamper."

"Before you said it was in the laundry shaft."

"It was in her closet."

"So you lied!"

"Answer the question. How did it get there?"

Aden threw up his hands and walked toward the window. "How should I know?"

"Blame me," Josie said. "I must have thrown it there while I was cleaning."

"Aden said he lost it over Thanksgiving." Duncan studied his son, who stood with his back to them. "Why did you go in her room?" Duncan said.

"Can't I even walk through the house?"

"Were you looking for something?"

"Like what?"

Duncan reached inside his wool coat and removed the Bee Gees tape, then watched for his family's reactions. Aden glanced at it then stared out the window blankly; Josie and Glynis betrayed only confusion.

"I found it in Lindsay's closet," Duncan said.

"So?" Aden said quietly.

"So is it yours?"

The boy shrugged, a pantomime of indifference.

"Glynis said Lindsay didn't like that kind of music."

When Duncan looked to his daughter, her skin looked pale, her lips almost blue. He paused to allow the evidence to percolate through them, then spoke again.

"I know it's yours, Aden. It's from that car you took, isn't it?"

"No, and if it was I wouldn't stash it in Lindsay's room."

"Who else would?"

"What difference does it make?"

"Because I defended you to the police. I knew you were having problems, but I never figured you for a thief."

"Then why'd you ship me off to military school?"

Josie walked to Aden and put a hand on his shoulder. "Because you always found trouble," she said. "You've got to control yourself."

Aden shook off her touch and faced the outside. "So what are you going to do, send me to jail and take away my parole?"

"Don't be sarcastic," Duncan said.

Aden traced a word in the steam on the window, circled it, then drew a slash through the middle. He studied it for a moment, then wiped it away so the others wouldn't see the text.

"That guy from the newspaper fingered you," he said.

"What guy?"

"The one who asked if you'd lock up your own family."

Josie tried to turn him to face them, but he resisted. "You're not going to prison," she said.

This time, he traced a square with vertical bars.

"Come on," Duncan said. "Let's settle this now so it's not hanging over us."

"Fine," Aden said. "I did it."

"You stole the car?" Duncan said.

"Borrowed it."

"And what were you planning?"

"Just drive around, see how it handled."

"Why?"

"Because we never had a choice car."

Duncan stepped toward his son whose face hid in shadow, his lean figure outlined against the frosted glass. He looked just as Glynis had described the burglar.

"Good. You're finally being honest," Duncan said.

Josie walked toward her husband, blocking his view of the boy, and said, "You done?"

"Not yet," Duncan said. "Two weeks before she died, Lindsay picked up a copy of your police report. Did she find your souvenir?"

"No," the boy said quietly.

"Then why?"

Duncan exhaled and watched the mist from his breath fade while he waited.

"She was my sister!" Aden finally said. "She was supposed to look out for me, not rat me out."

From the doorway, Duncan heard sobbing, but he wouldn't take his eyes off Aden. "Is that why you killed her?"

"Duncan, stop!" Josie said. "Aden, don't answer."

"We need to pack up all the secrets before we leave," Duncan said.

The boy turned and stared at his father, the .32 in hand. "Like this?" he said.

"Where did you get that?" Josie said.

"The electrical panel," Aden said.

"It's mine," Duncan said. He reached for it, but Aden drew away from him.

"Why are you hiding a gun?" Josie said.

"I meant to throw it out," Duncan said. "I forgot."

They stood immobile and silent while outside the wind threw snow against the windows.

"So maybe you killed her," Aden said.

"She wasn't shot," Duncan said.

"Then why bogart a piece?"

"For protection."

Duncan stepped toward him, trying vainly to recall if he'd emptied the cylinder. "I never thought I'd need it from you," Duncan said quietly.

He stood only feet from the boy, hand extended, watching his face as tears formed.

"You want me to say I did it?" Aden said. "Fine, then I'm guilty."

He tossed the gun at his father, ran for the door, and shouldered past his mother. Then his footsteps pounded down the stairs and a door slammed.

"What are you trying to do?" Josie said.

Duncan stooped to pick up the gun, then checked the cylinder: six bullets loaded.

"I needed to know."

"By persecuting your son?"

Duncan turned to Glynis, who held her hands over her face. With two deep breaths he removed the stress from his voice. "That night. You saw Aden, didn't you?" he said.

"I don't know."

"You can tell us. It will never leave this room."

"I couldn't tell. It was too dark."

"Satisfied?" Josie said. "Aden didn't kill her. How could you even think that?"

She wrapped an arm around her daughter's waist and steered her toward the hallway.

"Alright," Duncan said.

He walked to the window to see Aden's footprints in the snow-drifts, just like the sandy trail the police found three months before. It led to the lake's frozen edge. When he saw the boy step onto the ice, Duncan forgot his anger and ran after him.

Outside, Duncan's steps landed erratically. On some the snow held firm; on others it gave way, plunging him to his thighs. Already Aden stood ten feet from shore near the invisible line between solid and liquid. After clambering through a deep drift, Duncan reached the land's end. He took two steps onto the frosted ice flat and then paused, arm extended.

"Come back," he said.

Aden turned, looked over his father skeptically, then faced the endless lake again. "Why?"

"Because. We want to help you."

"By sending me to jail?"

"No!"

"You already told everyone that's what you want."

"Please, Son. Don't sacrifice yourself."

Waves slapped the ice rhythmically, and the wind blew snow into Duncan's eyes. The whiteout made Aden blur with the horizon. When Duncan looked up again, the boy sat crouched, arms around his knees, rocking on the thin crust.

"I'm sorry," Duncan said.

"For what?"

"For making you think we're enemies."

"You hate me."

Duncan hesitated. At times the last few days he had, but in that moment he could only imagine the pain of losing another child.

"Only what you've done."

"Same thing."

"No, it's not. I'll always care for you."

"Too late for that."

The boy lowered his head and convulsed as the ice beneath him bobbed in empathy. Duncan imagined it collapsing with a single crack, him watching Aden sink into the lake. Would he run after, knowing it would be futile, that they'd both be swallowed up?

From behind, Glynis said, "Please, Aden, don't."

Aden turned to see his sister and mother standing at the shoreline.

"I forgive you," she said.

Aden turned from them warily, as though some trick hid in this blessing, then lowered his gaze to the ice.

"Please, son," Duncan said. "Lindsay wouldn't want this."

The boy stared at the lake, then looked up to the sky. Finally he rose and moved cautiously toward shore, as though he'd just realized the danger and was attempting to backtrack in the same footfalls. Each step increased the risk. Snow swirled into Duncan's eyes, stealing his son again. He reached out blindly and waited. When he felt the boy's cold palm, Duncan yanked his son to land so violently that they fell into an embrace.

CHAPTER 37

THE STORM CONTINUED FOR HOURS, burying the city under two feet. After multiple attempts to excavate their car failed, the family returned to the house. They sat on the living room floor, still wearing their winter coats and hats, listening to the wind howl through the trees and crackle the stiff glass panes.

"Can't we go?" Glynis said. She curled into herself, thighs to chest, arms around legs, head on knees.

"How? No cabs are running." Duncan said.

"What about the Connolly's? They must be home."

He glanced toward his next-door neighbors, but couldn't imagine calling on the pediatrician again.

"Not until we settle this," Duncan said.

"What do you want?" Josie said. She sat cross-legged, head in hands, her breath escaping in visible puffs.

"To know *exactly* what happened."

Aden leaned against the wall, legs splayed, acting exhausted. He sighed and stared at the ceiling. Then he began. "Lindsay was snooping through my room and found my stash."

"So she confronted you?"

"Called me at school."

"And you said?"

"That the tape wasn't mine."

"She didn't believe you?"

The boy stared out the window to the grey square of sky. "She found other stuff too."

"What did she say?"

"That she'd tell you. She was totally on my case, but I got her to wait till I got home."

"The weekend of the fundraiser."

The boy looked down to his lap and nodded.

"Why did you go in her room?"

"I just wanted my stuff back. I figured she'd stashed it there, so I was looking while she slept. I had a flashlight, and I guess... I guess I scared her because she screamed. I figured you all must of heard."

Glynis sat, head down, hair covering her face, refusing to confirm anything.

"And then?"

"She tried to call you." He nodded to Duncan but glanced his way only momentarily. "Then she started talking about the fuzz. She wouldn't listen to anything I said."

"And?"

Outside, the wind threw snow against the windows like pellets.

"I reached out to stifle her, but she totally panicked. She was thrashing around like... I was going to strangle her." He shifted his weight and shouldered the wall as if it were a pillow. "I never meant to hurt her. If she'd listened..."

Duncan recalled the scene, her beddings thrown off, the pillow covering her face, the marks on her throat. Lindsay looked more shocked than scared, like the blow had taken her by surprise. No wonder.

"And your T-shirt, how'd that get there?"

"I thought I got blood on it."

"So you ran out back?"

"I... freaked. I just... ran."

"Why'd you break the back window?"

"Trying to open the door."

"And then?"

Aden stared along the wall toward the dark corner, avoiding his father's face. "Once I got outside, I hid the flashlight in the fuse box. Then I climbed the drainpipe to my room."

Silence filled the house. Outside, a snowplow scraped past, strafing the walls with its yellow lights. When no one else filled the lull, Duncan turned to Glynis. "You knew?"

"Not for sure."

"Why didn't you say something?"

When she dropped her head and cried, Aden put a hand on her arm.

"Thanks," he said.

"For what?" Duncan said.

"For backing me up. Nobody else here does."

Duncan shook his head and looked to his wife, who traced the lines of the wood floor.

"I don't believe you," Duncan said. "The coroner said Lindsay died from a blow to the throat. That couldn't have been an accident. You must have hit her with something."

"I didn't!"

The boy looked to each of them for support. Finding none, he threw himself back against the wall and folded his arms.

"Did you bring something from school?" Duncan said.

"No!" Aden's voice cracked and he began to cry, wiping the tears on his wrist.

"Then how can it be an accident?"

"That's what I do every day!"

"What?"

"Practice killing people. They teach us at school. How to kill someone with our hands."

"So you meant to kill her?"

"No! It just... happened."

Duncan had run out of questions. Finally, when no one else spoke, Josie did. "This can't be. My son wouldn't do such a thing."

She sat on her haunches, arms hugging herself, and rocked in place. When she shivered, Duncan reached to put an arm around her, but at his first touch she recoiled.

"I raised my children to love each other," she said. "We taught you all that nothing comes before family."

"Then why was Lindsay going to rat on me?" Aden said.

"Your sister protected you," she said. "She wanted to help."

"She was going to give me up signed, sealed, and delivered."

"What evil has infected this family?" Josie said. She began to cry. It was the first time Duncan had ever seen her weep, and he couldn't stand the sight, so he stood and walked to the window. Outside dusk lingered, but the streetlights remained dark. Without thinking, he grabbed a cigarette. After lighting it, he turned back to his family.

"Sorry," he said.

No one spoke, and the scent filled the room while the fumes narcoticized him.

"He has to be punished," Duncan said.

"You're not telling the police," Josie said.

"No, that would ruin everything. Even if we could persuade them it was an accident, it would be front-page news for weeks. We'd never survive the scandal."

He inhaled deeply and held the smoke in his lungs, which helped clear his thinking. "Any punishment will have to come from us."

"It was the campaign," Josie said. "It corrupted us all. The people we courted, the money we took, the promises we made." She wiped her tears but left behind streaks of dirt on her cheeks.

"We can't trust anyone else with this," Duncan said. "Only the four of us. And we have to seek normalcy. Tomorrow, Aden will fly back to school, and we'll go from there."

"That boot camp has only made things worse," she said. "He needs to be home with us."

"How could we supervise him?" Duncan said. "I'm too busy, and you never could."

"It's our fault," she said. "We failed him, so we have to repair him."

"I'd say just the opposite. If anything, he needs outside discipline."

Duncan turned to face them but took another deep puff before continuing. "He could enlist," he said.

"He's only sixteen!" Josie said.

"After he graduates. What better penance than serving your country? I knew a lot of men in Korea who chose the army over jail."

"Just don't ditch me," Aden said. "That's what started all this."

They fell silent as the streetlights flickered on. Duncan stared at the faces of his family in the dull glow and saw resignation mixed with dread.

"What about the man you had arrested?" Glynis said.

"What about him?" Duncan said.

"Are you going to let him go now?"

"We can't," Josie said. "That would force the police to look for someone else."

"You can't send him to prison for this," Glynis said.

"He's done plenty else wrong," Duncan said. "Besides, he hasn't even been charged, and I doubt he ever will be."

"How can you be sure?"

"It's in the hands of the state police now, and I... control them."

"You really think we can keep this on the q.t.?" Aden said.

"No one knows about it but us."

"How long can we hold something so... awful inside?" Glynis said.

"As long as we choose."

After sucking it down to the filter, Duncan crushed out the smoke on the hardwoods. "Right now, all we can do is maintain the status quo," Duncan said. "Aden will complete high school in New Hampshire. We'll support him until he's done. And he'll take summer classes to finish his degree early."

Outside, a car rolled past, chains slapping the asphalt.

"After that—"

No words could soften what he foresaw. Aden would become a shadow, unavailable if not unloved, and return only after he lost the egotism and recklessness that made his banishment necessary. His progress would determine the length of his sentence more than any measure of years. Meanwhile, Duncan could ensure that the law never prosecuted anyone and that the case remained unsolved. To outsiders, the family would be a symbol of unserved justice.

"Will I still see you?" Aden said.

"In time."

— THE END —

ABOUT THE AUTHOR

STORIES ABOUT CRIMES have always resonated with me, whether it was *Crime and Punishment* or *The Quiet American*. Maybe it's because I started my career as a police reporter, or because I worked for a time as a teacher in the county jail.

More than a decade ago, when I decided to finally get serious about writing, I started with short stories based on real misdeeds I'd witnessed. I wrote one about my next door neighbor, who'd been murdered by a friend, another about an ambitious bike racer who decides to take out the competition, and a bunch of others based on characters I met in jail. Over time these got picked up by various magazines online and in print. More than a dozen now exist, with most of the latest in Alfred Hitchcock's Mystery Magazine and Big Pulp.

For my debut novel, *They Tell Me You Are Wicked*, I drew inspiration from the most infamous event in the history of my hometown: the real life killing of a political candidate's daughter (though I made up all the details). Now I am at work on a second volume in the series, set two years later, after my hero, Duncan Cochrane, has become governor. He's haunted by the family secret that got him elected, and fighting a sniper who's targeting children in Chicago.

Please connect with me online at:
Website: **www.DavidHagerty.net**
Facebook: **www.facebook.com/pages/**
David-Hagerty-Author/1517793858476289
Twitter: **www.twitter.com/DHagertyAuthor**

WHAT'S NEXT?

Watch for the second book in the *Duncan Cochrane* crime mystery series, coming in the spring of 2017.

MORE FROM EVOLVED PUBLISHING

**For lovers of psychological/crime thrill-
ers, suitable for readers 17 and older:**

FORGIVE ME, ALEX
By Lane Diamond

Two personalities, two attitudes, two goals, two methods – one darkness. This
psychological thriller novel is now available. For more information on this
book, please visit the Evolved Publishing website at **www.evolvedpub.com**.

~~~~~

Tony Hooper stands in shadow across the street, one amongst many
in the crowd of curiosity-hounds gathered to watch a monster's release.
Seventeen years after Mitchell Norton, *the devil*, terrorized Algonquin,
Illinois on a spree of kidnapping, torture and murder, the authorities
release the butcher from psychiatric prison.

Tony longs to charge across the street to destroy Norton—no remorse—as if stepping on a cockroach. Only sheer force of will prevents
his doing so.

The devil walks the world again. What shall Tony do about it? Aye,
what indeed.

After all, this is what Tony does. It's who he is. *The devil* himself long
ago made Tony into this hunter of monsters. What a sweet twist of fate
this is, that he may still, finally, administer justice.

Will FBI Special Agent Linda Monroe stop him? She owes him her life,
so how can she possibly put an end to his?

Tony Hooper and Mitchell Norton battle for supremacy, with law
enforcement always a step away, in this story of justice and vengeance,
evil and redemption, fear and courage, love and loss.

~~~~~

Praise for *Forgive Me, Alex*:

"Lane Diamond has succeeded in bringing to the surface the dark and horrifying mind of a psychotic serial killer while at the same time bringing forth the desperate need for humanity and justice for the victims and their families." – *The Kindle Book Review*

"Psychological thrillers are my kind of books! Not only do I write them, but truly enjoy reading one that makes my skin crawl, my nerves skitter with fear and my heart thump a tad louder. This incredible novel by Lane Diamond handed me ALL of that, in spades!" – *Ashley Fontainne, Author of "Zero Balance (Eviscerating the Snake)"*

"With a deeply attuned attention to the nature of humanity and psychosis, Diamond delves into the darkest corners of the human mind and pulls out nuggets of horror and absolution that will leave you wanting more. I look forward to more books from this amazing author. This is a book to rival any of the great thrillers you've ever read and is a definite must read!" – *Kimberly (Karpov) Kinrade, Author of "The Forbidden Trilogy"*

"Lane gets you into the head of the characters and you feel this bond with them urging you to read faster to find out what happens next. You know you are reading a great book when you need to stop reading but keep telling yourself just one more chapter, then one more leads to half the book. I felt so bad for Tony and all his loss. I wanted to murder Mitchell Norton myself. I wish I knew old Frank personally. I was caught off guard by the ending and can't wait for the next book! Well done!" – *Jennifer @ Can't Put It Down Reviews*

"...Lane's writing makes you really care about these people and what's going on. Lane excels in this area of sympathetic characters." – *Tim C. Ward, Book Blogger & Podcaster*

"I have actually read this story twice, yes twice! There are new things to discover each time you read it and I would encourage you to pick it up again, see what you can discover about Tony Hooper the second time around ... and see what you can maybe discover about yourself. I was able to understand my sick fascination with serial killers and horror gore a little better with the aide of *Forgive Me, Alex* — it is the only media representation of such a horrific character type that effectively goes beyond the curtain." – *Marie Borthwick*

"I think what struck me the most about the story, and what I really enjoyed, was the way Diamond explored the depths of the main characters, Tony Hooper and Mitchell Norton. It would be easy in this type of story to get caught up in the action. But correctly, I think, Diamond recognizes that the strength of the book lies in the characters, and he does an excellent job of helping the reader understand the inner workings of their minds. ... That is not to say that the "action" scenes were not well done. In fact, I found myself drawn to the most disturbing scenes, which I think is a real compliment to the manner in which they were presented." – *Rich V.* at Amazon

For lovers of suspense thrillers, for readers 16 and older:

SHATTER POINT
By Jeff Altabef

A gripping glimpse of the near future, in which a twisted serial killer finds power in a corrupt political culture, this psychological thriller is a stand-alone follow-up to Jeff Altabef's first novel, the political thriller *Fourteenth Colony*. For more information about this book, please visit the Evolved Publishing website at **www.evolvedpub.com**.

~~~~~

Maggie met Cooper at a young age, but even then she sensed something was wrong with him. His charm, good looks, and wealth could not hide the danger that burned in his sapphire eyes.

Some nightmares don't go away. He'd been haunting her from a distance for as long as she could remember.

Now things have changed.

When her sons Jack and Tom discover she's been taken, they set out to rescue her and uncover nefarious family secrets, explosive government conspiracies, and a series of horrific murders along the way. Only their colorful great aunt and a covert resistance group can help them navigate the dark underworld full of political subterfuge and class warfare.

All the while, Maggie struggles to outwit her tormentor in a life and death psychological battle of tense desperation. Will Jack and Tom arrive before Cooper reaches his shatter point?

~~~~~

Midwest Book Review has described Jeff Altabef as an "articulate and engaging storyteller" and "a contemporary novelist of considerable merit and imagination."

~~~~~

Praise for *Shatter Point*:

"*Shatter Point* by Jeff Altabef was an amazing read. There were two separate stories here fully entwined together. The story started on a high note and never dropped a beat the whole way through. Excellent thriller, a scary one because the experimental drug side of it is something that could possibly happen, or may even be happening today. This is one of those books that no reader will be able to part with until they reach the end, I guarantee it." - *Anne-Marie Reynolds, Readers' Favorite Book Reviews and Awards*

"From the moral and ethical dilemmas posed by drug testing to the control of violence in a society dominated by privilege, *Shatter Point* reveals much food for thought. Add the overlap of romance, murder mystery, and political thriller and you have a truly multifaceted read that grabs a hold with powerful protagonists and issues and won't let go till its logical, satisfyingly unexpected conclusion: a neat wrap-up perfect for a precisely-evolving thriller." - *Donovan, eBook Reviewer, Midwest Book Review*

"I found the flow of the book to be fast paced and perfect for this kind of story. Jeff Altabef has truly created a gripping story that is full of suspense, thrills and drama. If you enjoy this genre, *Shatter Point* will tick all of your boxes and give you even more than that. I had trouble setting this one down and I think you will do too. I give this book two thumbs up and suggest it for a fantastic read." - *Kathryn Bennett, Readers' Favorite Book Reviews and Awards*

**For lovers of noir mysteries or old-fashioned
gumshoe detective stories:**

HOT SINATRA
By Axel Howerton

This quirky, often hilarious noir mystery, featuring the adventures of the memorable Moss Cole, is now available. For more information, please visit the publisher's website at **www.evolvedpub.com.**

~~~~~

Moss Cole is a private detective, the kind you thought only existed in old movies and afternoon reruns. He's smart, talented, sometimes even charming. You'd think he could find a better gig than carrying on his grandfather's legacy as a 'Private Dick.'

Cole is out of money, out of ideas, and out of his league. That's why he's stuck looking for a stolen Sinatra record... a record that may be just a figment of an old man's imagination.

Of course, if that were true, Moss wouldn't have so many people busting down his door. A vivacious redhead, a foul-mouthed Irish rock star, and a whip-smart little girl only complicate the job, when all Cole wants is a good cup of coffee and some Hot Sinatra.

If only he can stay alive — and in one piece — long enough to find it.

~~~~~

Praise for *Hot Sinatra*:

"Axel Howerton is one of the best new crime fiction writers out there — hell, one of the best writers, period. Do yourself a favor and settle into Axel's groove." - *Scott S. Phillips, Author of* Squirrel Eyes *and* Tales of Misery & Imagination, *and Writer/Director of* Stink of Flesh *and* Gimme Skelter

"Moss Cole sizzles hotter than bacon." - *Red Tash, Author of* Troll, Or Derby *and* This Brilliant Darkness

BROOMETIME SERENADE
The Oz Files – Book 1
+
INTRIGUE AT SANDY POINT
The Oz Files – Book 2

The *Oz Files* series of suspense/crime thrillers, featuring grisly cases from the Australian Security Intelligence Organisation, is now available. For more information, please visit the publisher's website at **www.evolvedpub.com**.

~~~~~

Broometime Serenade:

When authorities fail to identify human remains uncovered after a cyclone ravages the Western Australian coastline, Martin and Claire are sent to Broome, a popular holiday destination far from major population centres. The SOC (an offshoot of the Australian Security Intelligence Organisation) agents pose as new arrivals and attempt to merge with the locals in an effort to solve the baffling case and bring the killer to justice.

Lulled by the soporific influences of the sun, sand and surf—known by the locals as the 'Serenade of Broome'—time seems to have no meaning for the two agents, and the investigation drifts from one location to another as they follow a trail of bodies designed to confuse and distract them from their real business in this tropical paradise.

Little do they know their every move is being watched by an enemy who is both ruthless and deadly—a powerful, sadistic enemy who enjoys toying with others' lives before despatching them in the most horrifying manner imaginable. As the clues lead them first one way and then the other, they fall deeper and deeper into the trap set for them.

By the time they uncover the truth, they will begin to doubt everything they know and face their greatest challenge to date.

Praise for *Broometime Serenade*:

"Wonderful story; mystery, suspense and some romance portrayed by captivating characters in a tropical paradise. Very well written, I could easily place myself in the story along with Martin and Claire as they pieced together the puzzle and once again foiled the witch Wanda Jean attempt at world domination." – *Madhatt*

"The author has created an intriguing mix of suspense and the supernatural in a breathtaking tale that left this reader wanting more. The vivid descriptions of Broome and its surrounds made me want to pack a bag and fly there--and I would have but for other constraints. Dialogue was exceedingly well used and served to drive the action. An excellent read." – *PWindInspirations*

~~~~~

Intrigue at Sandy Point:

When an undercover CIA agent is murdered at the idyllic seaside resort of Sandy Point, Martin and Claire are despatched to delve into the matter. Before their investigation can gather headway, they discover there is more going on in this laid-back beach community than meets the eye, and they are threatened with death and worse than death by men who will stop at nothing to achieve their goals.

Eventually, the duo uncovers a devious plot that compels them to travel from one end of the country to the other in an attempt to stop those responsible. Fast cars, planes and hot air balloons are utilised in their race against time to avert disaster.

Just when they think they have the situation in hand, a new menace emerges — one that will have ramifications beyond Australia's shores. The problem is, they have no idea where or when this new threat to world peace will be carried out.

As if this wasn't enough to contend with, an old enemy reappears. Although she is in a weakened state, she is hell-bent on exacting revenge — as soon as her powers are fully restored. Will Martin and Claire overcome this new danger before their lives can be terminated once and for all?

CPSIA information can be obtained
at www.ICGtesting.com
Printed in the USA
FSOW03n1151240216
17326FS

9 781622 536177